WHILE SHE SLUMBERED

The Murder Blog Mysteries #5

PAMELA FROST DENNIS

WHILE SHE SLUMBERED
The Murder Blog Mysteries #5
Copyright © 2021 Pamela Frost Dennis
All rights reserved.
ISBN: 978-0-9993494-3-4

Printed in the United States of America
First Printing: 2021
For permission requests:
pamelafrostdennis@hotmail.com
Cover: Bookfly Design

PROLOGUE

Soft footsteps crept towards her bed. A shadowy figure loomed over her.

"Is that you?" she whispered.

There was no answer.

"Is it time for my medicine?" she asked.

"No. It's time to say goodbye."

WELCOME TO MY BLOG

Hi there! I'm Katy McKenna and this blog is a daily journal of my life: the good, the bad, and the boring. Only a select few have access. If you're new to my blog, let me share a little about myself.

I'm a thirty-two-year-old unemployed freelance graphic artist. Happily divorced and financially solvent due to a stash of gold coins I found in my attic a while back. No kids. Two pets—Daisy, a sweet yellow Labrador I adopted at the pound, and Tabitha, a gray tabby cat who adopted me.

I live in Santa Lucia—a quaint, quiet college town on the California Central Coast. I have a great relationship with my folks, Kurt and Marybeth Melby, who live nearby. Mom owns a hair salon, "Cut and Caboodles," so I get freebies. My step-dad, Pop, was a cop who took a bullet in the knee while answering a domestic disturbance call several years ago. That forced him into early retirement. Now he repairs appliances in his shop, "Pop's Fix-It Shop," next door to Mom's salon.

My younger sister by nine years, Emily, lives in Santa Monica with her significant other, Dawn, and works at Roxy Studios. My bio-dad, Bert McKenna, is a plastic surgeon in Palm Springs. He was a non-existent father to me—Pop raised me from the age of two. Now Bert is married to a woman half his age, and they have a toddler. Recently, he and I have forged a friendly relationship. I'm happy he's a devoted daddy to my baby brother.

I have a small circle of good friends and a bestie since grade school. Samantha lives in Santa Lucia and is married with two kids and one on the way. Sam is my rock.

That brings me to my other rock. What can I say about my glamorous, vivacious, and sometimes extremely exasperating grandmother, Ruby? She's not a cookie-baking kind of grandma— she's my partner in crime.

Eventually all things fall into place.
Until then, laugh at the confusion,
live for the moments,
And know everything happens for a reason.

~ Albert Schweitzer ~
1875-1965

CHAPTER ONE

Posted by Katy McKenna

Yesterday
Lunch at the Clamshell Café

We were sitting outside on the deck, enjoying the ocean view and eating fish tacos, when Ruby said to me, "I have a little confession to make."

"Oh, God. What did you do?"

My grandma pulled her cell phone out of the side pocket of her red organizer bag. "I need to show you something, and I want you to keep an open mind." She scrolled through the umpteen apps on her phone. "Here it is." She held the screen in front of my face, looking guilty as hell.

It was a dating app called "30-Something."

I dropped my taco. "Oh, God, what did you do?"

"I may have signed you up."

I thought she was joking until the "♥ *Thanks For Signing Up For Love* ♥" message arrived in my email inbox last night.

This Morning

When I called to chastise Ruby, she wasn't the least bit apologetic. "I don't know why you're so upset, Katy. I told you at lunch yesterday that I did this."

"You said you *may* have signed me up, Ruby. But I sure didn't believe that you'd actually done it."

"You know what they say. It's easier to ask forgiveness than it is to get permission. Honey, you're moping for a man who's living with his ex-wife."

"Nicole has cancer and Josh feels responsible for their marriage breaking up. Helping her is a way for him to make amends."

Ruby continued. "I get that. He's a great guy, but that ship has sailed. I'm not getting any younger, you know, and I—" She paused for a melodramatic sniff.

Oh, here it comes.

"Forgive me for wanting to see my granddaughter happily married before I cross the rainbow ridge and join your grandpa."

"It's Rainbow Bridge."

"Ridge, bridge. Whatever."

CHAPTER TWO

Posted by Katy McKenna

This morning

I was lounging on the couch, sort of watching a recorded *Beat Bobby Flay*, and bored out of my mind. To prove to you how bored I was, I decided to do some yard work. I changed into my ratty gray sweats and was heading out the French doors to the patio when my cell phone rang. Grandma's smiling face lit up the screen.

"Hey, Ruby. Kind of busy right now."

"What're you doing?" she asked.

I sat on the chaise lounge and kicked my feet up. "Working in the yard. Pulling weeds. Trimming bushes. It's hard work, but somebody's got to do it."

"Well, you deserve a break. Come over for coffee in the bistro and spend some quality time with your grandma."

"I suppose I could use a break."

"What are you wearing?" asked Ruby.

That should've warned me she was up to no good.

9

Shady Acres Senior Community

Ruby lives on a tree-lined lane in a charming, two-bedroom cottage with a perfect sized yard for a small dog. There are nice apartments if you don't want the fuss of a yard, and there is also assisted living. The complex has its own theater, a gourmet market, a bistro, several pools, and a fitness club. Twenty-three more years and I'll be eligible to move in!

Still dressed in sweats, I pulled up to the security entrance and rolled down my window, ready for my usual grilling from Gate Keeper George. The skinny middle-aged man stepped out of his booth, looking authoritative with a clipboard and pen. "State your name and purpose of business, please."

"George!" screamed Ruby, marching down the street, waving her fist. "Dammit, George. I've had enough of this. Always harassing my family and friends."

George looked wild-eyed—torn between his sworn duty to protect and serve the citizens of Shady Acres, or run for his life.

"Seriously, George. She's nuts." I tapped my skull. "Certifiable, and getting worse every day. No telling what she'll do."

George scrambled into the glass booth, slammed the door, and ducked. The gate went up a split second before Ruby reached the car. Looking like a senior fashion model in teal capris and a lime green top, she smacked the hood of my 1976 orange Volvo wagon, and pointed a menacing finger at bug-eyed George, who was peeking through the window. "Final warning, George!" She hopped into the car. "Let's roll."

"Oh, my God. That was priceless." I turned the corner towards the bistro.

Ruby shot me a disapproving glance. "Is that what you're wearing?"

"No. Why would you think that?"

She huffed an exasperated sigh. "I wish you would take more pride in your appearance."

"I didn't realize this was a formal occasion."

We parked in the lot next to the main building where the bistro is located. After locking the car door, I did a red carpet pose for Ruby. She shook her head and headed to the building. I dashed ahead and opened the glass door for her with a big grin.

In the glass enclosed atrium entrance, Grandma scanned the room—a cozy blend of sofas, tables, and original art done by talented residents. "Oh look! There's Betty with someone. We should say hello." She grabbed my hand, dragging me across the room. "Betty! Fancy meeting you here."

Attired in her trademark caftan and matching turban, Betty removed her big round black glasses and gave me an obvious once-over, which compelled me to brush imaginary dirt off my baggy pants. "I've been doing yard work."

"I'm glad you're taking a break, dear. You must be exhausted. Do join us."

When I was a kid, I watched *Golden Girls* repeats with Ruby. Betty's commanding voice reminds me of Bea Arthur. Low and husky. She scooted her chair over and patted the seat next to her. "Ruby, you sit here. Katy? Sit next to my grandson, Royce."

Looking very GQ-casual in his half-tucked button-down, he stood to shake hands. "Hi, Katy. It's a pleasure to meet you."

I noticed how much nicer his nails were than mine. "Great to meet you, too."

The grandmothers grinned at us like Cheshire cats who'd scored a quart of cream.

"Isn't this delightful," said Betty. "My *single* grandson is a C.P.A. with a big-time firm in San Francisco. He's down here going over my finances. Such a sweet boy."

"How old are you, Royce?" asked co-conspirator Ruby.

He ran a hand over his male-model stubble, obviously trying to smother a chuckle. "Thirty-five."

Ruby smacked the wood table. "What a coincidence. Katy is thirty-two."

"Wow!" I smacked the table. "That *is* a coincidence. We're both in our thirties." My chair screeched on the tile floor as I pushed it back. "I'll go order. What do you want, Granny?" She hates it when I call her that.

"A regular dark roast." She rose from her seat. "But I'll get the coffees so you two can keep talking."

Royce jumped to his feet. "Ruby—please allow me to help Katy."

"Well, aren't you a courteous young man." She sank back into her chair and winked at Betty.

Royce trailed me to the counter. After I placed my order, he said, "You realize what's going on, right?"

"It's pretty obvious." I leaned an elbow on the marble counter-top. "Truthfully, I'm not into dating these days. I just got out of a serious relationship. Or I think I'm out. Not quite sure. It's complicated."

"Actually, I'm *in* a serious relationship," he said.

"You haven't told Betty? How come?" I gazed across the bistro at the gleeful grandmas gawking at us.

With a serious expression, Royce touched my arm lightly. "Matthew and I just celebrated our six-month anniversary."

"I take it Betty doesn't know."

"She doesn't. My folks are not thrilled about it. They've known I'm gay for years, but refuse to acknowledge it. I don't want to lose Nana, too."

"The only thing Betty will care about is whether Matthew is good enough for you."

He sighed heavily. "I hope you're right, because I'm tired of keeping secrets. I'll tell Nana later."

The barista set my order on the counter. I doctored mine, and had turned to head back to the granny barracudas when Royce said, "How about we have a little fun with this and pretend we're going on a date?"

"Good idea. They deserve it." I noticed my neighbor, Nina,

from two doors down, across the room. "I have to say hello to a friend." I handed Ruby's coffee to Royce. "Tell my grandma I'll only be a minute."

Nina held out her arms for a hug. "My favorite neighbor. So good to see you. Sit for a moment."

I moved an orange pillow and sat next to her on the gray loveseat. "Are you visiting a friend?"

"No. I'm hoping to move here. I put my name on the list for an apartment."

"Hold that thought." I waved my Grandma over. She smiled and nodded at several people as she made her way across the room. "Ruby? Do you remember my neighbor, Nina Lowen?"

She perched on an easy chair facing us. "I certainly do. Nice to see you again. You changed your hair. I love it. It reminds me of Judy Dench's signature hairstyle."

Nina smiled, running her fingers through her short silver pixie. "That's what I was going for."

"Nina wants to move to Shady Acres," I said.

"Why on earth would you want to leave your beautiful home and garden? Don't get me wrong, I love it here, but every time I drive by your house I slow down to admire it." She chuckled. "I was thinking about asking if my ashes could be scattered in your garden."

Nina laughed. "What a lovely thing to say. I doubt I'll still be around by the time you pass. The truth is, maintaining the yard is too much work for me now. I'm ready to have some fun. You know, make new friends. Have a social life." She held up her coffee cup. "The coffee here is good, too. There's another reason for moving. I'm not thrilled with how our neighborhood is changing. Like those boys across the street and their loud music and crude language. It stopped after you talked to them, Katy, but started up again while you and Ruby were in England. That house has become a hangout for the town's lowlifes. Frankly, I've had enough."

"I've heard it, too. I'll go talk to them again."

"I hope you can convince them to stop, Katy. No one is going to want to buy a house across the street from that racket."

Ruby stood. "I better get back to Betty, or I'll never hear the end of it. Nina? If you have questions, please call me. I'd be happy to give you a tour."

"I'm going to miss seeing you on my walks, Nina."

She patted my hand. "It won't happen overnight. But I'm tired of being alone. My Edward has been gone for over twenty years now."

I leaned closer, giving her a coy look. "Are you by any chance looking for love?"

That sparked a hearty laugh. "Good grief, no. I don't need that complication at my age."

"Might be fun. How old are you, Nina—if you don't mind my asking?"

"I'm eighty-seven. And a half. Other than a few minor aches and pains, I feel pretty darned good."

I caught Ruby giving me the stink eye. "Uh-oh. Gotta go. She looks like she wants to strangle me."

"That's a good-looking young man sitting at your table." Nina cocked her head. "Are you being set up?"

"Yes we are. However, he's gay. But the scheming grandmas don't know it. So we're going to have some fun with them."

She picked up her mug. "I'll get a refill and stick around to watch the show. Oh! I almost forgot! When I move, I want to give you my stove. I remember how much you liked it."

"Like it? I love it!" It's a 1951 O'Keefe & Merritt Aristocrat Town & Country in mint condition. I have an old O'Keefe that came with my house, but Nina's stove is the Cadillac of vintage stoves. Two ovens, two broilers, six gas burners, and a griddle. It's a beauty.

"Are you sure?" I asked. "It's probably worth a fortune."

"Yes, I'm sure. I doubt the buyer of my house would appreciate it like you do."

"Nina, I will cherish that stove forever. If I move, it'll go with me. How can I ever thank you?"

"You can cook me a good dinner on it. The poor thing hasn't been properly used in ages."

"It's a date!" I pecked her cheek and returned to my seat, feeling giddy about my new old stove.

"Katy, Royce expects to make partner in his firm this year," said Ruby. "Isn't that wonderful?"

I nodded. "Yes, it is. Congratulations, Royce."

He set his cup down and laughed modestly. "It just means I have no time for a personal life."

"Royce, you're not getting any younger, you know," said Betty. "Tick-tock."

It was time for me to rescue the poor guy. "Royce? Do you like pizza?"

"Love it. Who doesn't? Do you know a good place?"

I propped my elbows on the table, looking like I wanted to devour him. "As a matter of fact, I do. Are you free tonight?"

Ruby choked on her coffee, coming very close to doing a classic sitcom beverage spew across the table.

I patted her back. "You okay, Granny? Coffee too hot?"

She coughed a few more times, sputtering, "I'm fine."

"Maybe we can go to the movies, too." Royce arched a brow, winking seductively. "You know… Make a night of it."

———

When I got home, it was quiet across the street. I went over anyway. I'd rather state my case when I'm not fuming. No one answered the door. I wrote a cordial note and put it in their mailbox. With hope, they'll get the message.

CHAPTER THREE

TUESDAY • JUNE 2

Posted by Katy McKenna

Guess who called first thing?

"How did your date go?" asked Ruby, without even a "hello."

I moaned. "Ooo. It was magically romantic."

"Tell me everything."

"We shared a pizza. Turns out, we both love vegetarian pizza."

"Ooo. How *romantic*," she said, sounding snarky. "Then what?"

"He loves kids and so do I. He wants to have at least five or six." I was gushing at this point. "Wouldn't it be wonderful to have that many kids?"

"It costs a lot to raise a child these days, you know."

"Not a problem. Royce makes like half a mil a year, and will make even more when he makes partner."

"Really?"

"Yup." I sighed. "It's amazing how much we have in common. We both drive Volvos, although his is new. And here's something really funny. Wait—hold on a sec. It's really noisy here. The jerks across the street are disturbing the peace again." I went into the hall bathroom, shut the door, turned on the fan, and sat on the toilet lid. "That's better. Where was I?"

"You said, 'Here's something funny.'"

"Oh, yeah. You'll never guess what else we have in common."

"What?"

"Men."

"*What?* What did you just say?"

"You heard me. Today he's coming out to his Nana." Before Ruby could muster a reply, I said, "Gotta go. Someone's ringing the doorbell. Bye!"

I peeked through the peephole and saw Nina, looking summery in a yellow dress. I opened the door, hollering, "Wow! Can they turn up the music any louder?"

"I hope not."

"You want a cup of coffee? I have a fresh pot on the stove." In the kitchen, I brandished the glass Pyrex percolator. "This was my Aunt Edith's pot. I brought it home from England."

"I haven't had real, honest-to-goodness percolated coffee in ages. You know, I used to have a pot like that way back when." She laughed. "I think everyone did."

I poured our coffees, cleared the mail off the kitchen table, and we sat.

After a few sips, Nina sighed. "Sure beats coffee pods."

I told her about the note I left in Randy and Earl's mailbox yesterday. "Obviously no one read it."

"Or they don't give a hoot." She set her mug down. "I just tried to talk to them before I came here, and they told me to—" She dropped her voice to a whisper. "F-off."

"Are you kidding? That doesn't sound like something Randy or Earl would say to you."

She shook her head. "It wasn't them."

I topped off our mugs, and then peered out the window over the sink. "I don't know who those guys are. Did Randy and Earl move out while I was in England with Ruby?"

"No, they still live there. I have no idea who those ruffians are."

"Well, I'm going to have a little chat with them."

"Maybe you shouldn't, Katy. No telling what they might do if you rile them up."

"We can't be afraid to live in our own neighborhood. If you want, you can stay with me until you move to Shady Acres, so you won't be alone. I have a spare bedroom."

"What a thoughtful girl you are. But I'll be fine. In fact, my niece, Donna, is coming on Tuesday from Ketchikan, Alaska for a few days."

"Isn't that where your sister, Linda, lived?"

"Yes, Linda, and her husband had a business way back when— sightseeing plane rides." She pressed her lips, looking solemn. "Bob and their younger daughter died in a plane crash in the early seventies. Donna was one of the few survivors." She stopped, shaking her head. "His body was never found, and little Trudy's washed ashore a day later."

"That is so heartbreaking. How old was Donna?"

"Ten. Luckily, she has no memory of the crash. The last time I saw her was at Linda's funeral. Ten years ago. She had emphysema. When it got bad, Donna moved in to take care of her. Donna is widowed, but that's a story for another day." She sighed. "This will sound awful, but I was relieved when Linda passed away much sooner than expected."

"I don't think it's awful. You didn't want your sister suffering. Has your niece ever been here for a visit?"

"Not since she was twelve. I took her to Disneyland and Knott's Berry Farm. Oh, my goodness. We had such fun! That was at least fifty years ago. Where does the time go? These days, she's so swamped with her writing that it's hard for her to take time off. I am really looking forward to her visit. She's the daughter I never had."

"Donna is a writer? How exciting. What does she write?"

"Murder mysteries. *The Ketchikan Kulinary Kapers*." She tilted her head, lifting her eyebrows. "They're an interesting read, to say the least. To be honest, they're not really my cup of tea." Nina took her mug to the sink. "I need to go home and let you get on with your day."

I walked her to the door. Before I opened it, I said, "Sounds like things have quieted down across the street, but I'm walking you home anyway."

"I won't say no."

I opened the door and she slipped her arm through mine.

Warning to Mom if you're reading this post!

I know you hate vulgar language.
So you might want to skip the rest!
It's bad!

We were on the porch when loud, offensive language erupted in the house across the street. "My fucking old lady is so fucked up. I'm fucking going to break up with that fucking bitch."

"Hey!" I yelled at the top of my lungs. "Close your damned windows. Nobody wants to hear your foul language."

They didn't, and several more lines seared our ears. I couldn't help marveling at how many clever ways they could insert the "f" word into a single sentence.

"I fuckin' hate your fucking guts, you big fat fuckbutt."

"That's it!" I stamped my foot. "Nina, why don't you sit on the porch swing while I deal with this? It may get ugly."

"Katy, we're in this together!" She looked expectantly at me. "What's the plan?"

"Wait here." I high-fived her, then went into the house, and grabbed my dictionary off the bookshelf. The big old Webster's Dictionary. Hardback. Four inches thick. Over six pounds of glorious words that makes an ideal toddler's booster seat.

I took her arm, and we marched across the street, halting midway in the front yard weeds. Another vocal stream of vulgarity assaulted us, and then I let loose. "Hey! We are fucking sick and tired of hearing the word fuck! And all your other bad words, too." Then to my sidekick, I said, "I'm sorry."

She grinned at me, and then yelled, "Is fuck the only fucking word you lowlifes know?"

The screen door creaked opened, and a paunchy slob in a sleeveless dirty white t-shirt stepped onto the porch. "You bitches gotta problem?"

That knocked the air out of me for a moment, and then I exploded. "Oh, yeah! We gotta problem, all right. A problem with you! You and your friends use the f-word as a noun, a verb, and an adjective. And you share it with everyone on the block, whether we like it or not. And believe me, we don't like it! There are kids in this neighborhood. There are sweet old ladies on this block. *I'm* on this block! And we are all sick and tired of listening to your fucking, foul, filthy language."

Nina shook her fist. "Yeah! Sick of it!"

We were on a roll and it felt so good! I climbed the wood steps and got in his face. "You must be the big, fat fuckbutt we all heard about earlier." I slammed the giant dictionary into the man's flabby gut, and he doubled over. "Here, take this. You obviously need it more than I do. There are thousands of words in this book. Try learning a few." Fearing he might clobber me, I hastily retreated to Nina's side.

"And another thing," said my friend. "You can't repair motorcycles in a residential neighborhood. It's against the law. So stop that, too, or we're calling the cops, you mother-fu—"

"I think we've made our point, Nina. Time to vamoose."

Like the bad-asses we are, we swaggered over to Nina's house and had a nice cup of tea.

After Dinner

I got on Amazon to hunt for Donna's mystery series. I searched

"Ketchikan Culinary Capers," not realizing it all started with a K. How "klever."

There are nine books in her series, and she has thousands of five-star reviews. Her name is Donna Baxter, and she's drop-dead gorgeous. I ordered the first one—*The Kupkake Kaper*. I'm excited to meet a real author—so I thought it would be nice to say I'm reading her book. Too bad she can't autograph an eBook. I would've ordered the paperback if she were staying longer than a few days.

I poured a glass of wine and got cozy on the couch with Daisy to begin the book.

The Kupcake Kaper
Chapter One

Patsy Kramer was a very pretty, petite young woman with thick wavy brown hair that she was always tucking behind her pixie ears, and she had been in love with her husband Larry since the first time she set eyes on him in freshman chemistry class.

The doorbell rang. Daisy scrambled to the entry, woofing. I checked the peephole and saw Randy and Earl. *Great. Not in the mood for another confrontation.* "Daisy! Quiet! Sit." I opened the door to two very shamefaced brothers. Randy, the older and taller of the two, held out a pretty bouquet of orange and yellow gerbera daisies, and Earl gave me a bottle of white wine and my dictionary.

"We heard what happened this morning, and we want to apologize," said Randy. "We didn't realize how bad things had gotten when we're at work. It won't be happening any more. Right, Earl?"

Earl shoved his hands in his pockets, looking downcast. "Yeah. It's my fault. I let a friend hang out because his parents kicked him out of the house, and I guess he took advantage of the situation."

Randy jabbed his arm. "Cody isn't a friend. He's a freeloading slacker and so are all of his loser friends."

"Randy's right," said Earl. "Anyway, we told them they aren't welcome anymore."

I set the gifts on the entry table, and gave them both a hug. "That's good to hear."

Earl knelt to give Daisy a love, then glanced up at me. "If you ever need help with anything. You know, like lifting heavy stuff."

Randy pointed at Veronica, my 1976 Volvo wagon sitting in the driveway. "We can do car work, too. No charge, except for, you know, parts."

"Thank you, guys. Your apology means a lot. One of these days, I might take you up on your offers."

"We apologized to Mrs. Lowen, too," said Earl. "I mean, Nina. She told us to call her that."

"She said it sounds like we're turning over a new leaf," said Randy. "I've never heard that before, but I think it's a good thing."

Bedtime

I climbed into bed, propped myself up with pillows, and opened my iPad to start *The Kupcake Kaper* again.

The Kupcake Kaper
Chapter One

Patsy Kramer was a very pretty, petite young woman with thick wavy brown hair that she was always tucking behind her pixie ears, and she had been in love with her husband Larry since the first time she set eyes on him in freshman chemistry class.

Patsy's grandmother had taught her to bake when she was just a little girl, and she was always joking that that was the reason that Larry had fallen in love with her.

One day, a few years after they were married, while making a batch of chocolate-coconut cupcakes in the kitchen of their cozy cottage up on a hill overlooking the quaint town of Ketchikan, Alaska, she told Larry that she had always wanted to open a bakery, and he thought that was a great idea. So great, in fact, that he decided he would quit his job at the grocery store that very day, and be partners with her.

"*Oookaaay*. Is it me, Daisy? Or is this bad?"

Daisy lifted her head and gave me her solemn, wise Yoda look.

"Listen to this. Patsy Kramer was a very pretty, perky, petite young woman with thick wavy—"

My astute pooch scratched her ear, and then settled her head back down with a long sigh.

"So it's not just me."

I read the Amazon reviews for the book and was shocked at all the four and five-star reviews. 1,294 reviews—and most were five stars.

- *I can't wait to read the other books in this new series!*
- *If I could give this book 10 stars, I would.*
- *Already bought all the books in the series!*
- *My new favorite author! And the chocolate-coconut cupcake recipe in the book is yummy!*

CHAPTER FOUR

WEDNESDAY · JUNE 3
Posted by Katy McKenna

Did you know you can lose a pound of fat a week just by walking 10,000 steps a day? I'd like to shed about ten pounds, so I bought a FitTrim Step Tracker. I figure I can easily knock the weight off in about ten weeks—no sweat. That's seventy days times 10,000 equals 700,000 steps. There are approximately two thousand steps in a mile, so that's 350 miles. No sweat!

After a shower, I tousled my layered bob bedhead with a blast from the hairdryer and dressed in my everyday uniform—jeans, T-shirt, and canvas slip-ons—and strapped on the FitTrim.

I cleaned up the kitchen, didn't make my bed, watered the limp houseplants, then checked the step tracker. "517 steps? Is that all?"

My phone tinkled a text alert. My heart flipflopped when I saw it was from Josh. I feared it was bad news about Nicole.

Hi Cookie. Have you met my cousin, Dillon, yet? He's a college student and is housesitting for me. Let me know if he's throwing wild parties. Every-thing the same here. Miss you more than I can say.

I sank into my big comfy chair by the French doors feeling

flummoxed. I was relieved it wasn't bad news. However, it is amazing how a few words can tank a good mood. As if on cue, my dog sauntered into the room and nuzzled my legs.

"Hey, Daisy. Wanna go for a walk?"

She dashed to the basket by the front door where I stow her harness.

"I take it that's a yes." On the porch, I commanded, "Daisy, sit."

Clearly not pleased with the command, she took her own sweet time setting her rear end down. I inhaled a deep breath, willing my lousy mood to fade away. The sky was a brilliant blue, and the air was perfumed with honeysuckle. A soft breeze caressed my face like butterfly wings. How could I be gloomy on such a beautiful, sunny day?

"Okay, let's go." She catapulted off the porch and dragged me to the sidewalk where we hung a right. I'd been avoiding that direction for a while, but if Josh and I are going to be friends, then I need to be a good neighbor and keep an eye on things for him.

"Slow down, Daisy. This isn't a race." She took the hint and started sniffing the dandelions popping through the sidewalk cracks, while I inspected Josh's two-story redwood shingled Craftsman. Nothing looked amiss. After texting a photo to him, we crossed the street and headed back down Sycamore Lane. We passed by Randy and Earl's and all was quiet. I saw Nina, dressed in jeans, a blue striped blouse, and a straw hat, standing in her front yard next to a large woman wearing a sleeveless orange muumuu. Nina beckoned me over.

I opened the gate into her charming picket-fenced English garden. A small dog yipped at us from behind the front screen door.

Nina took my hand. "Katy, I'd like you to meet my niece, Donna Baxter Morgan."

The older woman looked nothing like the glamorous young woman on her Amazon author's page. I hoped the shock didn't show on my face as I shook her rough, beefy hand. I'm 5'9", and it's not often I meet women taller than me. She had to be pushing six feet.

"I'm Katy McKenna. It's a pleasure to… Daisy, stop pulling! Sit! Sorry about that, Donna. I live two doors that way." I pointed down the block. "The yellow house."

She patted Daisy's head. "It's nice to meet you, Katy. Actually, I dropped the Morgan and am using my maiden name now. Baxter."

Nina looked surprised. "You didn't tell me you changed your name."

"I did it recently, Auntie."

"Well, good for you."

The yapping dog in the house was pawing furiously on the wood framed screen door, making it rattle on its hinges.

"Did you get a dog, Nina?" I asked.

"No, that's Donna's dog, Baby Girl."

"Excuse me?"

Nina smiled. "The dog's name is Baby Girl."

"Oh. Got ya. Cute. How's your cat, Mr. Snickers, doing with Baby Girl?"

She huffed a sigh. "At the moment, he's hiding in my closet."

Donna dismissed her with a wave of her hand. "Your cat will adjust. Before you know it, they'll be best buddies." She moved to the brick porch steps and sat with a grunt. "My feet and ankles are swollen, probably from the long flight." I glanced at her puffy feet jammed into ratty-looking, open-toe sheepskin slippers. "Can't get my shoes on."

"Nina told me you write murder mysteries. In fact, I have the first one on my tablet. *The Kupcake Kaper.* I'm really looking forward to reading it. It has a lot a great reviews." I failed to mention that I'd already read the first chapter a couple days ago and had not read any further. "How exciting it must be to be a writer."

Her florid face lit up with a broad smile. "Thank you. Although I don't know if exciting is the right word to describe the life of a writer. More like exhausted hermit. That reminds me. Aunt Nina, is it okay if I use your desk? I need to work on my latest book—*The Kannoli Kaper*." She mopped her drippy brow on her hairy forearm. "Is it always so hot here?"

It wasn't hot—low eighties at the most. Maybe that's hot for a Ketchikan resident.

"Let's get out of the sun." Nina led the way up the steps to the white wicker chairs on the covered porch.

Donna opened the screen door and scooped up her wiggly, long-haired black dog. "Baby Girl. Calm down!"

"She's so cute," I said. "What is she?"

"A malti-poo mutt." Donna sat and cuddled her bouncy dog.

Daisy strained on her leash towards the dog.

"My girl wants to meet her. Is that okay?" I said.

She looked reluctant. "Baby Girl isn't used to dogs. But I suppose she needs to learn."

While the pooches indulged in a get-to-know-you-sniff-a-thon, Donna said, "I wonder why I'm so hot? I can't even blame menopause because I had a hysterectomy over twenty years ago while in my forties."

"You're probably still worn out from the plane ride," said Nina. "Do you want to lie down for a while?"

"No, I'm fine."

I was hungry for lunch and ready to leave, but that might have seemed rude. I tugged Daisy's leash. "That's enough sniffing. Come and lie down." Snapping my fingers, I pointed at the painted wood floor in front of my chair. "Are you married, Donna?" As soon as I said that, I felt like a dope, remembering Nina telling me she was widowed.

She shook her head. "No. My husband passed several years ago. Car accident."

"I'm sorry." Those words always sound so empty, but what else could one say?

"Don't be. Gary was a bastard. For starters, I wanted kids, and that turd got a vasectomy without telling me."

"That's awful!"

"Tell me about it. I had no idea why I wasn't getting pregnant. When I found out, I felt so…so betrayed. I wanted to kill him. I should've divorced him right then and there."

As if on cue, a very pregnant mother strolled by on the sidewalk, escorted by a cute towheaded toddler on a squeaky red tricycle. With one hand cradling her swollen belly, the mom waved at us.

"Why didn't you?" I asked.

She shifted in her chair, gazing after the passing mom and child. "We had a long history that stupid me wasn't ready to give up on. We'd been high school sweethearts—voted cutest couple in our senior year." Donna snickered, fluffing her straggly bleached-out hair. "Look at me now. Hard to believe I was ever half of the cutest couple, huh?"

"I can see it." *No, I can't.*

"We had a thriving bakery. Splitting up would've meant selling the business. I didn't have much love left for Gary, but I did love the bakery, so I tried to make the best of a bad situation. However, over time, things went from bad to worse."

Nina shook her head with a grimace. "You can sure say that again. The man should have been shot. I remember how upset my sister was."

A blue jay screeched in the towering old sycamore tree that shaded the yard.

"Sorry to interrupt, but duty calls." Nina opened a plastic container that was under her chair, and placed a row of peanuts on the porch rail. "Jasper! Come get your peanuts!"

With a loud squawk the bird swooped down and landed on the rail. After a cautious glance at us, he carefully studied his choices, then grabbed one of the peanuts and flew off.

"He hides them around the yard," said Nina. "I'll miss that rascal when I move. I'm sorry I interrupted your story, Donna."

"No worries." She snuggled her dog. "Thank goodness I have you, Baby Girl." Her phone rang in her muumuu pocket. She glanced at the screen. "I've got to take this. I'll keep it short."

Donna walked to the far end of the porch before answering the phone. I don't know why she did that, since we could clearly hear her.

"Hi, honey," she said.

Nina glanced at me with a quizzical look and whispered, "Honey?"

Donna went on. "I'm in the middle of a conversation with my aunt and a neighbor. We're talking about Gary." She paused. "I miss you, too. I'll call you later, okay? Bye-bye."

Donna returned to her seat and settled Baby Girl in her lap. "Sorry about that."

"Who was it?" asked Nina.

"My best friend, Michelle. We've been besties forever. She was never a fan of Gary."

"My best friend couldn't stand my ex, either," I said.

"You know what they say," said Nina. "Love comes and goes but true friendship lasts forever."

"I like that," said Donna. "So where was I in my Gary saga? Oh, yeah. When I was in my forties, I started having pelvic pain, which I mistook for bad cramps. I figured I was going into my peri-menopausal years, so I didn't worry about it."

"My mother is going through that now," I said. "Definitely not something I'm looking forward to."

She shook her head. "Oh, how I wish it had been peri-menopause."

My stomach was growling, but I had to hear the end of her story. "What was it?"

"Pelvic inflammatory disease. My darling husband had given me chlamydia. If I'd gone to the doctor sooner, it probably could have been treated with antibiotics. But it had spread, and I had to have a hysterectomy."

Given everything this guy had done, I was surprised they had maintained a physical relationship. I've heard of people having horrible marriages but staying together because the sex was good. Wouldn't be my choice, though.

Donna continued. "That's when I finally went to see a lawyer. He assured me that I would get everything: the bakery and the house."

"The story gets even worse, Katy," said Nina.

"How is that possible?"

Donna snorted and got another kiss from her dog. "After I filed for divorce, he moved in with his girlfriend."

"Sounds familiar," I said. "My ex moved in with his girlfriend after I nursed him through cancer. But you win for worst betrayal."

"Lucky me. Anyway, one day I get a call from my lawyer, and he says he has something to tell me, but I better sit down first." Arching a brow, she took a dramatic pause, and I leaned forward in my seat. "Turns out he'd gambled all our retirement savings away and incurred a mountain of credit card debt. Of course, it wasn't long before the debt collectors went after me because we were still legally married."

Her outrageous story was like something out of the soap opera my mom and Ruby watched for decades. *All My Family*.

Jasper returned to the railing. Before selecting another peanut, he monopolized the conversation for a moment, squawking and ruffling his feathers, and then off he flew with his stash.

Nina removed her hat and ran her fingers through her flattened hair. "Tell her about the girlfriend."

"You'll love this. Tami—that was her name—came a-knockin' on my door one day a few weeks after Gary died."

"Wait, a sec. Were you still married when he died?"

"Yes. The divorce wasn't final yet. Anyway, this Tami bitch says she wants a memento of her darling Gare-Bear. Well, I gave

Tami a memento, all right." She eyed me, waiting for me to say…

"What did you give her?"

Donna beamed triumphantly. "His ashes in an old Vlasic pickle jar. You should've seen her face. As I handed it to her, I said, 'I hope you and Gare-Bear will be very happy together.'"

I cracked up. "I wish I could've seen her face."

While listening to Donna's astonishing tale, I kept trying to place where I'd seen her before. She looked familiar, but I knew we had never met.

She patted her pup's back. "Sorry about all that. It's been quite a while since I've talked about it."

"No problem," I said. "It makes my own bitter saga seem not quite so awful."

"There is a silver lining to the story," she said smiling.

"What could there possibly be?" I asked.

"I collected his life insurance—"

"Which certainly helped," said Nina.

Donna nodded. "Yes it did. We both had policies. Never in a million years did I think I'd collect that."

"You probably wouldn't have, if the divorce had been final," said Nina. "He undoubtedly would have made his girlfriend the beneficiary. Timing is everything, isn't it? You earned that money!"

"I suppose I did." Donna stroked Baby Girl's back, looking a hundred miles away for a moment. "Anyway, my heart was no longer in the bakery at that point, so I sold it for a healthy profit and paid off all of Gary's debts. I had plenty of money in the bank, and was ready for a new chapter in my life. I'd always enjoyed writing in high school and my best friend suggested I turn my Gary saga into a murder mystery. Of course, Gary wasn't murdered, but it was sure fun fantasizing about it. And even more fun making money from that fantasy."

"Now, I can't wait to read it," I lied. "How long are you staying? I'd love to have you both over for lunch, but the rest of this week I'm totally slammed." I expected a turn-down, since Nina had said the visit was only for a few days.

"Not really sure yet. I hope to do a few excursions if my aunt is up to it."

That doesn't sound like a few days. "Such as?"

"Go to Santa Barbara. Disneyland." She poked Nina's arm. "You up for that, Auntie?"

———

This evening I marched around the living room, racking up steps on the FitTrim, and watching a recorded show on The Food Channel. It went to commercial and when I fast-forwarded through the ads, a woman caught my eye. Curious, I rewound. It was a commercial for a show called *Ranch House Grub*, and the chef-host of the show reminded me of Paula Deen. I realized that's who Donna looks like. Paula Deen—if Paula didn't wear makeup, had ruddy skin, bristly eyebrows, weighed a lot more, and her hair was a straggly bleached out white-blonde bob with half-inch roots.

At bedtime, I still had 772 steps to hit my goal. So close and yet so far.

CHAPTER FIVE

THURSDAY · JUNE 4
Posted by Katy McKenna

Since Nina's niece will be hanging around for a while, I felt obligated to follow through on the invitation that brilliant me made yesterday.

I found my friend sitting on the porch cradling Mr. Snickers in her lap. Usually, Nina is very pulled together. Makeup, stylish clothes. But today, she wore a baggy T-shirt, faded black pants, no makeup (I had no idea her eyebrows and lashes were white), and looked gloomy.

"Hey, Nina," I called as I passed through the gate. I climbed the porch steps and sat next to her, stroking the leashed ginger tabby's soft fur. "You don't look very chipper."

"I'm a little pooped, that's all."

"How's the visit going?"

She blew out an exasperated sigh. "To quote Ben Franklin—guests, like fish, begin to smell after three days."

"It's only been two."

"Feels more like two months."

At the next house on the block, a yard service crew was blowing leaves into the street. They moved to the edge of Nina's property, and I had to yell to be heard over the machine. "What's she doing now?"

Nina shouted back, "She's out running errands, then getting a pedicure."

That poor pedicurist, I thought, remembering Donna's gnarly toes peeking out from her slippers.

"I had no idea she was bringing her dog. This morning I found Snickers cornered in the bathtub, shaking like a leaf. Donna thought it was funny. Funny!" She inhaled deeply and blew it out. "I tell you, this visit can't end soon enough for me."

The yard dudes finished and were stowing their equipment into their truck. I could still smell the gas fumes from the blowers, and they hadn't bothered to clean up the leaves they'd blown into the street.

"Donna should have asked before she brought her dog," I said.

"Yes, she sure should've. She says she goes nowhere without her *comfort* dog. Well, my *comfort* cat shouldn't be terrified in his own home."

"Where's the dog now?" I asked. "Getting a pedicure, too?"

"Taking a nap." Nina patted her cat. "She was worn out from chasing Snickers all morning."

"Not to change the subject—"

"Please do." Her gaze drifted across the street. "Will wonders never cease? There's Earl and Randy working in the yard. Such nice boys." She chuckled softly, looking more like the Nina I know. "What a difference a day makes, huh?"

"I'll say. Anyway, I came over to invite you two for brunch on Sunday."

"That sounds delightful, but I'll have to check with Donna. What time?"

"Does eleven or eleven-thirty work for you?"

"Better make it eleven. She's a late sleeper."

Nina's old, faded green Subaru Outback pulled into the driveway. Donna got out and lifted the back hatch.

I hollered, "Need some help?"

She waved. "No, I'm good."

I went to the car anyway. Donna was wrestling with a long, flat box, and the box was winning.

"Looks like it's stuck," I said. "I'll open the backseat door and see what it's caught on." I climbed in and heaved the box towards her. I got out and went to the back of the car. "You got a dog door?"

"It was on sale at Home Depot." She patted the cardboard box. "This is one of those dog doors that sit inside a sliding glass door. I have one at my house and love it. It'll make life so much easier if Baby can run in and out whenever she wants."

I glanced at Nina on the porch. "She's okay with that? I ask because I know her cat isn't allowed loose outside."

"He's so timid; I doubt he'll ever even try to go through the flap. Personally, I think it's awful to keep a cat cooped up in the house like a prisoner."

I have a dog door so I can leave without worrying about Daisy needing to go outside and do her business. My cat, Tabitha, uses it too. I worry about her safety, but I've never seen her leave the back yard. The bottom line is: it's my house and my choice to have the dog door.

Trailing her up the steps, I held one end of the heavy, cumbersome package, feeling like a traitor. "Nina. Look what Donna bought."

Her face froze when she saw the label, and she clutched Mr. Snickers tighter.

Donna said, "Baby Girl tends to have accidents in the house if she can't get out, so this will really help."

I furrowed my brow at Nina and cocked my head, trying to convey—*"You need to say something."*

She grimly shook her head, looking away.

We toted the box to the slider in the living room, and laid it on the floor. Her little furball raced into the room, all wiggly and delirious to see her mommy.

"Der's my sweet, widdle baby-waby. Mommy missed ooo." The dog jumped into her arms and Donna nuzzled her. "Give Momma some sugar."

"I'd offer to help install the dog door, but I have to go." I fled the room without giving her a chance to answer. Then I knelt in front of Nina on the porch and set my hands on her knees. "You need to say something. I mean, who does something like this?"

"Apparently, my niece does." She patted my head. "You're a good girl, Katy. If I had a daughter, I'd want her to be just like you."

Late Afternoon

I needed about a billion more steps to reach my daily goal, so I clipped on Daisy's harness, and we headed out the door. Across the street, Randy was stoking the rusty oil drum BBQ that has been in the yard since the day they moved in. A boombox sat in the recently whacked weeds, softly playing new-age yoga music. He waved, and then with palms pressed together at heart center, he bowed. I returned the wave, thinking, *Did he just namasté me?*

Cars were lining up on both sides of Sycamore Lane, with all occupants streaming into Josh's house. I saw Randy do his "namasté thing" to anyone who glanced his way. One of them yelled, "That's cool. Whatever, yoga dude."

I patted Daisy's head. "Looks like there's gonna be a party, and we weren't invited."

We walked for several blocks, then returned home to find the next door festivities had spilled out into Josh's back yard. Hip-hop and rap tunes were cranked up to ear-splitting, with everyone shouting to be heard over the music. Namasté Randy had adjusted his yoga music volume in retaliation. Let me tell you, it was an annoying mashup.

I had a couple of options.

One: call the cops and probably get told to do the neighborly thing and ask them to turn it down. The thought of pounding on Josh's front door yelling, "Turn down the damned music!" did not appeal to me. I doubt they would have heard me, anyway.

Two: pour a glass of wine, put on my headset, and watch a Netflix movie.

Guess what I chose?

CHAPTER SIX

SUNDAY · JUNE 7
Posted by Katy McKenna

Brunch

When I opened the door to greet my guests, Nina said, "Sorry we're a little late."

Her niece, outfitted in an ankle-length red-flowered sleeveless muumuu, hung back on the sidewalk, clutching Baby Girl under an arm, and chatting on the phone.

"Donna's talking to her best friend, Michelle. Those two never seem to run out of conversation." She sighed. "Makes me miss my best friend. Shirley. Oh, how we could gab. The two of us would lose all track of time."

I held the door wide and waved her in. "I know what you mean. Samantha and I never seem to run out of things to talk about."

Nina yelled at Donna, "I'm going in."

She waved. "Be there in a sec."

I hollered, "The door's unlocked," then began to shut it. I

stopped when she dropped her phone into her purse and headed up the walk.

In the entry area, Nina sneezed a couple of times. "Excuse me."

"Gesundheit. Gotta cold?"

"Either that or hay fever. Hard to tell. Probably allergies." She tugged a tissue from her sweater sleeve to dab her nose.

Donna stepped inside and I gave her a hug. "Good to see you again."

"Thank you for inviting us over." She set down her wriggly mutt.

Baby Girl spotted Tabitha loitering in the hall and tore after her, shrieking like a crazed banshee. I chased after and found my freaked-out cat perched on my dresser yowling at the dog. Donna entered the bedroom just in time to see Tabitha reach down and wallop Baby Girl's snout. Score one for Tabitha!

Glaring at me like it was my fault, Donna sat on the bed, cradling her bawling dog like an infant. "Did that nasty old cat hurt my widdle pwecious?"

The commotion brought Daisy bursting into the house through the laundry room dog door. She beelined to my bedroom, leaped onto the bed, and shoved her nose into Baby Girl's tush.

"Stop that, you nasty dog," shouted Donna, twisting away. "Leave my baby alone."

With the promise of a cookie, Daisy trailed me to the laundry room. I grabbed a cookie from the jar on the shelf above the washing machine and tossed it through the dog door. She followed, and I slid the cover in place. I was fuming and would have preferred to be in the back yard with my pooch, but I behaved for Nina's sake and joined the ladies in the living room.

"Who's ready for a mimosa? I know I am."

Donna was now sitting on the sofa, still cuddling her whimpering mutt. "We could use a mimosa. Couldn't we, Baby?"

Nina rolled her eyes in my direction and followed me to the kitchen. "Let me give you a hand."

Acting jovial, I mixed a batch of mimosas in a glass pitcher, tasted it, added more orange juice, and tried it again. "Works for me."

Nina whispered, "I told her not to bring her dog, but would she listen?"

"Don't feel bad. It's not your fault."

I filled a champagne flute and offered it to her, noting the slight tremble in her hand. "Are you sure you're up to being here?"

"Yes. I took some daytime cold medicine, but it tends to make me jittery." She tasted her mimosa. "Mmm. Delicious. I'd better take a few more sips before walking with this, so I don't spill."

The oven timer dinged, and I pulled out a sizzling frittata.

"Oh my, that looks appetizing. What's in it?"

"Roasted veggies, eggs, and cheese," I said. "It's an old *Barefoot Contessa* recipe."

"I rarely cook these days. Usually I nuke Stouffer's or Healthy Choice frozen meals. Donna's been cooking since she arrived so I'm eating well." She sneezed a few times and pulled her lavender cardigan closed. "It must be a cold. I hope you don't catch it. Better take some vitamin C just in case."

"I will. Has Donna said anything about how long she's staying?"

Nina shook her head. "No. We better get back in there or she's going to wonder what's happened to us."

I led the way into the living room. "Here ya go, Donna. Enjoy."

"Thank you." She sipped her drink. "De-lish. Baby Girl, try this."

"Donna? It has alcohol in it. Not sure that's good for her." Watching the dog slurp the cocktail, I sat on an easy chair across from the sofa.

"She's fine. I always share my drinks with her. Every night, we watch the evening news and drink a Jack and Coke. It's the only way we can stomach the news."

"Maybe stop watching the news?"

"I need to know what's going on in the lower forty-eight." Donna drained her glass and smacked her lips. "Ketchikan can feel very isolated at times. I love it there, but it's nice to get away for a while. The weather here is glorious. I checked the forecast back home, and it's raining all week. Ugh." She brandished her glass and said in a baby voice, "More, please."

I stood. "I don't know about you two, but I'm starving. I'm going to put the food out now. It'll just take a minute. I'll put the mimosa pitcher on the table so you can help yourself."

After setting the meal on the dining table, I refilled everyone's glass and placed the pitcher near Donna.

Nina yawned noisily. "I probably shouldn't drink another mimosa."

"Enjoy yourself, Auntie Nina," said Donna. "You can take a nap when we go home."

My neighbor sighed. "Seems like all I've been doing the last couple days is snooze." She chuckled. "Maybe I'm getting old."

"Maybe you should get a blood test," I said. "You know, check your thyroid, iron levels."

"You're fine, aren't you, Auntie?" mumbled Donna, through a mouthful of food. "I can only hope I'm as fit as you are when I'm your age."

Ha! That train has left the station. "Me, too. But still. I think it would be a good idea. You know, be proactive rather than reactive."

"I don't want to make a fuss," said Nina. "I'm sure it's just a cold."

"This frittata is de-lish." Donna shoveled a forkful into her mouth, then pushed a bite to the edge of her plate for her dog to lick up. "Baby Girl thinks so, too."

CHAPTER SEVEN

MONDAY • JUNE 8
Posted by Katy McKenna

The secret to happiness is low expectations.
~ Barry Schwartz ~

I took Barry's advice and lowered my step count to 4,500. But I swear I'll add steps every week until I'm back to 10,000. Oh, who am I kidding? Probably not.

My Morning Walk

Beer cans were strewn across Josh's lawn. I took a photo to send to him and made a mental note to pick them up after my walk. I zipped around the block and was passing by Nina's house when I spied Mr. Snickers prowling under the bushes in the front yard.

"Uh...oh. What are you doing out here, buddy?" I carried the docile feline to the front door and rang the bell. Donna opened the door. "Look who I found out front."

"You naughty cat. How did you get out there?"

All wide-eyed and innocent, I said, "The dog door, perhaps?"

My sarcasm was lost on Donna. She nudged open the screen door with her hip and reached for him. I tried to hand him over, but he'd attached his claws to my shirt. She drew him towards her while I disengaged each snagged nail.

"Is Nina here?" I asked, watching the cat squirm in her firm grasp.

"She's napping. Let's keep this between you and me. I don't want to agitate her. She's got a bad cold and—"

"Oh. So it was a cold and not allergies?"

"It really hit her last night. She's old and frail, and she has a weak heart, you know."

No, I didn't know that.

"So I don't want to take any chances. The last thing she needs is to get pneumonia again. At her age it could kill her. I've got her loaded up on vitamin Cs, zinc, Echinacea, and cold medicine."

"She's had pneumonia in the past?" I said.

"Yes. She has a tendency to get bronchitis and a couple times it turned into pneumonia. So we don't want to take any chances now."

"Shouldn't she go to the doctor? I'd be happy to take her."

"No point in that. There's nothing a doctor can do. Antibiotics don't work for a cold. She just needs plenty of bed rest and healthy food."

I shook my head. "She's never mentioned heart trouble to me."

"Auntie is a very private person and likes to keep personal matters like that in the immediate family." Donna was closing the door. "Thanks again for the lovely

brunch yesterday. I have to get back to work now."

I raised my voice. "Tell Nina I'll be by later to say hi."

"Will do." Click. Lock.

———

Afternoon

I kept my promise to drop by Nina's. Looking as unfashionable as ever in a plaid muumuu, Donna informed me that Nina was napping.

"Another nap?" I said.

"With her cold, she needs all the rest she can get." Donna bent over with a groan and picked up her dog. "Isn't that right, Baby Girl? Auntie Nina has a nasty cold and is vewy, vewy tired and needs her nappies."

"Please tell her I dropped by."

As the door swung shut in my face for the second time today, she said, "I will."

I shuffled out of the yard, slamming the picket fence gate behind me. "I can't wait for that rude woman to go home. Alaska can have her."

Randy called from his porch. "Are you all right, Katy?"

"No!"

He beckoned me over. The tattered sofa that had graced the yard for so long, now sat on the porch. The boys were lounging on it, sporting matching tie-dye shirts. A lavender-scented candle burned on a small round wood table, and a muscular brindle pit bull was wedged between them. As I approached, her beady cold gray eyes narrowed on me.

"This is Violet." Randy scratched her head, and she leaned into him with a happy groan. "We rescued her from the pound this morning. She'd been there for over a year."

Earl continued, "Yeah, her elderly owner died, and no one in the family would take her in. Can you believe that? She's twelve, which made it even harder for her to find a home. That's why we chose her."

"That was kind-hearted of you. May I pet her, Earl?"

"Sure. She's a big old love."

I reached out, wondering if I were going to lose my hand in

one big chomp of her massive jaws. She leaned towards it, took a sniff, and then slurped it. I moved closer and ruffled her ears. "You're a big old cuddle bear, aren't you? I'm glad you have a home now." She nuzzled my hand, and I took that as my cue to rub behind her ears. Daisy loves that.

"Would you like a cup of green tea?" asked Earl.

"That would be nice." *Am I in an alter-universe? Wasn't this the guy I saw smashing a beer can on his head not too long ago? Now it's lavender candles, green tea, and sweet old Violet.*

He uncrossed his legs and stood. "What do you take in your tea?"

"Sugar, and don't be stingy. I like it sweet." *Plus, I don't like green tea.*

"We don't have sugar. Is stevia or honey okay?" asked Randy.

"Honey. Lots."

"I'll be right back," said Earl.

"Why no sugar, Randy?"

"After you pointed out how shitty, oops, sorry, our language had become, we took a long, hard look at ourselves. Our lifestyle, eating habits, choice of friends—and we realized how toxic our lives were." He stroked Violet's massive head. "So, we've got our new friend here, dumped most of the old, and we've taken up yoga, meditation, and healthy eating. No more sugar because it inflames our bodies and is the root of all diseases. No caffeine, alcohol, gluten, grains, meat, dairy."

"That's a lot to give up all at once." I started to sit on the filthy couch in Earl's spot next to Violet, then thought better of it and perched on the porch railing. "So what does that leave?"

"We now eat a healthy, plant-based diet. I feel…" Randy took a long, cleansing breath. "Fantastic."

I eat a plant-based diet, too. Plus sugar, caffeine, wine, gluten, grains, dairy, fish, cake, pie, cookies, ice cream, and chocolate. Did I forget anything?

His brother returned with my tea. "Is the old lady across the street all right?"

"Earl, her name is Nina," said Randy. "You know that. Be respectful."

"Not really sure," I said. "She's got a cold."

"Who's the fat chunker stayin'—" Earl stopped in mid sentence. "Sorry, not cool."

"Nina's niece from Alaska. Donna Baxter."

"You don't sound like you like her," said Randy.

"Not so much." I drained my cup and slid my butt off the rail. "This has been lovely, but now I must run." I cupped Violet's enormous face in my hands. "It's been a pleasure meeting you. You and Daisy will have to have a play date."

The boys unfurled their crossed legs and stood. My first thought was they were going to hug me, but instead, they namastéd me, and in unison said, "I bow to the divine in you."

Yup, I definitely had stepped into the *Twilight Zone*.

CHAPTER EIGHT

TUESDAY · JUNE 9
Posted by Katy McKenna

My call to Nina's cell phone this morning immediately went to voice mail, so I dialed her landline. Of course, Donna answered.

"What?" she said.

Her cranky, abrupt answer ticked me off, but rather than answer in kind, I set my tone into snotty-hyper-chirpy mode. "Top o' the mornin' to you, Donna. It's Katy callin'. So good to hear your cheerful voice. Gorgeous day, huh?"

"Uh-huh. What do you want?"

"How's your darling Baby Girl?" *Gag. Really can't stand that name.*

That comment hit the right note and her tone softened. "She's good." Her voice veered away from the receiver. "Aren't you, Baby? You're such a good widdle girl. Yes, ooo are. You're mama's pwecious widdle baby." Then back to me. "You should see her. She's lying on her back in a sunny spot on the floor. So cute."

"Ahh. How adorable. Take a picture of the cutie and text it to me. How's Nina doing? May I say hello to her?"

"She's taking a bath right now. Normally she doesn't take baths

47

because there's no one to help her out, so this is a real treat for her. Me? I'm a shower girl. In and out."

Her dog started yelping in the background. I heard a familiar thwack-thwack sound that I couldn't place, and the barking faded.

"Uh-oh," she said. "Baby Girl just chased the cat out the dog door." Click.

I dashed to Nina's house in case Donna needed help catching the cat. When I got to the front gate, she was coming round from the back yard. I unlatched the gate and entered the garden. "I thought you might need some help. Do you know where the cat is?"

She pointed at an enormous blooming rose bush. "Baby Girl got him corralled under there. Good girl, Baby!"

The hysterical dog was poking her head into the bush, snapping and growling at the yowling cat.

"Donna! If you'll hold your dog, I'll try to get Mr. Snickers out."

She lumbered over to her crazed mutt and picked her up. "Do not scare the cat away, Katy, or there will be hell to pay with Aunt Nina."

I couldn't believe she'd said that to me—like it was my fault the cat was loose. Shaking my head and keeping my lips zipped, I got down on all fours and tried to coax the freaked cat to come to me. But he wasn't having it.

Donna pointed at the bush. "You need to get under there and grab him before he runs off."

"Easy for you to say," I muttered.

"What?"

"Nothing." I flattened to the ground, shimmied in close, keeping my eyes nearly shut to avoid having a thorn pop an eyeball, and reached out both arms. My hands were still several inches away from him.

Snicker's eyes were dilated to the point of looking cross-eyed. "It's okay, buddy. I'm not going to hurt you." I wriggled closer and grabbed the scruff of his neck. He struggled and scratched my arms as I dragged him out. Once free from the rosebush, I rolled onto my back, pinning him to my chest. I lay there for a moment, catching my breath.

"What're you waiting for?" snapped Donna, heading to the porch steps. "Let's get him in the house before he gets away from you."

I struggled to a sitting position. Snickers had gone limp, so I was able to stroke his body. "I'm so sorry. I know how scared you must be."

Donna had the front door open. "Come on!"

My back was to her and I yelled over my shoulder, "Not until you tell me the dog door is closed."

The screen door slammed. I got to my feet and climbed the steps to the porch.

Donna returned. "It's closed. Give me the cat."

I tightened my grip on Snickers. "I can bring him in."

"*Donnnaaa!*" called Nina from the bathroom. "I'm freezing. Where are you?"

"Coming, Auntie!" She snapped her fingers at me. "Cat, please? Hurry up. My aunt needs to get out of the tub."

I reluctantly handed over the miserable feline. "Please tell Nina I'll drop by later for a visit."

"Not a good idea."

A split second later, I was staring at the mahogany wood door.

CHAPTER NINE

WEDNESDAY · JUNE 10

Posted by Katy McKenna

It seems like all I'm posting about lately is Nina. I'm probably worrying way too much. If I had a job, or a life, I'd have other things to blog about.

Nina is an early riser. Usually she's puttering in her yard by eight. I figured that since she was feeling well enough to take a bath yesterday, she might be out this morning. I got halfway to the sidewalk and remembered the FitTrim. After strapping it on, I started again for Nina's.

I decided to loop around the block to rack up some steps. Passing by Josh's, I did a visual check. Everything looked in order. The cool morning air was invigorating, and I zipped along, thinking about my annoying experience with Donna yesterday. No wonder Nina was ready for her to go home just one day after she had arrived. So far, that woman has not earned any Brownie points with me.

I arrived at Nina's garden gate in record time. I didn't see my friend in the yard, so I rapped on the door—praying she'd be the one who answered.

The door opened and Donna took one look at me and rolled her eyes, not even attempting to hide her irritation. "Your little friend isn't up yet. And before you ask, the answer is no. Her cold is worse and she can't come out and play today."

I held out my hand to stop the inevitable slammed door. "Wait! You say her cold is worse? Do you think she has bronchitis? Maybe she should see her doctor."

Donna tilted her head and spoke to me like I'm a moron. "It's just a rotten cold. Nothing more. If I think she needs to see a doctor, I will take her." She began to close the door. "So go home and mind your own business."

————

While cussing up a storm, I poured a cup of coffee, dumped in three teaspoons of sugar, a splash of half and half, and a squirt of whipped topping. Still madder than hell, I went out on the front porch and slumped on the glider to call Sam.

"Hey, what're you up to?" she said.

"Not much. How about you?"

"Trying not to throw up."

My pregnant buddy sounded pathetic.

"That sounds fun. Not. Does that mean you're not up for going to lunch? There's something I want to pick your brain about."

"I'll be fine by then, but Casey will be with us. So it won't be a leisurely lunch. I have a long list of errands to do afterwards, anyway."

————

An hour later, Sam tooted her car horn in the driveway. I opened the passenger door and got a surprise when I saw her.

"I thought you were growing your hair out. You finally had the sides covering your ears, which is the hardest part when growing out short hair."

She ruffled the top. "It was driving me nuts. Last night while getting ready for bed, I thought I'd just trim the sides a little. The next thing I knew, there was a bunch of hair in the sink."

"You did a good job." I said.

"Meh. I called your mom this morning and made an appointment to clean it up and freshen the blond."

Before buckling in, I turned to say hi to her six-year-old son.

"Hi, Auntie Katy," he said solemnly.

"Hey! What's up, Gloomy Gus?"

"I'm not Gus. I'm Casey! And I want to go to the park, not do dumb errands."

"We can't always do what we want. Hey! We'll have fun because we're together."

Sam put the car in gear. "First stop, lunch."

"Where?" I asked.

"Benny's."

"I wanna go to McDonald's!" said Casey. "We never get to go there."

Sam calmly said, "We're going to Benny's because you can get a grilled cheese and I can get a salad. And Aunt Katy doesn't eat burgers."

"I hate grilled cheese."

I looked at Sam, silently mouthing, "Since when?"

She shook her head with a "who-knows" look. "Then you can get a burger or a PBJ, Casey."

"McDonald's!" yelled the six-year-old.

"One," said Sam.

He kicked the back of my seat hard. "McDonald's!"

"Two."

A softer kick, and he mumbled, "McDonald's."

"Two-and-a-half."

The kid clammed up.

I was dying to find out what would have happened if she had said, "Three."

———

Before launching into my Nina concerns, I waited until our lunches arrived. Sam usually reads my blog at bedtime, so the only encounter she didn't know about was this morning's. I briefed her on that and finished with, "What do you think I should do?"

Sam had just forked a big bite of romaine lettuce dripping in Ranch into her mouth, so I had to wait for her to chew and swallow. "How many days since Donna arrived?"

"A week ago Monday." I counted on my fingers. "Nine days."

"The last time you saw Nina was at your Sunday brunch? Right? So it's only been three days since you've talked to her. She was fine then, right?"

"She was tired and coming down with a cold."

"I'm tired, too. But I'm coming down with a baby."

"Aunt Katy?" mumbled Casey through a mouthful of grilled cheese. "I'm too tired to run errands."

"You probably need a very long nap," I said.

His face lit up and he giggled. "Just kidding! I'm not really tired."

We were seated by a window that overlooked the busy street. "Wow, Casey. Check out that truck driving by. It's huge."

"I'm gonna be a truck driver when I grow up, and drive a big truck just like that one," he said.

"I thought you were going to be a firefighter."

He nodded enthusiastically. "*And* a truck driver."

I reached across the table and tousled his blond hair. "What was I talking about, Sam?"

"You're worried about Nina."

"Right. I haven't *seen* her since Sunday, but I did *hear* her calling from the bathroom yesterday."

"Then you know she's okay. Nina is in her eighties and she's got a bad cold. So it is understandable why Donna keeps putting you off. But I gotta say, she is a real b-i-t-c-h."

"Ummm," said Casey. "You said a bad word, Mom."

"Spelling it doesn't count, Mr. Smarty Pants," she said.

"But why won't Donna let me see her?" I wiped the wet ring under my water and drank half the glass.

"*Uh, because* Nina is under the weather and is resting a lot?" she said.

I scowled at her.

"Don't give me that look."

"Yeah, Aunt Katy. Mom will put you in time out." Casey pushed his plate away. "I'm done eating. Can we go now?"

"Not until Aunt Katy and I are done talking." Sam pulled a coloring book and crayons from her bottomless mommy-purse. "Color me something pretty."

I continued. "My intuition tells me something is not right."

"I think you're looking for trouble where there isn't any."

I didn't like her answer, but I pondered it while I sipped my chocolate milkshake. "You're probably right. This is what happens when you have nothing going on in your life. You overthink everything."

"After all your horrible adventures, I can understand why you would worry. I also believe we should pay attention to our intuition. So, while I think you have nothing to worry about, I do think it would be a good idea to write everything down. In chronological order. Just in case this does turn into something."

"I have. In my blog."

"I mean a timeline from day one. On paper. No goofy stuff like in your blog. Just the facts."

"Okay." I nodded. "I can do that. Then what?"

"Keep trying to see her, and in another week or so, if that

woman is still putting you off, then I'd say it's time to do something," she said.

"Like what?"

"Like call social services."

Evening

I did what Samantha suggested. Wrote a timeline, starting from the day I met Donna. On paper, it didn't appear to add up to much. As things occur, I will continue to update the timeline.

CHAPTER TEN

THURSDAY · JUNE 11
Posted by Katy McKenna

Breakfast With Ruby
Benny's two days in a row! Lucky me!

"Scrambled eggs. Hash browns, crispy. Rye toast, extra toasty," I said to our server, Sheila, who looked years beyond qualifying for Medicare.

"Coffee? Orange juice?"

"Coffee with cream, please." I checked the sugar packet caddy. "I'll need more sugar, too."

"You got it." She grabbed the menus and said to Ruby, "I love your glasses. Be right back with your beverages."

Ruby took off her turquoise cheaters that hung on a southwestern-style beaded chain around her neck.

"Lately, you seem to have a pair of glasses to match every outfit," I said.

"There's a site online that has the cutest cheaters and chains for cheap. I figured that since I can't read a darned thing without them, and I'm always searching for them, I might as well make them a fashion accessory." She waited while Sheila placed our drinks on the table. "How's Nina doing?"

"Did you read yesterday's blog?"

Ruby sipped her black coffee and grimaced. "Wonder how many hours this has been sitting on the burner." She dribbled some cream into her cup. "I did read your blog."

"Then you're up to date."

"With Nina's history of pneumonia, she needs to be careful. When I was a little girl, my uncle Harold died from it. Aunt Eloise found him. Dead. In his recliner. She'd just got home from the annual Tupperware Jubilee in Florida. She was a top seller and made scads of money. I remember when she showed me the mink coat she'd earned." She shook her head with a wistful look. "I was only ten, but I knew I'd found my calling."

"So multilevel sales is in your DNA. That explains all the marketing schemes you've gotten into. Like E-Z Lips Stencils."

"Oh, God. Don't remind me. What a fiasco." She sighed. "Uncle Harold had contracted polio as a child, so he walked with crutches, but it never slowed him down. Such a delightful man. He was only fifty-six." She cleared her throat. "Anyhoo, considering Nina's age, I applaud her niece for taking good care of her." She took a swallow of coffee. "Yuck. You may have noticed I brought my laptop."

"I noticed. What're you up to? As if I can't guess."

She placed the computer on the table and slipped her glasses back on. "Maybe we'll find you a charming prince." She scooted over and patted the empty seat next to her. "Sit here and take a look at your profile."

"You're kidding. You set up my profile?" Feeling a little miffed, I shoved my silverware across the table and moved to her side of the booth.

"Somebody's got to get the ball rolling. You can change it if you don't like it."

Sheila set our meals on the table. "Anything else I can get you girls?"

"Tabasco would be great," said Ruby.

She extracted a bottle from her apron. "Enjoy."

Ruby scrolled on the track pad and clicked a couple times. She'd used my Facebook photo. I read my profile out loud while she doused her eggs with hot sauce.

"I love sunset walks on the beach. No, I don't. It's usually too cold. *I like a man who can make me laugh.* Oh, brother. *I'm a glass-half-full kind of gal.* I guess. Maybe. *I enjoy going out and staying in.* At least I'm flexible."

Feeling a tension headache coming on, I opened a grape jelly packet and spread the contents on my toast.

"Look! You already have three messages." She clicked the first one. "Okey-dokey. Let's see what Groovy Guy has to say."

"The fact that he calls himself Groovy Guy is a big enough turnoff for me. And he looks like he's in his fifties."

She read his tagline out loud. "Loves music, loves to dance."

I dropped my toast on the plate. "Where do I know that line? And why is it giving me chills?"

"Because we both read the book years ago. It's a Mary Higgins Clark about a serial killer who uses personal ads to lure his victims. Remember?"

"Oh, yeah. I wonder if this guy realizes this."

"We'll never know. Moving on. This next one is from Steve McDreamy." She was silent for a moment. "Never mind."

"Hold on. I want to read what McDreamy said. *I want to be your friend. Do you like friends with benefits?*" I wrinkled my nose. "He's got a mullet."

"Here's one more. You know what they say." She crossed her fingers. "Third time's the charm."

Shaking my head, I slowly closed the laptop. "I'm sorry, Grandma, but you have to admit, this is a little weird. Even for you."

She picked up her coffee, then set the cup down, looking contrite. "All right. I screwed up."

"I know you want me to be happy." I searched for words that wouldn't hurt her. "Here's the thing. I *am* happy. Yeah, I don't have a love life at the moment, but I don't need a man to be a happy, contented person. I never have. I have an amazing family." I looked her square in the eyes. "I have an unbelievable, wacky grandma whom I love with all my heart, even though there are times I'd like to strangle her."

"Like now?"

"Yes. Like now."

She shook her head with a half-smile. "But I was right about you being a glass-half-full kind of gal."

Afternoon

I was in the bathroom, organizing the makeup drawer when my FitTrim vibrated, pestering me to do 250 steps. "I hate this damned thing." I glanced at my girl, snoozing on the bathmat. "Hey, Daisy. Walk?"

Daisy was her usual delighted self at the mention of a walk. At least one of us likes the step tracker.

We halted at Nina's gate while I vacillated whether to knock on the door. Knocking won. Maybe I'm a glutton for punishment. Or maybe I'm a half-glass full kind of girl. Halfway up the walk, Daisy ripped out of my grasp and tore through the shrubbery. I chased after her and caught up in time to see Mr. Snickers leap over the fence that borders the vacant house between our homes.

"*Nooo!* Come back, Snickers!" I grabbed Daisy's leash and we raced next door to the yard gate. It was locked. I could see the slide bolt through the crack between the gate and the post.

In my back yard, I dragged a bench to the fence and climbed on board. "Mr. Snickers. Here, kitty-kitty-kitty." I listened for meows or rustling in the bushes. "Please, Mr. Snickers. Please come out. I know you're scared." *What was that?* I cocked my head, trying to crank up my hearing. "Was that a meow? Kitty?"

"Rrrraugh."

"All right, sweetheart. I'm coming in, and I'll take you home to your mama."

I flung my right leg over the top of the capped fence and shimmied myself into a sitting position, feeling sharp splinters dig through my jeans. Death-gripping the wood, I hoisted my left leg over. Directly beneath was a thorny scarlet bougainvillea that ran the length of the fence. With any luck, I could fling myself far enough to clear it and land on my feet.

I realized if I got hurt, no one would know where I am, so I called Samantha. "You will not believe this. I'm about to jump into my neighbor's back yard."

"*Ooo-kaay.* Why?" I told her, and she said, "You're going to kill yourself. I know you. You're a total klutz."

She was right about that. When we were kids, she'd climb a fence, and I'd crawl under. "Well, I'm going for it."

"All right, but if I don't hear from you in three minutes, I'm calling an ambulance."

"Give me twenty. Once I'm in, I have to find that darned cat." I jammed my phone deep into my padded bra. Then, holding my breath, I flung myself into the yard, landing my butt smack in the center of the spiky bush with a loud shriek.

Mr. Snickers tore out from under the deck, and catapulted over the back fence. I limped to the gate to discover I was trapped in the yard by a padlock hanging from the slide bolt. "This day keeps getting better and better."

I called Sam.

"You okay?" she said.

"Yes, and no. Do you have a hacksaw?"

———

Before reporting the cat's disappearance to Nina, I visited the owners of the yard he'd jumped into. The friendly folks escorted me into their gorgeous *Better Homes and Gardens* yard. We searched for him, but he was long gone.

On my way to Nina's, I peered under every bush and surveyed every tree and roof, continually calling his name. I arrived at her front door with a heavy heart.

"What do you want?" Donna's hair was freshly bleached to brassy-white, and styled into a hideous spiky do.

"First off—your hair! Wow!" I said.

"Thank you." Looking pleased with the uncompliment, she mopped her damp brow on her forearm, and I spotted her long stiletto-sharp purple and green plaid acrylics.

I grasped the screen door handle and pulled it wide open. "The reason I'm here is that I need to see Nina. It's terribly urgent."

"Sorry. No can do. She's already in bed. We had an early dinner, and she was exhausted."

"Is she doing okay? How's her cold?"

"Much better. The zinc really did the trick. Or maybe it was just allergies. Anyway, we had a big day." Donna furrowed her black bushy brows. "Hopefully, we didn't overdo it. We went shopping at Walmart. Then had our hair and nails done. Then a nice dinner."

"Your nails are really something. Very eye-catching." *Very hideous, too.* "Where'd you have dinner? It must have been early because it's only quarter after five now."

"Burger King. We love their Whoppers."

"Hey—who doesn't? Now that she's over her cold, I would imagine you'll be going home soon."

She shrugged. "As long as I have access to the internet, I can work anywhere, so I'm in no hurry. I can stay indefinitely." She started closing the door. "I'll tell her in the morning that you came by."

I put my hand on the door. "Wait. You need to know what I was going to tell Nina."

Donna widened the gap, gazing at me expectantly.

"I saw Mr. Snickers jump over the fence into the yard next door a little while ago."

"Oh, for crying out loud. That damned cat got out again?" Looking irate, she crossed her arms and leaned against the doorframe. "Say, does this have anything to do with your dog? I heard a dog barking out front earlier."

"We were walking by, minding our own business, and then Daisy spied Mr. Snickers in the front yard. So, yeah, she acted like a dog and barked."

She narrowed her eyes. "So it's your fault the cat is gone, huh?"

"No, it's *your* fault." My brain was screaming, *Shut up, Katy!* "You're the one who put the dog door in. Without Nina's permission, I might add."

"Okay, we're done here." The door was closing. I stopped the action with my foot.

"No, we're not. I need a photo of the cat so I can make flyers to put up around the neighborhood."

"I'll see what I can do. Now, if you don't mind," she glanced down at my doorstop foot, "I'd like to get back to work."

This Evening

I didn't want to wait until Donna scrounges up a photo of Snickers, which will probably never happen, so I found an image online that could be his doppelganger and posted it in the "Santa Lucia Lost and Found Pets" group on Facebook. I also posted on Craigslist. Fingers crossed!

CHAPTER ELEVEN

FRIDAY • JUNE 12
Posted by Katy McKenna

If at first, you don't succeed, try, try, try again.
~ *William Edward Hickson* ~

Afternoon

I figured that needing a photo of Snickers was a good excuse to try and see Nina again; however, standing at her front gate, I hesitated. I stood a good chance of getting rejected again.

Maybe if I had a treat. That's a neighborly thing to do.

I had a plastic bag of baked chocolate chip cookies stored in the freezer for cookie emergencies. I hurried home and dug them out. They looked like they had frost bite, but after prying them apart and heating in the toaster oven, they smelled delicious. I nibbled one and it was pretty good for a cookie that had been frozen for over a year.

Back at Nina's house, I rang the bell and plastered a cheery smile on my face. Donna took her sweet time. Just as my grin was wilting, she answered, holding Baby Girl and wearing a yellow terrycloth strapless romper that made me miss her muumuus.

"Hi, Donna. I thought I'd drop by and see if Mr. Snickers came back."

"Nope."

"Oh, no. I was so hoping. How is Nina handling it? She must be absolutely devastated."

"I haven't told her."

"You're saying she hasn't noticed that her cat is gone?"

Donna snuggled her dog. "Aunt Nina's memory is fading. I think she may have Alzheimer's."

My hand involuntarily scrunched the cookie bag. "She was sharp as a tack when you came for brunch."

"Was she? Really? Maybe you chose to ignore the obvious signs. She's elderly, so it's inevitable."

No it's not! I held up the mangled, greased stained paper bag of warm cookies. "I brought a treat. Fresh baked chocolate chip cookies. Maybe we could all have coffee?"

Donna shook her head. "Aunt Nina is a little under the weather today. Upset tummy, so no cookies for her. She's napping now." She opened the screen door wide enough to snatch the bag. "I'll give them to her when she's feeling better." She pulled a cookie out and tasted it. "Not bad."

"Did you find a photo of Mr. Snickers I can use for the flyers?"

"Not yet."

Did you even bother to look for one? "What's a good time to come back for one?"

"There isn't one." She shoved the rest of the cookie in her mouth and shut the door. Once again, her rudeness shocked me. You'd think I'd be used to it.

Across the street, Randy was waxing his car. I watched from the curb for a moment, thinking, *wax on, wax off.* He waved, so I crossed the street to say hi.

"Any luck seeing Nina?" he asked.

I shook my head. "No. Her niece seems to always have a reason why I can't. Today she says Nina is under the weather with a sick stomach. Yesterday it was all about how tired she was from getting her hair and nails done, shopping, and a *fancy* dinner at Burger King. She was so worn out that she was already in bed when I went over just after five. And the days before that, she had a cold."

Randy shook his head with a peculiar expression on his face. "Are you sure about the shopping and all that?"

"What do you mean?"

"Yesterday, I saw Donna leave in the morning and not return until late afternoon. I noticed that her hair was different when she got back. And she was carrying a Burger King bag. But Nina wasn't with her."

The minute I got home, I added everything to the "Nina and Donna Timeline."

CHAPTER TWELVE

SATURDAY · JUNE 13
Posted by Katy McKenna

Josh's housesitting cousin, Dillon, and his college buddies partied till dawn. Again. This morning I read the local noise ordinance online.

The noise ordinance for the City of Santa Lucia is a 24/7 regulation. Between 10:00 p.m. and 7:00 a.m., it is a violation to make or allow any loud noise that can be heard across your property line. Loud noise includes music and other sounds such as a TV, music, power tools, or voices at a gathering.

Evidently, Dillon thinks that three a.m. is a perfectly acceptable time to be blasting music. If you can call it that. Sorry, hip-hop and rap are not my thing. These thoughtless kids only think of themselves nowadays.

Whoa. Who am I? Where did cool Katy go?
She grew up, that's where. Just call me "Geezer Katy."

CHAPTER THIRTEEN

Posted by Katy McKenna

Lunch

Sam and I met at Suzy Q's. It's a vegetarian restaurant with a boho vibe, and the food is so good that even an ardent meat-lover like my dad enjoys eating there. We usually sit on the patio, but it was borderline hot, so we sat inside by a window.

Samantha sighed. "I needed a break. Spencer took the kids to the beach. Hopefully, he'll wear out Casey. I miss the days when he took an afternoon nap."

"You can always plunk him in front of the TV and let him play video games all day. That's what the cool parents do," I said, knowing I'd get a rise out of her.

"No! Are you crazy? It's not healthy for his developing brain." She stopped, giving me a peeved look. "Okay, you got me. Although there are days when I'd sure like to. I think kids should be outside playing. The Parks and Rec summer program starts tomorrow and he's signed up."

"He'll love it. We sure did."

"I hope so. Let's order first before we launch into a talking marathon," she said. "I'm starving. I've dropped a couple pounds, so I need to feed this baby." She patted her belly and opened the menu. "Let's see. What looks good?"

"Stand up a sec. Let me see your baby bump."

Sam stood, turned sideways, arched her back, and held her bright lime green top close to her body. "Not much to see yet."

A server came for our order. "Ladies! How's it going today? Did you see the specials on the chalkboard?"

"We did, and I'll have the avocado toast and the microgreens salad," I said.

"Excellent choice. The pickled onions on the toast are incredible."

"What? No fries?" said Sam. "I'm shocked. I'm going to have the grilled tuna burger with a dinner salad and an order of garlic fries."

The waiter took our menus and said he'd be back in a jif with our drinks.

"I'll split my fries with you." Sam leaned forward, elbows resting on the mosaic tiled table. "I read yesterday's blog this morning. Anything new today on Nina? Did her cat come back?"

"If he did, I wouldn't know." I beamed adoringly at her. "Sam? Best friend of mine? Did I tell you how great your hair looks?"

She rolled her eyes. "What do you want?"

"I have a huge favor to ask you."

"What?"

"The other day at Benny's, you said it's too soon to call social services, but Donna doesn't know that."

She grimaced. "Oh, boy. What kind of scheme are you concocting?"

"I want you to go to Nina's house and say you're a nurse—"

"Which I am."

"A geriatric nurse—"

"That's a pretty big stretch from maternity nurse."

"You're with social services, and you're doing your once-a-month check-in with Nina."

Her eyes darted around the crowded restaurant, probably trying to think of a nice way to say no. "When do you want this caper to go down?"

I felt excitement bubbling up. "You mean you'll do it?"

"Yes. There are so many cases of elder abuse that go undiscovered until it's too late. We need to be proactive." She glanced up at our approaching waiter.

"House-made lemonade for you," he said, with a smile of approval to Sam. And then plunked a water in front of me. "Flat tap for you."

"Thank you. Our city water is great!"

"If you say so. Your orders will be out soon."

I watched the water snob scurry away before resuming our conversation. "Could we do it this afternoon, Sam?"

"I love how you say, 'we.' I'll make you a deal. I'm willing to do it but not yet. I know I said it was too soon to call social services the other day, but what do I know? How many days has this Donna person been here now?"

"Let me think. She arrived on a Tuesday." I scrolled on my phone to the calendar. "We're at twelve days now."

"And the last time you actually saw Nina was your brunch?"

"Correct."

"So, it's only been a week since you've seen Nina. I often go months without seeing some of my neighbors. Plus, you heard her calling from the bathtub a few days ago, and other than being cold, she sounded fine, right?"

"Yes. But generally, if the weather is nice—"

"Which is pretty much all the time here," she said.

"True. Anyway, I usually see her out in the front yard when I walk Daisy. Puttering in the garden or sitting on the porch—reading a book, or talking to friends on her phone. Unless I'm in a rush, I always stop to say hi. A few days ago, Donna said she's pretty much over the cold, so why isn't she back to her normal routine? All I can think is Donna is—"

"What? Holding her prisoner?"

I shrugged, realizing how crazy that sounded.

"All right. I think it's definitely time to call social services and make a report about your concerns. Have you been writing everything down like I suggested, so you have something to refer to. Especially, if they ask a bunch of questions?"

"Yes, I have. Dates, times, all of it."

"Good. It'll make you sound credible rather than just a nosy neighbor."

"Good to know I'm a credible busybody."

"You know what I mean." Sam picked up her phone. "Hold on, I'm looking up elder abuse on the social services site." She scrolled the screen. "Here it is. Adult protective services. Types of abuse." She read for a moment. "I assume she is not being sexually assaulted or beaten."

"I can't imagine she's been sexually assaulted, but who knows about being beaten?"

"Lack of clean, appropriate clothes or linens?"

"I have no idea."

"Here's one that probably fits the bill. Caretaker isolates victim by restricting visits and phone calls—may not want to let someone into the home to speak to the victim."

"That's definitely happening."

She continued. "Caretaker is violent."

"Not to my knowledge, but who knows? She sure is rude with me."

"Rude is not violent. What about—medications used to restrain victims?"

"That certainly would explain the naps," I said.

"Or, she's resting because she is still recovering from a cold."

Sam plucked the mint leaves from her lemonade and sipped. "When you get home, call social services and make a report."

"It's Sunday, so I doubt anyone will answer."

"There's a number for after business hours. I'll text it to you now. If in a few days, you're still worried, we'll try it your way. Deal?"

"Do you think they'll call me after they check on her?"

"Not likely."

"Will they tell Donna it was me who called?"

She shook her head. "The website says all calls are confidential."

"All right, I'll call. But I doubt it will do any good."

I saw the server coming and put my hands in my lap. After he set down our meals and left, Sam said, "I have a favor to ask you, too."

I snatched a fry and doused it in the aioli. "Name it."

"Chelsea needs to practice driving. I get too freaked out. Plus, I don't want Casey in the car with that maniac, and Spencer is gone too much for her to get in enough practice to ever pass the test. So, you're it—Auntie Katy."

"No problem. Should be fun teaching the maniac."

She snickered. "Famous last words."

"I sure hope not!"

———

As soon as I got home, I called social services. As I relayed my concerns, I realized that I did sound like a busybody neighbor with too much free time on my hands. Next thing you know, I'll be sitting at my front window policing the neighborhood through binoculars.

They assured me they would look into the matter as soon as possible. Did that mean today? Tomorrow? Sometime this year?

CHAPTER FOURTEEN

MONDAY • JUNE 15
Posted by Katy McKenna

Earsplitting jack-hammering roused me this morning. After peeling Tabitha off the crown of my head, I checked the time. Seven-fifty. I threw on some clothes, then set out on a recon mission to discover the source of the annoying racket and wound up at Nina's.

The scene I beheld left me completely gobsmacked.

The picket fence and gate were flattened to the ground. A tree removal truck with a wood chipper hitched to the backend and a cherry picker crane on top was parked in the yard. A man wielding a chainsaw stood in the basket, sky-high in the tree, sawing off the stately sycamore's leafy limbs. Nina's blue jay pal, Jasper, squawked his disapproval from a high branch.

The heirloom roses had been dug up and tossed on top of a pile of rubble in a commercial dumpster. A heavily tattooed, muscular man in a sleeveless t-shirt was jack-hammering the mossy brick walk into crumbling chunks.

A rusty white van with a faded logo on the side sat in the drive-way. *The Final Touch Home Remodeling. Quality Work Done Cheap!*

Three men sat on the porch steps, staring at their phones and sipping takeout coffee.

Donna slammed through the screen door, hollering, "I'm not paying you to sit there slurping your fancy-schmancy lattes. I'm paying you to work! So get to it!" Her eyes flicked in my direction. She crossed her arms, and narrowed her eyes, daring me to say something.

I kept my mouth shut and went home to ponder this new development.

———

After a shower and breakfast, it was pushing nine-thirty—time to go back and ask what's going on. Yes, it was obvious what was going on—but why was Nina's award-winning garden being demolished? Why would Nina allow this to happen? Maybe she really does have Alzheimer's.

Hand on the front door handle, I hesitated. *Maybe I need another cup of coffee before confronting Donna.* I had started for the kitchen, when I heard paws scratching on the door. Not knowing what was on the other side, I cautiously cracked the door to peek out. Baby Girl barreled through, wagging her feathery tail with a guilty grin that revealed a healthy set of choppers.

"Uh...oh! What're you doing here?"

She rolled over, submitting her furry tummy for a rub that I lavishly bestowed. "You naughty girl. Your mother must be having a panic attack. Well, at least I have a good excuse to go over there now. Your timing couldn't be better."

Daisy strolled into the house through the dog door. When she saw Baby Girl sprawled on her back, she rushed in for a sniff. The little dog scrambled to her feet, and the two of them raced through the house having a blast. Donna's dog probably never has "doggy fun" so I went ahead and made myself a cup of coffee while they romped.

Steamy mug in hand, I sat on the easy chair in the living room and watched the dogs play tug-of-war with an old slipper. I sipped my coffee while savoring the thought of Donna panicking about her missing dog. Then, in no rush to relieve her misery, I poured another cup.

———

Nina's front door was wide open. I stepped in and called hello. After my second "Hello!" I moved into the living room and yelled, "Nina? Donna?"

Donna came down the hall. Her eyes bugged out when she saw Baby Girl in my arms. "Oh, my God! What the hell're you doing with my dog?"

"Instead of yelling at me, you should be thanking me. She showed up on my doorstep." I handed the dog to her. "You're welcome for me rescuing her before she got hit by a car."

Donna clutched Baby Girl. "With all the commotion here, I didn't realize she was gone."

Darn it! I had hoped she was losing her mind with worry.

She held the dog out at arm's length facing her, and sharply said, "Shame on you! Why did you run away?"

"Uh, maybe because the door is open and the noise and machinery scared her." I shrugged. "That'd be my guess, but what do I know?"

I was rewarded with a scowl.

"So, what's going on here?" I made a big show of looking out the front door. "Nina hasn't mentioned a thing about demolishing the yard. Her garden is the envy of the neighborhood, so I'm surprised, to say the least. Last year they did a feature on her garden in the *Santa Lucia Living* magazine. They had a contest and her yard won first place."

"If you must know, I'm helping my aunt get the house ready for sale. We're updating to appeal to a younger demographic. Families are not interested in a high maintenance yard. Plus, those old bushes and trees were blocking light into the house."

A couple, maybe in their mid-forties, dressed in white coveralls, entered the room and spread a measuring tape across the wood floor. "Fourteen, six," said the tall, lean man. "Okay, Karen. Let's run it the other way." He snapped up the tape measure, eyeing me. "Would you mind stepping aside, please?"

I shuffled to the opposite side of the mahogany wainscoted room, and Donna followed.

Karen, a big-boned curvy redhead, wearing a blue bandanna wrapped around her head like Rosie the Riveter, said to her partner, "Joe? Do you know if we're keeping the fireplace?"

Before he could answer, Donna said, "No, it's dated. We're bringing this house into the twenty-first century."

"It's not dated. It's vintage," I blurted. "The house was built in the early 1930s, and the fireplace is classic Craftsman style. It goes with the period of the home. Buckingham Palace is dated, too, you know, by several hundred years, and you don't see the royal family updating it to the twenty-first century, do you? No. You don't. Because that would be nuts."

"Who cares?" said Donna. "We're taking out that wall anyway to open up the space. That's what buyers want nowadays. People want to be able to see everything from the kitchen."

I took a deep inhale, struggling to calm myself before I said too much. "Nowadays, most folks are restoring these old bungalows. You could save a lot of money selling it as is. It's in perfect condition. Don't you ever watch any of the restoration shows on TV?"

"I know what I'm doing. I redid my mother's old house after she passed and made a ton of money."

"Well, excuse me. I didn't realize you're a remodeling expert." I checked my sarcasm, and continued in a quiet NPR monotone. "How about I take Nina over to my house. You know, get her out of all this commotion. It's got to be driving her crazy."

"She's fine." Donna snuggled her dog. "Isn't she, baby? Auntie

Nina is just fine." Then to me, "In fact, she's taking her morning nap, now."

"She can sleep through all the racket?"

She shrugged. "What can I say? She's ancient, she's worn-out, and her hearing isn't what it used to be. So yeah, she's sleeping like a baby. Wish I could sleep like she does. Must be nice."

The other day Nina told me she hasn't had a decent night's sleep in decades. "How is she feeling?"

"She's doing much better. Still taking lots of vitamins and zinc."

The dog struggled in her arms, and she held him tighter. "Baby! Stay still. I can't put you down. The door is open, and I might lose you."

Again. "Speaking of losing a pet, did Mr. Snickers come back?"

She shook her head with an unconcerned half-shrug like she couldn't care less, and then herded me towards the front door. "I'll tell my aunt you dropped by."

At the door, I stood my ground. "Not so fast, Donna. I don't believe you're telling Nina anything about my visits. I also do not think anyone could sleep through all this commotion. I want to see my friend. Now!" I shoved past her, heading for the hall. "Nina!"

"You're trespassing," screamed Donna. "Time for you to get out!"

Karen rushed to block the hallway. "I think you need to leave, lady." She stretched her arms wide, setting a hand on each wall. Her short sleeves inched up to reveal well-muscled arms. One bore a USMC Death Before Dishonor tattoo. The skull was a nice touch. She cocked an eyebrow that clearly said, *Try it. I dare you.*

Back at home, I was boiling mad and called Ruby to vent.

After listening to me rant for a couple minutes, she calmly said, "Katy, maybe this woman is on the up and up and actually trying to help her aunt. Not everybody is sinister, you know. Just because you don't like her doesn't make her a bad person."

That statement pissed me off, and I struggled not to lose it. "I was threatened by a Marine."

"Donna had told you to leave, so that woman must've thought you were a threat to Nina."

"Whose side are you on, Ruby? I'm telling you, this isn't right. First off, other than the sniffles, Nina was fine the last time I saw her. Second, just because she's eighty-seven doesn't mean she's ancient or has Alzheimer's. Everyone ages differently—like you! I think of you as youthful."

"How youthful?"

"Like in your fifties, not seventies."

"Well, thank you, although I like to think I'm in my forties, even though my wrinkles and the calendar say otherwise."

"I don't trust Donna, and you wouldn't either if you met her."

"Then I tell you what. I'll do just that."

"What?"

"Meet the woman. How about I come over on my lunch break?"

———

Ruby halted where Nina's picket fence gate had been and surveyed the torn-up yard. "You said it was bad, but I didn't expect it to be this bad."

"I don't know how you're going to make it to the front door in those heels, Ruby."

"Oh, poo. I could climb Mount Everest in heels."

I followed her to the front door, ready to catch her if she stumbled. She rang the bell, and we waited. She jabbed it again, and Donna yelled, "Hold your horses. I'm coming."

I poked Ruby's arm. "What are you going to say to her?"

"Not sure. I'll wing it."

A long minute later, Donna opened the door. When her eyes landed on me, she did not look pleased. "What is your problem? I told you she's napping."

"That was hours ago."

"Exactly. Auntie Nina had a nice lunch, and now she's napping." She swung her cold gaze to Grandma. "Who are you?"

"I'm Katy's grandmother, Ruby. Nina and I are good friends." Ruby's tone was bubbly. "We go way back. She invited me for lunch today. By the way—love your muumuu. Very trendy." She turned to me. "Sweetie, thank you for walking me over. You can go home now." And to Donna, "This will give you a laugh. Katy didn't think I could walk through the yard in my heels."

Donna crossed her arms, looking suspicious. "When did my aunt invite you?"

"The other day," fibbed Ruby. "In the bistro at Shady Acres. We were having coffee."

"That couldn't have been just the other day, because I've been here for two weeks, and she hasn't been out of my sight since I arrived."

"Then it was right before that. I put the date on my phone." She brandished her phone at Donna. "What can I say? I'm ancient, and these days everything is just the other day for me. Thank goodness for my calendar alerts, or I'd always be a day late and a dollar short." She patted my shoulder. "It seems like yesterday that my dear granddaughter was born, and here she is, thirty-three."

I smirked. "Thirty-two, but who's counting?"

"The thing is, today is the day." Ruby glanced at her cell phone. "It's Monday, twelve thirty-three, so I'm three minutes late. If she's already had lunch, we can just visit." She turned towards the yard and spread her arms to encompass the mess. "This is sure a surprise. Nina never mentioned anything about all this. Her garden was her pride and joy. Did some kind of deadly disease invade the yard?"

While she nattered on, I tried to see if Nina was in view, maybe sitting in a chair, but Donna's bulky frame blocked the line of sight.

Ruby continued. "Let's go wake up my lazy gal-pal." She placed a pointy toe on the threshold.

Donna didn't budge. "Wow. You Californians are sure a pushy bunch, aren't you? As I said, my aunt is sleeping, so—no lunch for you."

"Tell you what, hon," said Ruby. "Be a sweetheart and let Nina know I'll be back later."

———

I warmed up the iron skillet, then placed two buttered Swiss and cheddar cheese sandwiches on the hot surface. While I grilled, Ruby used the bathroom, gave snacks to the furry kids, cleared off the kitchen table, and then sat gazing out the window until I set lunch on the table. "You want chips?"

"No, this is plenty."

After a couple bites, I put down my sandwich. "So? You gonna say anything?"

"Two words. No. Make that three words." She pointed at her sandwich. "Delicious. Elder abuse."

"I think so, too. That's why I called Adult Protective Services a couple of days ago and made a report. Who knows what will come of it, though."

She sipped her sparkling water. "Elder abuse is more common than you'd think." Another sip, and she set down her glass on the placemat. "Listen. I could be totally off-base about this Donna person, but given everything you've told me and what I saw... Something is definitely not right over there. I don't know what we can do, but ignoring it is not an option."

———

When it was dark outside, I went over to Nina's with a stepstool and plucked several of the heirloom rose bushes out of the dumpster. I'm going to plant them in pots and save them for her. If I'm lucky, maybe I saved her mother's roses.

If it turns out she doesn't want them when she moves to Shady Acres, then I'll have to learn how not to kill roses. I wonder if there is an app for that.

CHAPTER FIFTEEN

My "missing cat" post on Facebook has been shared twenty-seven times. So far, no one has found him. I've also been checking the pound online twice a day for any new cats brought in. I feel responsible for Mr. Snickers' disappearance.

Late Afternoon

I stretched out on the patio chaise lounge to read more of *The Kupcake Kaper* on my tablet. I skimmed through the little I'd read and got to:

Suddenly, Patsy's usually perpetually perky, happy-go-lucky smile drooped, and she burst into uncontrollable tears.

"What's wrong?" questioned Larry, looking very distraught.

"My dear grandmother always dreamed of owning a

bakery. Remember, I told you it was her who taught me how to bake?"

"I remember. She taught you to bake to make you happy after your father and baby sister died so tragically when you were a little girl," said Larry.

"Yes. It was front page news, remember?" said Patsy. "It was even on the network news. They blamed my father."

Nina had told me the tragic story about the plane crash that killed her sister's husband and child. Curious to learn more, I dug around online for old Ketchikan news stories.

In the search box, I typed *tragic death of father and child in the 1960s in Ketchikan, Alaska*. First up: Alaska Shipwrecks. 1750 to 1850. Then a memorial page for the 1964 Alaska earthquake.

I'm more efficient with a keyboard, so I went in the house to get my laptop. I wound up in the living room where I could watch HGTV while searching for information. My research assistant, Daisy, jumped on the couch and got comfy next to me.

"Okay, Daisy. Let's try Bob Baxter death in Ketchikan, Alaska. No, probably would be Robert Baxter."

- *We Found Baxter | View Public Records Online.*
- *Ketchikan Records Free Search | Enter a Name & Search For Free: Find Out Everything You Want to Know About Anyone for FREE!*

I scrolled beyond the ads and did something I rarely do. I clicked on the next Google page. Halfway down, I found this:

September 14, 2004. A man was found dead when his partially submerged car was discovered in the George Inlet by a passing bicyclist on the S. Tongas Highway. Gary Morgan, 54…

"Wasn't he Donna's husband?"

… drowned when his Ford Explorer went off the road and landed in the water sometime in the early morning hours. Emergency services were called, and Morgan was pronounced deceased at the scene of the accident.
Officers say the death is not being treated as suspicious. Morgan's wife, Donna Baxter Morgan, was devastated by the news, saying, "He was a good man and a devoted husband."

"Uh, no. You said he was a bastard."

Donna Morgan was at the epicenter of another heartbreaking tragedy when she was a child. In 1971, several passengers from the cruise ship Pacific S.S. Princess Beatrice were killed when the Ketchikan-based sightseeing plane they were aboard crashed into the George Inlet waters.
The airboat, built by Admiral Skyways in 1936, and originally used for commercial transport, held 22 passengers. Among the dead were Donna's father and pilot of the plane, Robert Baxter, 38, and his four-year-old daughter, Trudy. Donna Baxter, 10, and four other passengers were the only survivors of the crash. After a thorough investigation, they ruled the cause of the crash pilot error.

I read the story three times, trying to absorb the enormity of the tragedies. Donna is lugging around a heavy load of baggage. Not only did she lose her father and sister—her dad was blamed for the crash. I'm sure she had to deal with a lot of hostility from community members and cruel ridicule from classmates.

Her husband betrayed her several times and then drove off the road and died, although I doubt she was very broken up about that. After all of that, she nursed her ailing mother until she passed from emphysema.

Maybe I need to cut her some slack. Maybe all she is trying to do is take care of Nina. And perhaps she's simply overly cautious.

———

Last Thoughts

I updated my Donna-Nina timeline, then had a long thinking session about everything that has happened since Donna had arrived. I decided I can't allow myself to be swayed by her sad history. I may be dead wrong about Nina's welfare, but until I see my friend and feel assured she is all right, I can't turn a blind eye to what's happening over there.

Tomorrow, it's time for Sam's spy mission to Nina's.

CHAPTER SIXTEEN

WEDNESDAY • JUNE 17
Posted by Katy McKenna

Samantha and I stood at the edge of Nina's property peeking around the bushes at the demo team scurrying like busy bees.

"You told me what's going on, but seeing is believing," said Sam. "Her yard was the yard of my dreams. Why would anyone do this? It's so strange."

"Speaking of strange."

I spun around to Randy and Earl lurking behind us. "Holy crap. You scared the-you-know-what out of me."

"Me, too," said Sam, patting her chest. "I'm lucky I didn't pee my pants."

"Sorry," said Randy. "Didn't mean to scare you. We're wondering if you've noticed the homeless-looking dude staying at the Miller's house?"

The Millers were the family who'd lived in the house between Nina's and mine. They moved out while I was in England with Ruby.

"No." I scanned the yard and realized the "For Sale" sign was gone. "Maybe he bought the house." I set my hands on Sam's shoulders. "You ready?"

"Ready for what?" asked Earl.

"I'll tell you later." I adjusted Sam's hospital ID hanging around her neck. She was wearing navy blue scrubs, and her stethoscope and medical bag made her appear hospital-official. "Ready?"

She nodded, looking nervous. "I am."

"No, you're not." I handed her the clipboard tucked under my arm. "Now, you're ready. Almost." I tugged my phone from my back pocket. "I got an app that records phone conversations. I'm going to call your phone now, and you answer, so I can listen to everything that Donna says. Plus, we'll have a recording in case she says anything incriminating."

"That's brilliant, Katy." She slipped the phone into her breast pocket.

"Now, you're ready." I felt like I was sending my firstborn into battle. "Wait! You should park your car in front of her house."

"You're right. Good call."

Violet yelped frantically through the boys' open living room window.

"Uh-oh. I bet she saw that mouse again," said Earl. "Mice terrify her."

"We gotta go," said Randy. "We've been trying to catch it so we can release it back into the wild where it can live a happy mouse life."

As they trotted across the street, Earl called to me, "In our former life, we would've offed the mouse with a shovel."

Sam parked her SUV behind a construction truck, then glanced in my direction, looking anxious.

I whispered into my phone, "Talk loud so I can hear you."

She squared her shoulders and started for the door. On the former Miller's property, I moved to a spot in the bushes that was parallel to Nina's front door. Then spread the branches apart to keep an eye on Sam.

She jabbed on the doorbell a few times before Donna opened the door.

"HELLO," said Sam. "I'm from ELDER CARE SOCIAL SERVICES."

"Why are you shouting?"

"SORRY. Sorry. It's noisy out here." Sam pointed at the yard activity. "I didn't know if you could HEAR ME OVER THE BULLDOZER. I can hardly hear myself think!" She paused a moment, standing on tiptoes, struggling to peer over Donna's broad shoulders. "AWFULLY NOISY IN THE HOUSE, TOO."

"I CAN HEAR YOU! So stop the shouting. What do you want?"

"I'm here to do my scheduled monthly check-up on Nina Lowen."

"Why? She's perfectly healthy."

"And we want to keep her that way. She is expecting me."

Samantha set a foot on the threshold and Donna's hand blocked her entrance. "What're you doing?"

Sam stepped back, waving her clipboard. "As I said. Mrs. Lowen's check-up."

"You'll have to make an appointment. My aunt is napping."

"Napping? Now? We have an appointment." Sam made a big show of checking her watch. "This is our regular day and time. You'll need to wake her up. I'm on a tight schedule."

"Like hell, I will. The woman is a viper. If I wake her from her beauty sleep there will be hell to pay."

"That doesn't sound like the sweet Nina Lowen I know," said Sam.

"Well, then she's got you fooled. Give me your card and I'll have her call you to set another appointment."

My scalp tingled. *What will Sam say?*

She didn't miss a beat. "I left them in my car. I'll jot it down for you."

I saw her writing on the paper attached to the clipboard. She tore off the number and handed it to Donna. "I'd like to hear back today. Otherwise, I'll have to report this to social services."

Donna did not look pleased.

Samantha glanced at her watch again. "Tell you what. I think I can squeeze her in around four o'clock. Please make sure she's awake." She turned her back on Donna and practically jumped down the steps.

Donna waved the scrap of paper. "Wait a minute!"

Sam ignored her, hastily picking her way through the dirt clods and ditches to the pavement. Keeping her head down, she jumped in her car and sped to my house.

I backed out of my hiding spot and ran home. We didn't say a word until we were in the kitchen.

"Oh, my God, Sam—you were brilliant!"

She puffed her chest. "I was, wasn't I?" Then her bravado sagged and she slumped onto a kitchen chair. "Except now I have to go back. That woman is scary. And what's up with the hideous orange muumuu? Not a good look on her. Or anyone."

I sat next to her. "Who knows? She's always dressed like she's in the middle of a heatwave." I gave her a hug. "Thank you for doing that, but I don't expect you to go back—especially in your condition."

"I'm pregnant, not dying from a rare tropical disease. I need to go back. I agree with you. Something really strange is going on over there."

"At least you don't think I'm crazy."

"I always think you're crazy, so what else is new?"

"Yeah, yeah. Very funny. But I don't want you going alone. So, who can go with you?"

"Not you," she said.

"Obviously. Not Ruby either."

Sam snapped her fingers. "How about Ruby's boyfriend, Ben?"

"Hmm. That could work. He's a retired hotshot L.A. lawyer, so he can spout legal jargon that no one understands, but it sounds threatening. I'll call him."

I did, and, being the dear man that he is, he agreed.

———

In my entry area, Ben held open his suit coat. "Do I look official enough for you in my three-piece?"

"Love the watch chain," I said.

"Belonged to my grandfather. He gave it to me when I passed the bar. It's been a while since I've worn my work clothes. I'm relieved this suit still fits considering how spoiled I am by Ruby's excellent cooking." He winked at Sam and me.

"Ha! That's rich!" snorted Ruby. "You're the chef, not me."

"If anyone wants coffee, I've got a fresh pot on the stove," I said. "Let's go sit in the kitchen."

Everyone accepted a cup except Sam, and we sat at the table

Ben gleefully rubbed his hands together. "What's the plan?"

While I briefed him, Sam researched Social Services house calls online to gain more verbal ammunition. A few minutes before four, they got into Ben's shiny silver Mercedes, drove around the block, and parked in front of Nina's house. Ruby and I crossed the Millers' lawn to the spot in the shrubbery where I had viewed Sam earlier.

Ben pressed the doorbell and stood back, looking professional and authoritative. After a reasonable wait, he rang again.

After the third ring, he asked a construction worker if Donna was home. The young man shrugged his shoulders and spoke in Spanish.

Ben replied in what sounded like a perfect accent to my ear. "*Está ella en casa?*"

"Si." The man said a lot more that was way beyond my two years of forgotten high school Spanish.

Then Ben pounded on the door, hollering, "I am the legal counsel for social services. You are required to let us in to see our client, Nina Lowen. If you do not…"

The door swung open.

"It's four o'clock, and I'm back as promised." Sam gestured at Ben. "This is Ben Burnett. He's the legal counsel for—"

"Yeah, I heard." Straddling the threshold, Donna crossed her arms. "You already reported me?"

"My concern is for my patient above all else. Unfortunately, earlier today, you were not amenable to my visit, so Mr. Burnett is here to ensure I have access to Mrs. Lowen. Once I'm satisfied that she's in good health, I can file my report."

Donna didn't budge.

"We'd like to come in now," said Ben.

"Unless you have a warrant, I don't have to let you in."

Sam moved closer to her. "I'm also required to do a safety evaluation given the state of disrepair the home is now in."

"I did a little research after you left. The only way you're getting into this house is if you can show me a warrant signed by a judge, or I invite you in, which sure ain't happening."

Ben drew his phone from his pants pocket. "That can be arranged. By not cooperating with us, this will go on file and will cause considerable problems for you if we are forced to take you to court." It looked like he had dialed a number, then paused. "Are you the legal guardian of Nina Lowen?"

"Yes, I am," she snapped.

Since when? I wondered.

"I'd like to see that documentation, please," said Ben.

"Oh yeah? Well, document this!" Donna slammed the door.

Sam shouted, "You better clean up the place because you can bet we'll be back."

Ben took her arm and hustled her down the steps. The yard workers gaped at the pair weaving their way through the yard.

"What are you staring at?" yelled Sam as she climbed into Ben's car. "Take a picture. It'll last longer!"

Ruby and I rushed home to meet them in the driveway. When Sam got out of the car, she took one look at me, and we both cracked up.

"I haven't heard you scream like that in ages," I said.

"Then you need to spend more time at my house. Raising a teenage girl brings out the beast in me all the time."

We gathered on the porch. The ladies sat on the glider, and Ben leaned against the rail.

"So now what, Ben?" I asked.

He shook his head. "Unfortunately, that woman is right. We would have to show a warrant."

"Obviously, that's not happening," I said.

"Sometimes I really hate the internet," said Ruby. "If she couldn't have checked the rules online, she probably would've let you in."

"Actually, it's better that she did that," said Ben. "If she'd called social services and found out we weren't who we said we were, she could have had the cops waiting for us."

Ruby stood and dusted her immaculate denim capris. "We gotta scoot. We have tickets to see *Forever…Patsy Cline* at the community theater, and I need to change my clothes. We're double-dating with your parents."

"Dinner first at The Red Door," said Ben.

"Ooo. I'm jealous. I love that place," I said.

Sam stood. "Time for me to go, too. I promised Casey I'd make his favorite for dinner."

"Mac and cheese?" I asked.

"No. He's broadened his culinary horizons and is into tuna noodle casserole now. Cheddar cheese is the magic ingredient."

CHAPTER SEVENTEEN

FRIDAY • JUNE 19
Posted by Katy McKenna

I ran errands this morning. The bank, hardware store, groceries. Returning home, it surprised me to see no trucks, vans, or workers at Nina's house. After parking in my driveway, I waved at Randy across the street, then strolled over.

Violet was on the couch next to him. She jumped down, wiggling her bum and lobbing doggy air-kisses at me. I sat on the top step and she nuzzled under my arm until I wrapped it around her. "Did you catch the mouse that was terrorizing poor little Violet?"

"No. Now we have three humane live traps in the house."

I pointed across the street. "None of the workers are at Nina's today. I wonder why."

Randy nodded. "They walked off the job about an hour ago. I was doing my morning salutations when it happened. That woman was screaming her head off at them—really foul language. Totally messed with my chi. Now I get why you were so pissed—I mean angry with us."

"What was she screaming?"

"Stuff like 'I paid you a thousand bucks last week, and I can't pay any more right now.'"

"So everyone up and left?"

He swept back his shaggy hair. "I heard the supervisor say she owed them $7,000 for materials and labor, and if she wasn't going to pay them, they had other jobs that would, and didn't need this shit—his word, not mine. Then the dudes working in the house came out and left, too."

I gazed at the house. "There's a toilet in the yard."

"The plumber was about to throw it into the dumpster when all this happened. He had a new one sitting on the porch. He grabbed it and left."

"Wow. Sorry I missed all the excitement." One more pup snuggle and I stood. "Thanks for the update. Let me know if any other weird things happen. I'm very concerned about Nina." I moved to the bottom of the steps. "Hey! Have you seen that homeless guy at the Millers' house again?"

"I saw him leave this morning."

"Was he acting sneaky, like he didn't want anyone to see him?"

"No. He came out the door carrying a backpack and walked down the street."

Randy namastéd me, and I went home to ponder these new neighborhood developments.

———

After Sam's bogus social services visits to Nina's house, I owe her big time, which means giving her sixteen-and-a-half-year-old driving lessons. I got my license the day I turned sixteen, but Chelsea pulled a stunt a while back that delayed her driving lessons.

Texting your friends that your folks are gone for the night is a recipe for disaster. Thank goodness for homeowner's insurance.

Not only did Chelsea have to wait to learn how to drive, she now has an embarrassing flip phone with no internet access or texting capabilities. If she wants to communicate with anyone, she has to talk to them. How humiliating is that?

Chelsea's First Driving Lesson.
And My First Gray Hair.

"Okay, Chelsea. Buckle up."

"Check."

"Can you see out the rearview mirror?"

She adjusted it, fluffed her hair, then reached to turn on the radio.

"Uh-uh. I want all your attention on the road."

"We're in the high school parking lot, Aunt Katy."

"This is where I had my first lesson. Sam, too. Now, turn the key."

"Our cars don't have keys. You just press the button."

"I know. And if you lose the remote fob thingie, it costs at least a couple hundred to replace."

She pulled out the metal key and scrutinized it like it was an archeological artifact. "How much does a key cost?"

"A few bucks."

"Maybe I'll save up for an old car instead of a new one." She inserted the key into the ignition. "Should I press the gas pedal?"

"No. It'll start without doing that."

She turned the key and Veronica's engine purred.

"Did you really learn how to drive in this car?" asked Chelsea.

I patted the dashboard. "Sure did."

"Wow. This car is so old."

"Hey! It was old when I learned, too. Now it's a classic, so treat Veronica with the respect she deserves."

She gripped the wheel, bouncing on the squeaky seat. "Now what?"

"Stop bouncing and put your foot on the brake. No, your right foot. In an automatic, we only use our right foot."

"What does my left foot do?"

"Nothing."

"That doesn't make any sense. I mean it's right there, and there's two pedals, so why can't I use both feet? It would be way easier."

"Do you want to pass the driver's test and get your license?"

"Yeah."

"Enough said." I released the parking brake. "Put it in drive. The D."

"D for drive. Duh."

I tapped the steering wheel. "Now, with both hands on the wheel like I showed you, take your foot off the brake and *ever* so gently press the gas pedal."

The elderly car lurched into supersonic warp speed. The G-Force snapped my head back against the headrest. "Stop! Hit the brakes! STOP!" My seatbelt anchored my body to the seat as Veronica screeched to a halt.

"Wow!" shrieked Chelsea. "That was awesome!"

Those few seconds wiped out several years of my life and any debt I owed Sam—now and forever.

This Evening

A party was brewing next door. As their volume climbed, so did my TV volume—and my blood pressure. I reached the tipping point when Daisy tried to bury her head under the cushions.

"Enough is enough." I paused the show, found the noise ordinance online, and printed it. Then stomped to Josh's door.

After ringing the bell several times, the door opened, and a guy holding a beer and reeking of weed stumbled past me, discharging a loud, rolling belch.

"Real cute," I said.

The idiot grinned stupidly and passed out on the lawn.

He'd left the door open, so I invited myself in. I'd seen Josh's cousin, Dillon, from a distance but had not yet formerly introduced myself. That was about to change. I finally located him lounging on the back deck. After edging a couple girls aside, I planted myself in front of his prone body.

"Allow me to introduce myself. I'm Katy McKenna." I pointed at our mutual cedar fence. "I live over there."

Dillon grinned crookedly. "Okay."

"There's a city noise ordinance that states that ten o'clock is the cutoff time for noise." I glanced at my phone. "Right now it's nine forty-two." I waved the ordinance at him. "You've got less than twenty minutes to wind down this party to a whisper, or every neighbor on this block will call the police." I tossed the document on his lap. "You've been warned."

As I made my way through the house to the front door, I spotted a skinny girl shrouded in waist length black hair sitting on the living room couch. She was petting a cat that looked a lot like Mr. Snickers. "Is that your cat?"

"No. It belongs to the guy who lives here."

I sat next to her. "Dillon?"

She shrugged her bony, bare shoulders. "If that's the guy who lives here."

"I love cats." I reached out. "May I hold him a moment?"

"Whatever."

I pulled the feline into my arms and checked his collar tag. "This isn't Dillon's cat."

My fury had resumed tenfold. My first inclination was to confront Dillon. Instead, I left the house clutching Snickers. It was too late to knock on Nina's door, so I took him home.

I closed the laundry room dog door before setting Mr. Snickers down for Tabitha and Daisy to inspect. After he passed the sniff test, I fed everyone a snack, then showed him the cat box.

Hoping that Dillon would clear out the party so I wouldn't

have to follow through on my warning, I topped off my wine and flopped on the couch to finish my show. Snickers jumped on board and settled on my lap. A moment later, Tabitha joined us and shoved Snickers off.

At ten-thirty, the party was louder than ever, and I was madder than ever. I didn't want to call the cops because they have more important things to do. Instead, I pulled a bench over to the fence in my back yard, mounted it, and videoed the revelry. Then, without a lot of thought, I texted it to Josh. *Here's a video of the weekly Friday Night Bash at your house.*

After that, divine inspiration hit me—please do not judge me until you have walked in my shoes. I got the hose, attached the sprayer nozzle, turned the water on full blast, and aimed it over the fence. The shrieks were music to my ears.

CHAPTER EIGHTEEN

SATURDAY · JUNE 20
Posted by Katy McKenna

I was drinking my first cup of coffee of the day while trying not to fall off the chaise lounge I was sharing with dead-weight Daisy. All was well with the world until my eyes landed on the hose by the fence.

"Probably not our finest hour, huh, Daisy?"

The chaise lounge hog climbed down, found a sunny spot on the concrete, collapsed with a groan, and stared at me.

I stretched my legs. "Okay—not *my* finest hour. But you gotta admit, hosing them was fun! At least I didn't call the cops."

"Maybe you should have," said Josh from his yard.

My heart pinged and Daisy went wild. She zipped to the cedar fence, barking joyously. Her boyfriend was back!

"Josh? What are you doing here?" I called.

"May I come over?"

"Yes, of course." *Geez. I'm a mess!* "Just give me a minute."

I hurried to the bathroom to fix my bedhead hair. Then a swish of mouthwash, a dab of lipstick, some blush. I tried to apply mascara, but my hand was shaking so hard that I smeared it across my cheek.

The doorbell rang.

Dammit. I should have said thirty minutes! I scrubbed the mascara off my cheek, reapplied the blush, then spritzed the air with perfume and ran through the misty cloud to the front door.

With heart pounding like a race horse at the finish line, I opened the door and beheld my blond Viking. "Hi." I tried to act nonchalant. "Long time, no see." *Long time, no see? Where'd that come from?*

"Hey, Cookie." He gave me a slow once-over that made my knees weak. "You got my favorite sexy pajamas on."

I clutched the collar of my Oreo Cookie print flannels. "I'm a little slow this morning."

He leaned a hand against the door frame. "You have good reason considering what was going on last night."

Daisy had figured out that her sweetheart was at the front door and was pawing frantically on the closed dog door.

"Hold on. Someone wants to see you." I dashed to the laundry room and let my besotted girl in. She raced to the entry and nearly knocked Josh off his feet. He knelt to hug her and got a face full of sloppy kisses.

"I missed you too, Daisy." He glanced up at me. "More than I can say."

"You want to come in?"

He stood. "I do."

We went into the kitchen. I poured him a cup of coffee without asking if he wanted one. He took a sip.

"This is good." He gazed at the antique Pyrex percolator on the stove. "My grandma had one of these. She always kept a pot on the burner that she'd reheat over and over, all day long."

"Sounds awful."

He laughed. "It probably was."

And then we both said, "About last night…"

"You first," I said. "No, wait. Me first. I'm sorry I texted you that video. I don't know what I was thinking."

"You were angry and rightfully so. I haven't talked to Dillon yet, but when he wakes up, I'll set him straight."

"He's going to hate me."

"He needs to understand that if he's living in my house, he has to respect the neighbors. Otherwise, he can go back to the dorms. This was a favor to him. A nice home and free rent. I should've known better. I was his age once, and I was a thoughtless idiot, too."

Mr. Snickers sauntered into the kitchen flicking his tail like he owned the place.

"New cat?" asked Josh.

We sat at the kitchen table, where I brought him up-to-date on the neighborhood news.

He hung his hand down low, and Snickers rubbed his nose against it. "I can't believe Dillon didn't take this guy home. What the hell is wrong with him?"

I shook my head. "Who knows? I'm taking him back to Nina today. Hopefully, Donna will let me in."

"After everything you told me about Donna, you want me to walk over with you?"

"Yes, I would. But don't you have to get back to Nicole?"

"She has a friend visiting. I'll go back tomorrow."

"How's she doing?"

He waggled his head, lips pressed tight. "Up and down."

"It's really nice of you to be taking care of her."

"I owe her big time. Hopefully, helping her will help me stop feeling guilty for wrecking our marriage."

I pushed away from the table. "I need to get dressed."

Josh stood and whispered in a husky voice, "Do you really have to?"

Stepping close, he reached out for my hand and pressed it against his broad chest. I could barely breathe. I felt his heart beating as he cupped my chin, lifting my face to meet his lips.

————

I was literally floating on air as we strolled down the street to Nina's house. Josh was cradling Mr. Snickers securely in his arms. At the edge of Nina's property, he shook his head. "How could anyone in their right mind do this?"

I rang the bell, and a long minute later, Donna answered. You should've seen her face flush when she got a load of Josh's captivating smile.

"Hi. I'm Josh Draper. I live on the other side of Katy."

She glanced at me and her dopey smile flickered out. Then her gaze returned to his blue-sky eyes.

"We found Nina's cat," he said.

"Oh?"

He held Snickers aloft and she noticed the cat for the first time. "Oh."

Josh tucked Snickers under his arm. "We can't wait to see Nina's face when we give this little fella back to her."

"You can't come in," she said. "She's napping. Dreaming of happier days when she was young and healthy, I would imagine."

I huffed a sigh. "Donna. Every single time I come over to see her, you say she's sleeping. Every single time—except for the time she was taking a bath. How can that possibly be? I bet I've been over at least ten times now."

"What can I say?" The woman shrugged. "She's old. She's sick. She's on her last legs."

Josh kept his tone neutral friendly. "I bet if the old girl sees her cat, it'll perk her up." He even tossed a wink at her.

For a moment, she looked mesmerized, then shook her head, regaining her equilibrium. "No. No, it won't. It'll just upset her. Please take the cat and go."

I lost it and screamed, "Are you kidding me? You don't want your aunt to have her cat? That's cruel!"

She pinned her sharp glare on me. "I want you to stop coming over here and butting into our business. You got that? If I have to, I'll get a restraining order."

Fists clenched, I stepped closer, dying to flatten her bulbous nose. "A restraining order? For what? Caring about my neighbor?"

Josh eased me back. His voice shifted into low and ominous. "Listen, lady. You might need to get two restraining orders because this isn't over. Got that?"

Eyes wide, Donna stepped backwards, gripping the edge of the wood door.

"Let's go, Katy." Still cradling the cat securely under his arm, Josh draped his other around my shoulders and led me down the steps.

The door closed softly behind us.

When we were back in my house, I took Mr. Snickers from Josh and snuggled him close. "You poor, poor baby. I promise we will get you back to your momma as soon as that awful person goes home."

Josh moved close and petted his head. "In the meantime, big guy, you're lucky to have Auntie Katy taking care of you. It's probably a good thing that Dillon didn't take him back. No telling what would have happened to him. But that still doesn't excuse his thoughtlessness." He glanced at his watch, and I instantly fixated on his blond, hairy, tanned arm. "I should get over there and talk to him. You okay?"

I nodded. "Give him hell."

He leaned in for a kiss. "You better believe I will."

CHAPTER NINETEEN

MONDAY · JUNE 22

Posted by Katy McKenna

Josh left last night. I tried to be cool about saying goodbye again, but I'm so not cool. I wish Nicole hadn't told me she's still in love with him. It makes me feel like "the other woman." Not a part I want to play.

I realize I've blogged this many times in the last few months, but hey—it's my blog, and I'll cry if I want to.

I know just the thing that will take my mind off my woes. Terror.

Driving Lesson #2

"Are you buckled?"

My student rolled her eyes. "Yes, ma'am."

"Today, we're going to drive on a paved road," I said. "But not here in your neighborhood. Too busy."

Chelsea rolled her eyes again. "It's a cul-de-sac, Aunt Katy."

"Do not roll your eyes at me again. It's rude, and I'm doing you a favor. Teaching someone to drive is really scary, and if I'm annoying you, we don't have to do this. But you get to explain to Sam why I quit."

The devastated expression on her face killed me, but I didn't retract my statement.

"I'm so, so sorry. I was just kidding around, Aunt Katy. Seriously."

"Seriously? You know, whenever my folks got annoyed with whatever I was saying, I always said I was just kidding. Like that made it all right."

"I was being a jerk. I really am sorry. I do appreciate you teaching me how to drive."

I leaned in for a hug. "Okay, back to business." I pointed beyond the circular street. "Past that stop sign, it's open road. Cross streets. Pedestrians, kids on bikes, city buses. Driving a car is like holding a loaded gun. If you're not careful, you will kill someone. That's why I'm taking us to a quiet road out in the countryside."

Twenty minutes later, Chelsea said, "We're in the boonies, now. How much further?"

We were heading to a county park that has a paved road running through it. Hardly anyone goes there. I figured it was a good next step for my pupil.

"You're in luck. There's our turn up ahead," I said.

"Hatcher Park? I haven't been here in a super long time. I love this place," said Chelsea. "But I thought I was going to drive on an actual street today."

"I said a paved road. This is a paved road." I parked next to a towering Blue Gum Eucalyptus tree. "Your turn."

We switched seats and my jaw was already clenching. I should have taken aspirin before leaving the house because I felt a tension headache coming on.

"All right. Start your engine, and let's roll. Really slow. Watch out for squirrels darting across the road."

We drove around the park, practicing parking and backing up.

After about half an hour, Chelsea said, "Can we stop now? My neck hurts, my arms are stiff, and I have a terrible headache."

You and me both, kid. "That's because you're tense and gripping the wheel really tight. How about you park the car and we go play on the swings?"

She grinned like the little kid she still is. "You're on!"

CHAPTER TWENTY

TUESDAY · JUNE 23
Posted by Katy McKenna

Last Night

I was sitting up in bed, reading *The Kupcake Kaper*, and trying to figure out why Donna's books have so many five-star reviews.

"Have I ever told you what cute cupcakes you have?" asked Larry, his voice throaty with sudden need.

Patsy giggled very coyly. "Many times, you bad little boy."

Larry moved in close, pinning his willing wife against the counter, then hoisted her eager body onto the cold, stainless steel counter in the bakery kitchen.

"Larry," moaned Patsy ecstatically. "A customer might come in to buy cupcakes."

He ripped her ruffled apron off and roughly slid his hand under her blouse. "Baby, these cupcakes are only for daddy."

"Yuck!" I yelled, startling the fur babies snoozing next to me. "Sorry, guys."

I logged onto Amazon to see what genre Donna's books are in. I had thought they were cozy culinary mysteries. I was wrong.

#3 in Culinary Mystery Erotica

#17 in Erotic Cozy Mysteries

#11 in Erotic Thriller Culinary Mysteries

"Okay, Donna. Now you have my attention." I breezed through several chapters. I have to admit that some of it was pretty titillating. But then I'd picture sloppy Donna in her hideous muumuus, gorging on cupcakes while she typed steamy sex scenes on a sticky, crumb-covered keypad. Talk about a buzzkill.

I knew my bestie was asleep, but I had to tell her about the book, so I texted:

You have got to read Donna's book! The Kupcake Kaper. It's sooooo good! I'm sending you the eBook now. My gift to you! Talk tomorrow.

This Morning

Construction commotion awakened me too early this morning. I assumed Donna had scraped up the money she owed the crew, and that's why they were back on the job.

While my coffee perked, I checked my messages. Sam had replied to the text I sent last night: *You're kidding, right? You want me to read that woman's book?*

I texted back: *I've read several chapters, and OMG—shocker! Read it!*

After chugging a cup of caffeine, I pulled myself together and went to check out the action at Nina's. Turns out, the construction work was next door at the Miller house. Workers were installing wind turbines on the roof peak. A fellow wearing a blue baseball cap stood on the lawn directing the installation.

I was observing from the sidewalk and he strode over. "Beautiful, aren't they?" The logo on his hat said *Catch the Wind*. "You live in the neighborhood?"

I backed up a step, shaking my head. "Just out for a walk."

"Be glad to give you a free estimate. You'd be shocked how much electricity these babies can generate. My name's Mel." He handed me his card. "And you're?"

Didn't want to share that, either, so I said the first name that came to mind. "Patsy. I'll do a little research, and if it's affordable, I'll give you a call." I turned to escape.

"You can't afford *not* to do it. This is the future of power."

Back home, I scrambled an egg, poured a glass of orange juice, and settled on the couch to watch TV. Mr. Snickers slinked into the room giving me a beseeching look that said, "Why am I here?"

"I'm sorry, baby. I can't take you home until that horrible Donna and her annoying dog leave." I sighed, thinking, *you may be here a long time.*

The Hallmark Movies and Mysteries Channel had offered a free thirty-day trial period, and I'd recorded a show called *The Mystery Blogger.* I blog, and I've accidentally solved a couple of mysteries, so the title had intrigued me.

The story's gist was: A cute woman in her early thirties, lives in a charming town, owns a quaint craft shop, and blogs about her daily life. This was the first episode in the series—originally broadcast two years ago, so if I like it, there are several more. In this one, she was concerned about an invalid neighbor who's not answering her phone, or her door.

When I got to the scene where Ashley is opening a window to sneak into the neighbor's house, I clicked pause.

Could I do that? Dare I do that?

I continued the scene. The heroine climbs through the sash window. Even though it's sunny outside, the room is dark and gloomy. She scans the room with her phone flashlight and the beam lands on a person in bed who is clearly dead. Ashley hears voices coming down the hall and hides in the closet.

A tall creepy guy with a spider web throat tattoo says, "What are we going to do with the old biddy's body?"

"The bigger question," says the dumpy, frumpy, short woman with him, "is, what're we going to do with yours?"

"Huh?"

Bang.

I paused the show again to think. The Nina situation isn't a TV mystery movie, so it's not like Donna will shoot me if she finds me in the house. I concluded that a Good Samaritan cannot let the law stand in her way.

———

Earl was sitting on the porch trying to get some decent sounds out of a didgeridoo and not having much luck. Looking embarrassed, he stopped when he saw me approaching.

"Please don't quit on my account. I've never seen anyone play a didgeridoo before."

"I watched a video on how to do it. I think I need to watch a few more." He set it down on the floor. "Woo. I am out of breath."

"I came over to ask a favor."

He nodded. "Name it."

"I don't want you to go to any extra trouble, but if you see Donna leave Nina's house, would you call me?"

"You bet. Why?"

I leaned against the porch rail. "I haven't been able to see Nina in over two weeks now, and I'm worried about her. I don't want to wake up one morning and get a call from my grandma telling me she just read Nina's obituary."

He looked baffled.

I shrugged. "What can I say? Some people watch the news with their morning coffee. My grandma reads the obituaries."

———

It didn't take long to realize I was too antsy to wait for a call from the boys that might never come, so I packed a lunch and asked them if I could park on their porch.

I was sitting on the steps, working on the second half of my tuna on rye, and listening to a true crime podcast, when Nina's front door slammed. I quickly hid behind the porch railing before Donna saw me.

She balanced a large cardboard box on her hip, while stumbling through the mounds of dirt, rocks, and debris to Nina's car parked at the curb. She popped the rear hatch, stowed the carton inside, and drove away.

After the car rounded the corner, I raced over and pounded on the door, shouting Nina's name. I heard her feebly call out, "Who's there?"

"Nina! It's Katy! Can you come to the door?"

No answer.

I pressed my ear against the carved wood. "Nina! Can you hear me?"

"Who's there?" Her usually vigorous voice sounded weak and wobbly.

I tried the knob and it was locked. I dashed to the dog door set in the glass slider facing the back yard. Temporary plastic orange mesh fencing bordered the dirt where the aggregate patio had been. Judging from all the poop piles, this was Baby Girl's potty area. I tried the slider. It was locked to the dog door insert.

Keeping my ears perked for the sound of the Subaru returning, I sneaked around the perimeter of the house, checking for open windows and unlocked doors. The kitchen door was locked. A bathroom window was open, but too high and small to climb through. I got lucky on a bedroom window that was open a few inches. I struggled to slide the sash window up, but it was stuck. There was a rolled-up towel stuffed in the gap.

I removed the faded yellow towel and peeked into the gloomy

room. Nina was in the bed, lying on her side, eyes closed, facing the window. "Nina? It's me. Katy. Do you need my help?"

Nothing.

Crap. Now what? "NINA! Tell me you're okay!"

Silence.

I stepped away from the window wondering if I should break it. It wouldn't be the first window I've shattered in recent times. While searching the yard for a good-sized rock, my gaze fell on the dog door. Could I fit through it? It was bigger than Donna's dog needed, but was it big enough for me?

"Only one way to find out." I got down on all fours, stuck my head through, and hollered Nina's name again.

No answer.

"Looks like I'm going in." I had wiggled my head and shoulders through the opening when I heard…

"Well, if it isn't little Miss Nosey Nellie. What the hell are you doing?"

Frozen in mid-wiggle, I heard the click of a phone-photo, and backtracked out the doggy door to face my nemesis. "Nina was calling for help." I crossed my arms, trying to look like a hero rather than a freaked-out trespasser.

"I very much doubt my aunt was calling for help. She was dead to the world when I left. Looks more like breaking and entering to me." She brandished her phone. "And I've got a photo to prove it."

"Technically, I was not breaking in. The dog door was open, and I was—"

"Breaking in, trespassing. burglarizing, whatever."

"Oh, please. Why would I break in to steal stuff?"

"You tell me. Aunt Nina has lots of nice things. Valuable things that you've no doubt noticed on past visits."

"Like what?"

"Jewelry, for one thing. She has some expensive pieces."

"Really? How would you know that?"

Donna tipped her head with a smug smile. "She's my aunt, in

case you forgot, and they're family heirlooms. She showed me, since it'll all be coming to me soon."

"Soon? Sure sounds like you can't wait."

She pointed her finger at me. "You need to leave now."

"I don't suppose you'd let me see Nina first, would you? You know—as a goodwill gesture. I promise to quit bothering you if you do."

"When hell freezes over." She gazed up at the crystal clear blue sky. "Doesn't look like that'll be happening today."

A Little While Later

Hidden from the street by the flowering trumpet vine hanging from the eaves, I sat on the porch glider, gently rocking and nursing a cup of tea. Daisy lay beside me, resting her head on my lap.

"Well, that's that, Daisy. I've tried to get in that house several times." I scratched behind her floppy ears, and her back leg thumped the cushion. "Even got Sam, Ruby, and Ben involved. And I reported my suspicions to Social Services. So now it's time to give up."

Daisy lifted her head, ears perked at attention. A car door slammed, and I peeked through the vine. A squad car sat at the curb, and a grim-looking officer was marching up the walk.

Oh, God. This can't be good. I stepped out into the open. "Hi there. May I help you?"

Daisy bounded down the steps to meet her new best friend. The cop smiled warmly and patted her head. "Hey, poochie. Aren't you a sweet thing?" Her smile flip-flopped when she set her cool gaze on me. "Are you Katy McKenna?"

I swallowed hard. *Please don't tell me someone has died.* "I am. Is there something wrong, Officer?"

Daisy escorted the woman to the porch, then watched the brunette as she pulled out her phone and aimed the screen photo at me. "Look familiar?"

I'd know that butt anywhere. "Yes. That's me. I was trying to check on my neighbor. Nina Lowen. I'm very concerned about her welfare."

"So, you broke into the house instead of knocking on the door?"

"This isn't what you think," I said.

"I think you were breaking in." She glanced at my jeans. My front thighs had snags and dust on them. "What do you think?"

I think I should've changed my pants. "Are you going to arrest me?" I held out my hands to be cuffed, then jerked them back. "Wait. I need to put Daisy in the house first."

"Lucky for you, your neighbor is not pressing charges, so this is only a warning." She held the phone photo up again. "Do this again, and I will arrest you."

There was no way I could promise that I wouldn't do it again without lying. "I won't do it again."

"Thank you. Have a nice day." She stepped off the porch.

"Wait!" I tailed her down the walk to her car. "Has Social Services checked on Nina? I called and made a report several days ago."

"I wouldn't know. You'll have to take it up with them."

"They won't tell me anything. A few days after that woman…" I rolled my eyes, hoping she'd get the message. "…Donna Baxter came to (I finger-quoted) visit, she started blocking me from seeing Nina. Every time I try, she says Nina is (I finger-quoted again) sleeping. This has been going on for over two weeks now."

"Ms. Baxter told me about your concerns. She knows you care, and that's why she isn't pressing charges. However, Ms. Lowen is in her late eighties, so sleeping a lot doesn't sound unreasonable to me."

"She wasn't sleeping all the time before her niece arrived."

"A person's health at that age can change suddenly. I saw it happen with my grandfather. He had a nasty fall and was never the same again."

"Nina hasn't had a nasty fall."

A dispatch came through her radio—a family disturbance.

"I have to take this," she said. "Please, don't do anything fool-ish, okay? You seem like a nice person, and I don't want to arrest you."

She got in her car, flipped on the siren and lights, and sped away. I glanced down the street and saw Donna on the sidewalk, arms crossed and looking smug. I resisted the urge to flip her off.

She didn't resist the urge.

CHAPTER TWENTY-ONE

FRIDAY · JUNE 26
Posted by Katy McKenna

Sam called while I was putting on my makeup. "Hi. I'm driving Casey to the summer rec program at the park."

She was on Bluetooth, so Casey joined in. "Hey, Aunt Katy! I'm going to the park. Are you going to do boring errands today?"

"Hey, Casey. Let's see. Let me think. Yup. I'm doing boring errands today."

I heard him gleefully giggling in the backseat.

Sam got back into the conversation. "What's up with you? Are you all right? You haven't blogged in a few days."

It was her idea that I start a blog when I was suffering through my miserable divorce from Cheater-Chad. She said it would be therapeutic, and she was right.

I set the mascara tube on the counter and perched on the toilet seat lid. "I'm fine. There's nothing to blog, that's all."

"Maybe that's a good thing."

"I dunno. I feel like I don't have a purpose." I gazed at the grooming clutter on the counter, thinking I should clean up that mess one of these days.

"Sure you do. You still don't know what's going on at your neighbor's house. Hold on a sec. Casey? You got your lunch?"

"In my backpack, Mom. Bye, Aunt Katy!"

"Bye," I hollered. "Have a super fun day. Say hi to your girlfriend!"

"*Mom!* You told her?"

"You didn't tell me it's a secret, honey."

"Her name is Isabella," said Casey. "She's eight and really, really good at soccer. Bye, Aunt Katy."

The car door slammed, and Sam immediately jumped on my case. "What's happened to my snoopy, caring, vigilante-wannabe buddy?"

"I'm still here, but since that cop warned me off with the threat of arrest, I've let the Nina thing go. Really don't want to wind up in jail."

"If anything bad happens to Nina, you'll never forgive yourself."

"I don't think anything really bad is going to happen to her," I said. "Like Donna murdering her or something. It's just that it seems her life has been taken hostage by her niece, and there's nothing she can do about it. I've accepted the fact that there's nothing I can do about it, either."

"Before Donna came into the picture, Nina was making plans for a new, fun chapter in her life. Now, in just a few short weeks, her life has come to a grinding halt. She's sleeping all the time—"

"According to Donna," I interjected.

"Her beloved cat is living with you because Donna didn't want him. And her lovely home is in ruins. I didn't tell you this, but when you told me she wanted to move to Shady Acres, Spencer and I were seriously thinking about checking out her house to buy. We could have been neighbors. But no way now. I wanted the vintage house it was, not the fixer-upper mess it is now."

"Oh, that would have been so fun."

"Listen. If you decide to continue your Nina crusade, I'm here if you need my help. I'll even bail you out of jail if need be." She laughed. "Unless I'm in there with you. Don't forget—you got a hotshot attorney in the family now."

"That's true. We've got Ben. Let's talk later, okay?"

I finished my makeup and didn't clean up the counter. While giving my coffee a warm-up in the microwave, I thought about Sam's pep talk. She's right. I can't turn a blind eye and say it's none of my business. Someone has to do the right thing. And that someone is me!

I threw back my slouchy shoulders, wishing I had a Super Woman cape, and strode out the front door. Then went back inside, drank my coffee, and strapped on the FitTrim. By then, my initial resolve to be a valiant vigilante had dissolved into a more reasonable level of caution.

I sat on the porch steps and ran through different scenarios about how to get in that house to see Nina and with hope, get her out of there. Finally, I came up with a plan that was pretty crazy, but doable. Unfortunately, it required breaking in again.

However, this time, I would make sure that Donna wouldn't be around to catch me in the act.

———

Private.
I have to keep this private.
Mom reads my blog and tells Pop everything.

———

The Plan

Uncle Charlie's Clunker Carnival used car lot features an ongoing carnival with a Ferris wheel, merry-go-round, carny food, loud calliope music, and salespeople wearing clown costumes. It's amazing that this corny gimmick still works in this day and age, but it does.

Every year, they hold a contest to win a shiny used car. Usually it's a drawing, but last year they tried a new gimmick. The winner was the final person to still have a hand on the prize. I was hired to design the promotional poster for the contest. The contest went on for several grueling days and didn't go well, so this year they are back to having a simple drawing.

Donna wouldn't know about the contest, but she is definitely aware of the car lot because it's next to Home Depot where she bought the dog door. I was asked to do the poster again, but I was in England with Ruby when they contacted me. The winning name hasn't been drawn yet, so there are colorful posters and festive decorations around the lot right now.

My plan required a voice that Donna wouldn't recognize. But who? "Hold the phone! Betty! She's perfect."

Daisy had been snoozing on the porch next to me. She lifted her head, flicking her brows up and down quizzically. I gave her a little poke. "Grandma's friend. Caftan, turban—you know. She freaks you out."

She exhaled a long, belabored "whatever" sigh and settled her head on my lap.

I called Ruby. "Say 'hi' to your great-granddaughter. She misses you."

I held the phone by Daisy's ear, and Ruby screamed, "Hi. Grammy loves you, and I guess you're the only great-grandchild I will ever have!"

Daisy did a perfect down-dog yoga stretch, and moved to the porch swing.

"Whatcha doing?" I asked.

"I'm at the fitness center, and you just rescued me from the dreaded stair-stepper machine."

"Ooo. I hate that thing. By any chance is Betty around?"

"She's sitting on a recumbent bike chatting with the girls. Why do you ask?"

I outlined my plan to her. When I concluded, she said, "Oh, good! I was upset that you were giving up on Nina. I think I can safely say Betty will be thrilled to do it. We'll call it an acting gig."

Betty is a volunteer usher at our community theater. She's also active in the Shady Acres yearly stage productions. A few years ago, she played the lead in *Mame*. That's when she started wearing caftans full time.

Ruby went on. "You'll need to write a script for her because you do not want her ad-libbing. You should download some carnival music for background ambiance, too. When do you want to do it?"

"Tomorrow. The sooner, the better."

CHAPTER TWENTY-TWO

SATURDAY · JUNE 27
Posted by Katy McKenna

The Con
Private

The grand dames arrived at ten. Betty, attired in a purple, gold-trimmed caftan, matching turban, and gold sequined sneakers, regally swooshed through the door, trailed by a breeze of Elizabeth Taylor's White Diamonds and a hint of weed.

"Dah-ling." She held my hands, and air-kissed my cheeks. "So good to see you."

Daisy took one look at her and beelined to my bedroom. Mr. Snickers sidled up to Betty and sniffed the air, then joined Daisy. Tabitha, however, hung out with us.

I led the ladies to the kitchen table and offered coffee.

"I'll have a cup," said Ruby. "Got any cookies?"

I set a pink box on the table, and opened it to reveal an array of danishes. "Still want cookies?"

The ladies helped themselves while I poured coffees.

"Where's my script?" said Betty. "I need to rehearse my lines. Ruby explained the role I'm playing, but what's my inspiration? My motivation? What drives my character? What's her backstory?"

Ruby mumbled through a mouthful of apricot croissant. "Oh, good grief."

I sat opposite them and handed a one-page script to Betty, then flipped open my laptop. I'd already downloaded a long looping soundbite of carnival sounds. People screaming on fun rides, a barker enticing people to play a game of chance, and calliope music.

Betty lifted her long chin, her fake lashes fluttering as her hand floated back and forth in the air. "Ah, yes. Coney Island. Cotton candy. The funhouse." She opened her eyes wide and flashed me a smirk. "Yuh want me tuh do a Brooklyn accent, or what?"

"Wow," I said. "That's great."

Ruby wiggled in her seat. "Oh! Oh! Do the Muppet's Swedish Chef!"

Betty picked up the script. "Helluuu. I'm calleeng frum Kluunker Kernifel cer deelersheepa. Mey I speeka tu Nina Lowen-a, pleese-a?"

"Now do your Southern drawl," said Ruby.

"What state?"

"I don't care. Just give us your worst."

"Howdy. I'm callin' from Clunker Carnival caw dealership. May I spake to Nina Lowen, pelayze?"

I smacked the wood table. "I love it! That's the one I want you to do."

Ruby nodded. "It's my favorite, too."

I refilled our coffee cups. "The only problem with trying to follow a script is, Donna won't be following one so you may have to ad-lib a little."

Ruby widened her eyes at me, and I widened mine back at her with a shrug.

"All right, ladies. Let's do this," I said.

I picked up my phone and Betty shook her head. "Let's use mine just in case Nina's phone has caller I.D." Before Betty dialed the number, she said, "Friday's Five Fresh Fish Specials. Twixt this and six thick thistle sticks. Red leather, yellow leather."

Thinking Betty was having a breakdown, I glanced at Ruby.

"She's warming up," she said.

"Red leather, yellow leather. High roller, low roller, lower roller." Betty took a swig of coffee, gargled, and cleared her throat. "Ready now." She dialed, then hummed a catchy little tune as she waited.

"What's that song?" I asked.

Ruby grimaced. "The Doublemint Gum" commercial song from way back when I was a teenager. Now it's going to be stuck in my head all day."

I whispered to Betty, "Put the call on speaker."

She nodded, then held up a hand to shush us. "Howdy. I'm callin' from Clunker Carnival caw dealership. May I spake to Nina Lowen, pelayze?"

Donna: "Mrs. Lowen is napping and cannot come to the phone."

Betty: "Ah'm sorry. But it's imperative thet I spake to her. Would yawl be so kind as to wake her up?"

Donna: "Give me a message, and I will make sure she gets it."

Betty: "Is yawl the housekeeper?" Improv Betty was already off-script.

Donna (sounding snippy): "No. I'm her niece, and I take care of her. Anything you need to say to my aunt can be said to me. I'm her legal guardian."

I clapped my hand over my mouth to keep from screaming, *What a damned liar!*

Betty: "All righty then. I'm pleased to be the bearer of some exciting news. Nina Lowen has won a brand new previously owned caw in our annual caw give-a-way contest. She sent in her entry three months ago, and we drew her name tuhday. Isn't that wonderful?"

Donna (sounding excited): "Really? What kind of car?"

Betty widened her eyes at me, and I whispered, "A BMW SUV." I figured that would really get Donna going since she's been driving Nina's 1996 rusty Subaru Outback.

Betty: "Hold on to yer hat, honey. It's a one-year-old BMW SUV valued at $85,000. Only five thousand miles on it. Premium leather interior with all the bells and whistles yawl can imagine."

Donna (squealing now): "Are you kidding? $85,000?"

Betty: "Thets raht, sweetheart. But there's gist one little old hiccup. The caw must bay claimed tuhday, or we will draw a new winner. Now do yawl wanna wake up your auntie?"

Donna: "I can't. She's very old and weak and sick. I know! Since I'm her legal guardian, I can claim the car for her!"

Betty: "Hold on a little minute. Ah need to run thet by mah boss."

She put the call on hold and bobbed her head as she hummed the *Jeopardy* tune three times. Ruby and I nearly giggled our heads off.

Betty: "Hi. Ah'm back. Ah hope Ah didn't keep yawl waitin' too long. Mah boss said that would be fine as long as yawl git here within the hour. Please bring your driver's license and your aunt's, too."

At this point, Betty was totally off-script. "That's so we can make sure you're who yawl say you are. It's not that way don't trust yawl—it's gist a legal formality, yawl understand? Please bring your checkbook cuz there is a small title transfer fee. And make sure yawl got your lipstick on, hon, cuz there will be a news reporter coverin' the event."

Donna (sounding giddy): "Of course, I understand. I'm on my way right now."

Betty: "We'll be preppin' the caw for transfer when yawl git here, so git yourself some complimentary cotton candy an' stroll around the carnival area. We'll come git yawl when we're ready. Bye-bye now."

Donna: "Wait! Hold on! How will yawl, I mean you, know me?"

Betty (with a chuckle): "Well, that's easy, hon. Yawl will be the happiest lookin' gal on the lot."

Betty set her phone on the table with a triumphant look as Ruby and I applauded her performance. "How'd I do?"

"If I could, I'd give you an Oscar," I said.

"Gwad I couwd be of assistance."

I clapped my hands. "Elmer Fudd!"

"That was fun," said Ruby. "Now it's time for the next phase of this con."

———

We hid behind the tall evergreen bushes bordering the former Miller property waiting for Donna to leave. Betty leaned out to sneak a peek, and Ruby yanked her back. "Geez, Louise. If she sees us, we're toast!"

"Shh! The door's opening." Through the leaves, I spied Donna, all gussied up and practically skipping down the steps, looking giddy. Halfway through the yard, she tripped and did a nose dive into a dirt pile.

She rolled around in the dirt, screeching a vast array of expletives, trying to get to her feet.

"Oh, crap," I muttered. "What if she can't get up?" It was hard not to run over and help her.

Donna finally got to her feet. Her legs, arms, face, and pink muumuu were filthy. She checked her watch and realized she didn't have time to clean up. After another colorful round of cussing and a quick brush-off, she stomped to the car, climbed in, and slammed the door.

When the Subaru was out of sight, we scurried to the dog door.

I got down on all fours, ready to enter, and Baby Girl poked her head out the flap and licked my face. "Yes, I'm happy to see you, too."

"Wait a minute," said Ruby. "Someone needs to stand guard out front. Betty? It has to be you. Donna would recognize me."

Betty was on her way to the front yard when she stopped. "We need a signal. You know, in case she returns while Katy is still in the house."

"Good idea," said Ruby. "How about hooting like an owl?"

"Too soft. You might not hear me. How about a crow? CAW! CAW!" Just as she "cawed," a crow squawked a response in a pine tree next door.

"Ladies!" I said. "We're losing precious time. How about if Betty sees Donna driving down the street, she yells, 'She's back!' Then Betty can walk away as if she were strolling through the neighborhood."

"Works for me," said Betty.

"What about you, Katy?" asked Ruby. "You might not hear her."

"Shout at me through the dog door, then run for it. I'll sneak out of the yard as soon as I can."

"You know what happens when I run," said Ruby. "Or sneeze, or—"

"I don't think it will come to that. We should have plenty of time to check on Nina and be out of here long before Donna returns. I'm going in now. Wish me luck."

The Craftsman fireplace had been demolished, along with the mahogany built-in bookcases on either side. The half-wall of shelves topped with stained glass that had divided the living room and dining room was gone, too. I knew it was going to happen, but seeing the end result literally made me feel sick to my stomach. Most of the furniture had been removed—no doubt to the Salvation Army or the dump. Even the gorgeous antique Persian rug that had to be worth a fortune was gone. All that remained was the green couch, the coffee table, and a brown leather recliner with a Tiffany lamp on a side table next to it, topped with a pile of Milky Way candy wrappers, a plate with a few chips on it, a Coke can, and a *People* magazine.

I entered the first bedroom in the hallway. Silk scarves draped the lamps, and in the corner sat a gaudy dog bed mini-throne: red velvet and gold trim. It had to be new because she couldn't have brought it from Ketchikan. On the bedside table lay a dog-eared Rosemary Rogers bodice-ripper paperback.

The next door down the hall was closed. Holding my breath, I opened it. In the dim light filtering through the closed curtains, I saw Nina in the bed, the covers up to her chin.

"Nina?" then louder, "Nina?" She didn't respond. With trepidation, I placed a finger on her neck feeling for a pulse.

"Is she dead?"

I screamed and spun around. My scream made her scream, too. "You scared the heck out of me!"

"You scared me, too!" said Ruby. "Thank God, I always wear a sneeze guard."

"What are you doing in here?"

"Making sure you're safe."

"What if Donna comes back? You won't hear Betty."

"Trust me. We'll hear Betty. She's not known for being subtle." Ruby edged me aside to inspect Nina. "She looks so peaceful."

At that moment, Nina snorted, rolled over, and released a long toot.

"She's definitely alive!" I said. "Thank goodness."

Her glasses were on the nightstand, along with a glass of water, a box of tissues, soda crackers on a dish, peppermint lifesavers, and a half-empty bottle of extra-strength SleepWell nighttime liquid cold and flu medicine.

"What're you thinking?" asked Ruby.

"I'm thinking maybe I let my dislike for Donna cloud my judgment. She seems okay, right?"

"I wouldn't call sleeping all the time *okay*." She picked up the purple cold medicine. "No doubt this has something to do with it." She shook her head. "However, I think we're at a dead end here. Nina doesn't appear to be in immediate danger, and you have gone above and beyond for her." She set the medicine on the night stand. "I don't think there's anything more you can do, short of kidnapping her." She saw the scheming expression on my face. "Don't even think about it. I'm too old to go to prison."

"I doubt we'd go to prison for taking her to my house. She could sleep off the cold medicine and then tell us what she wants to do."

"What about Donna?"

"We'll leave her a note," I said.

Ruby shook her head. "And then she'd know we'd been in the house, and she'd call the cops. Next thing you know, we're doing hard time."

I blew out a sigh. "Damn it. I wasn't thinking."

"Ca-CAW! Ca-CAW!"

"Is that Betty?" I said.

"Yup." She took my hand. "Time to skedaddle."

"I thought we weren't doing the crow thing."

Ruby shook her head. "Trust me. It's Betty. And that means the bitch is back."

"That was fast," I said. "I wonder what happened."

We dashed through the house to the dog door. Ruby wriggled through first, then Baby Girl shoved in front of me and joined her outside. As I was crawling through, the hem of my gauze cotton top snagged on a screw.

"Hurry!" said Ruby.

"I'm stuck! Save yourself! Go!"

She got down on her knees. "I'm not leaving without you." She reached in, yanking the shirt. The fabric ripped.

"Crap! This is my favorite top."

"I'll buy you a new one." Ruby tugged hard. "I can't get it undone. You need to take it off."

"How am I going to do that? I'm kinda stuck here!"

"CA-CAAAW! CA-CAAAAAW!"

"See if you can back up and pull it over your head," said Ruby. "Hurry!"

I squirmed my way backwards into the living room, keeping my arms stretched out in front of me as the shirt slid over my head. I wriggled free, and Ruby gave it a Herculean yank, ripping the shirt off the screw, along with toppling the entire dog door insert out of the slider frame. Ruby tumbled backwards onto her rear as it crashed to the dirt outside. I stepped through the opening just as Donna inserted her key into the front door.

Ruby held out her hands. "Help me up."

"Are you okay?"

"Yes! Just get me up!"

She groaned as I hauled her to her feet, but seemed all right. Holding hands, we fled the scene.

A few seconds later, Donna screamed, "WHAT THE HELL? You BAD, BAD dog."

I stopped on the side of the house to look through the side window of the dining room. Donna was holding a big cone of pink cotton candy and glaring at the broken dog door.

"As if I haven't had a bad enough day already—getting bamboozled by a crank call that made me look like a fool. Someone must've got a good laugh at my expense. That door cost me 150 bucks, you damned dog!" She put the cotton candy on the plate on the lamp table, grabbed the *People* magazine, rolled it into a bat, and swatted the innocent dog several times. "Stupid, bad dog!"

Without thinking, I turned to go back. Ruby grabbed my arm, whispering, "There's nothing you can do. Come on."

I slipped into my tattered shirt and we hurried home.

In the kitchen I said, "I know it's a tad early, but I could use a glass of wine. Who's with me?"

My partners in crime raised their hands, shouting, "Me!" While I poured us jittery ladies all a hefty glass, Ruby told Betty what happened in Nina's house.

After chugging half a glass, I announced, "Ladies? Nina appears to be all right, more or less. The truth we must face is we can't do a thing about her dismal situation. I must admit, I feel like a failure."

"Honey, don't beat yourself up," said Betty. "You've gone above and beyond what most people would do."

"That's right," said Ruby. "You accomplished the mission. You got in the house and found Nina—alive and well." She shrugged. "She's alive anyway, and looked okay. That has to be comforting to you."

"Thank you both for your help. It means a lot to me." I sighed. "But your attempts to make me feel better are not working. We may not be able to help Nina, but, there *is* someone we can save."

"Do you have another neighbor in distress?" asked Betty. "If so, count me in."

I nodded. "Yes. Baby Girl."

Ruby looked dumbfounded. "You can't stand that dog."

"It's her name I can't stand. I've never met a dog I didn't like, or cat, or horse, or bird, or any other animal for that matter." I snapped my fingers. "Oh, wait. That's not true. I've met plenty of people I didn't like."

"Amen to that," said Ruby. "Count me in!"

"Girl power!" said Betty, wagging her empty goblet at me.

CHAPTER TWENTY-THREE

MONDAY · JUNE 29
Posted by Katy McKenna

There's another project underway at the Miller house. I should quit calling it the "Miller house," since they're long gone. Solar panels now line the roof facing the street. And they're planting panels on half of the front lawn, too. Our homes sit on quarter-acre lots, so needless to say, the big panels look ridiculous in the smallish front yard.

I approached the man who looked in charge. "Hi there. I'm wondering about something."

He turned to me, and I realized it was the same guy who'd supervised the wind generators on the roof. Today, Mel wore a dark green cap with a "Polar-Solar" logo.

"Patsy! Good to see you again. Have you given any thought to installing a wind generator?"

He caught me off-guard for a second. I'd forgotten I'd fibbed about my name the other day. "Not really." I pointed at the panels. "Is it legal to have solar panels sitting in the yard?"

"There's no law that says you can't. Pretty soon, he'll be generating enough power to supply the entire block."

"Is he home now? I should introduce myself. I don't even know his name."

"His name is Simon Prichard. He's some kind of reclusive computer guru and prefers not to be disturbed. If I have questions, I just call or text him. For all I know, he could be on the other side of the planet."

"I'll ring the doorbell. Who knows, maybe he'll answer."

"Suit yourself." Mel's attention was diverted to a panel swinging from a crane. "Hey! Watch what you're doing! Someone could get killed."

I decided to go home and read rather than risk getting decapitated at the "Prichard house."

The Kupcake Kaper
Chapter 16

"A penny for your thoughts," said Larry to Patsy in the bakery kitchen.

The cute, curvy woman set her latest cupcake creation on a plate and sipped her steamy coffee, eyeing her husband over the rim and thinking, *I know what you've been doing. I hate you, and I wish you were dead.*

Larry set his hands on her hips, pulling her close, grinding his aroused man parts into her, and inquired, "Why so quiet, baby?"

"I'm just thinking about what a very lucky girl I am to be married to such a swell guy like you. That's what Shawna always tells me. She says she is so jealous of me." *Yeah. Shawna. My so-called best friend and your shag buddy.*

With satisfaction, she felt his boner instantly collapse.

Larry's smile grew wider as he backed away. "Oh? She said that? What else did she say?"

"She said I should watch out because one of these days, someone might steal you away from me."

His smile froze and he asked, "She did?"

"She sure did. But don't let it go to your head. You know what lousy taste she has in men. One loser after another." Patsy picked up the cupcake and smeared the creamy frosting across Larry's thin lips and bristly mustache. "Take a bite. It's a new recipe."

He chewed with a perplexed expression. "That's, uh, really different."

Patsy stiffened and frowned. "Oh? You don't like it?"

Larry plucked the cupcake from her fingers. "No, no. It's just, uh, very unique." He finished half the cupcake. "I can't quite put my finger on it." He nodded, looking at the cake. "Chocolate, but what else?"

"Curry. And the salted caramel cream cheese frosting has hot curry and ginger in it. Pretty crazy, huh?" said Patsy.

"Crazy good!" He exclaimed as he popped the rest in his mouth. "But, it might be a little too sophisticated for our customers."

"Shawna really loved them."

"She was here?" Larry swallowed, and his protruding Adam's apple bobbed up and down in his long skinny neck.

"A little while ago. She loved the cupcake so much, she ate two. I asked her to have dinner with us, but she had to scurry. You know what? She hasn't had dinner with us in a very long time. I wonder why."

Patsy watched her husband's guilty face flush, and then she held out another cupcake.

He shook his head. "Oh, I don't want to take the last one. You eat it."

"Nope, this one's got your name on it. I have another

batch in the oven." She peered at her watch. "They should be done now."

As she slid the cupcake baking pan out of the oven, Larry asked, "Why did she have to go?"

"She has a very hot date tonight. Sure hope he's not another loser." Then very slyly, she said, "I hope she's using protection. Did I tell you she has a STD? Tacky, huh?"

"STD? What's that?"

"You are so innocent, Larry! She's got chlamydia." She pressed a finger over his lips. "Do not tell her I told you. She would die of embarrassment."

Patsy stepped to the sink and started washing the big pile of dirty dishes in the sink. Larry grabbed a towel and dried the big glass bowl she handed him.

"I sure hope Shawna tells her date about her STD if things start to get hot and heavy—because, well, you know," said Patsy.

"Know what?" he questioned.

She watched him out of the corner of her eye. "Chlamydia causes erectile dysfunction."

Larry dropped the big glass bowl on the floor and it broke into a million sharp pieces. "Sorry. Clumsy me. I'll go get a broom."

"No, I'll clean it up. You have your Elks meeting, right?"

"I sure do—every Tuesday night for the past two years," he babbled. "Thursday is bowling night. Monday—Rotary. Wednesday afternoon is chamber."

"You're a very, very busy boy, aren't you," she said.

"It gets very tiring," he sighed. "But it's for the business, you know. Except for the bowling. You should join a women's team. It's really fun."

"No, thank you. I'm too tired from baking and taking

care of customers six days a week to go out at night and toss a twelve-pound ball at a bunch of pins."

"Don't forget, I have that big Rotary fundraiser meeting in Anchorage next weekend."

"I haven't forgotten. I had thought that Shawna and I could have a girl's night on Saturday. You know, order pizza, make popcorn, watch a couple old chick flicks, like *The First Wives Club*. I love those movies where the women destroy, or better yet, murder their cheating husbands." She heavily sighed. "But it turns out, she'll be out of town, too."

Larry's eyes got really wide and he stammered, "Oh, really? Where's she going?"

Patsy said, "To visit her mother in Fairbanks, poor thing. That woman is a monster, but Shawna is a very good, very devoted daughter and says it's her duty."

"Yeah, she's a very good girl, all right." He tossed the towel on a wooden peg and headed to the door. "I gotta get going, but hey — you know you could still order pizza and watch a movie on Saturday night."

She smiled broadly. "Oh, I intend to. I might even treat myself to some champagne. Like a little celebration."

"What will you be celebrating?" he asked.

"Life, liberty, and the pursuit of happiness."

CHAPTER TWENTY-FOUR

TUESDAY · JUNE 30
Posted by Katy McKenna

On our morning stroll, Daisy and I checked out the solar project next door. I'm thankful I have mature evergreen trees and bushes separating our yards so I don't have to look at them. Don't get me wrong; I am all for solar power. In fact, if Mel is right about the new neighbor producing enough electricity to power the whole block, I might sneak over and plug in a long extension cord. Think of all the money I could save!

Randy and Earl called me over. At the foot of the porch steps, I said, "You guys sure look glum. What's up?"

"Come up on the porch, and you tell us."

I followed their gaze across the street to the blinding glare from the solar lawn panels.

"We like sitting out here in the morning," said Randy. "Drinking tea, waving at the neighbors, and letting the peaceful vibes set our ch'i in harmony for the day, but this is a total buzzkill."

"I never would've thought this could happen," I said. "Have you talked to the guy?"

Randy shook his head. "We've gone over three times, but he's never around."

My gaze shifted to Nina's property. "Looks like Donna must've paid off the workers. What are they jackhammering now?"

Earl said, "That's our other buzz kill. They're removing the brick steps."

Randy said, "We're talking about selling the place. This was our grandparents' home. A lot of happy memories here, but this neighborhood is really going downhill."

"That's what Nina said not too long ago." *Although, at the time she was mainly complaining about the boys.*

He went on. "We're thinking about getting some land out in the countryside. Build a yurt. Grow our own vegetables. Get some chickens for fresh eggs, and a goat. Eventually, we could each have our own yurt for when we get married. Make it a family compound. Kids and dogs running around."

I smiled, feeling a bit wistful. "That sounds really delightful. I'll come visit you."

"You will always be welcome," said Earl.

"Ya better watch out. I may pitch a tent and never leave."

It was time to be on my way. Daisy and I strolled to the end of the block, crossed the street, and started back towards home. As I neared the dirt where Nina's concrete driveway had been, Donna came out clutching a large cardboard box. Spilling over the rim was a red, white, and black flowered blouse sleeve that looked like the one Nina had worn on her visit to Shady Acres. I dragged Daisy back to the house we'd just passed and hid behind a Hopseed bush to observe her.

After she stowed the carton in the Subaru, she left the hatch open and returned to the house. As soon as she was out of sight, I ran to the car and peeked into the box. I was right. It was the same blouse. In fact, everything in the carton looked like Nina's clothes.

The front door slammed. Daisy and I hustled back to our hiding place. Donna shoved another box into the back of the car. I was torn between confronting her and staying out of sight. Out-of-sight won. I breathed a sigh of relief when she sped off in the opposite direction.

This wasn't the first time I've seen Donna put large boxes in the car. All I can think is they're getting rid of stuff in anticipation of Nina's move to Shady Acres.

The Kupcake Kaper
Chapter 17

"Oh, honey-bunchkins," cooed Patsy. "I'm so sorry you have an upset tummy."

Larry groaned, clutching his belly. "Yeah. It's very bad." He stood, looking very alarmed. "Gotta go again!" He rushed out of the living room.

"I'll bring you something for your tummy ache," hollered Patsy through the bathroom door, smiling to herself. "I'm so sorry you didn't make it to your Elks meeting. I know how much it means to you. All the good works you do for the community."

"Must be something I ate," he said, whimpering pitifully.

Patsy could hear his stomach contents dumping into the toilet and said very cheerfully, "I just talked to Shawna, and she is really sick, too. She had to cancel her hot date. Maybe there's a nasty bug going around."

"Yeah, maybe," gasped Larry.

Patsy winked at their cat, who was curling around her legs, and whispered, "Or maybe it's all the chocolate flavored laxative I put in the cupcakes. Revenge can be sweet, huh Baby Girl?"

What? The cat's name is Baby Girl?

"What did you say?" called Larry in between wrenching groans and farts.

"Oh, nothing. Just talking to the cat. I'll go get the Bismuth. That'll make you feel *all* better."

Patsy took a cherry-flavored Magnesium Citrate bottle from the cabinet in the hallway where they stored medicine and first aid supplies.

Whoa. Wait a sec. Isn't that a laxative? I took a moment to check online, and sure enough, it is.

She also grabbed the cherry-flavored Nighttime Cold and Flu liquid medicine. In the kitchen, she poured a quarter cup of the nighttime medicine in a bowl and whisked in a quarter cup of the magnesium citrate. It was too thin, so she added cornstarch to thicken it to proper bismuth consistency. She poured the concoction into a juice glass and then went to the bathroom and tapped on the door.

"Can I come in, sweetheart? I have your medicine. It's a new flavor. Cherry." She opened the door and saw Larry sitting on the toilet, clutching his stomach. "Here, sweetie. Drink this," she said as she opened the window. "It's a double dose to get you started. We'll get that nasty diarrhea under control in a jiffy."

Larry tipped the contents into his mouth and wiped his lips on his sleeve. "Not bad. Better than the mint flavor. Could you bring me more TP? I think I'm going to need it." He flushed the toilet and pulled his pants up.

"Why don't you lie down for a while? Later on, I'll make you some nice bone broth. But right now, I need to frost a fresh batch of cupcakes."

"More of the new ones?" he said, clutching his stomach with a wince.

"No. Your favorite. Carrot-zucchini. It's a special order for the hospital auxiliary. I'll give you more medicine in an hour."

His eyes widened, and he grimaced. "Gotta go!"

Yeah, I know, she thought, stifling a giggle.

CHAPTER TWENTY-FIVE

WEDNESDAY • JULY 1
Posted by Katy McKenna

While running errands downtown that my little friend Casey would call boring, I passed by the defunct business I once shared with my ex: The Bookstore Bistro. Heather, Chad's second wife, sold it after she divorced him and moved away with their baby to live with her mother. We've kept in touch and she's doing well.

Half a block down, a parking enforcement officer was pinning a ticket under the windshield wiper of an old green Subaru. I slowed to a crawl to get a closer look, and sure enough, it was Nina's car.

I whipped around the block, parked, and fed the meter, then crept down the street towards the car, keeping an eye out for Donna. Two doors away, I stood under a covered entrance. I couldn't wait to see her reaction when she saw the $65 ticket. I know the dollar amount from bitter past experience.

Peeping around the corner of the brick wall, I gazed down the sidewalk. A shop doorbell jingled across the street. Donna, wearing a floral purple muumuu and flip-flops, stepped out. I shrunk into the shadows feeling wickedly gleeful and got out my phone, thinking a P.I. would record her movements.

"Godammit!" Donna ripped the parking ticket from the wiper blade and yelled for all to hear, "Sixty-five dollars? Are you kidding me?" She waved the ticket at a scrawny teenager wearing a gray beanie and toting a skateboard. "Sixty-five damned bucks! Can you believe it? Do I look like I'm made of money?"

The young guy dashed across the street and sped off on the skateboard.

She crumpled the citation, jerked the car door open, and tossed it in before settling her big bottom on the driver's seat.

After she drove away, I went over to the store she'd exited. Posh Jewelers—Consignment Estate Jewelry is our Specialty. Inside, I glanced around the shop, taking in the Victorian décor and glass jewelry cases.

"May I help you?" said a familiar-looking, dapper, bow-tied senior behind the counter.

I stared for a moment, trying to place him. "Do I know you?"

He bowed. "Cornelius Hembry at your service."

"That's right! You sell vacuums and are a Universal Life Church minister, too. I was there when you did a funeral ceremony for a cat."

"Good old Dave. Wanda's cat."

"Yes. At ACME Upholstery. I did a graphic art job for her."

"I remember the lovely logo you designed."

"Thank you. So, you're selling estate jewelry now?"

He tweaked his silver handlebar moustache. "I find it exhilarating after selling vacuums for so many years."

"I've never been in here before." I looked into the glass case. "The reason I came in is I saw a lady leave a few minutes ago, and she looked pleased."

"She brought in some exquisite pieces for consignment. I'm not ready to put them in the display cases yet. Would you like a little peek?"

He spread a black velvet cloth on the counter and arrayed the jewelry on it. I gasped when I recognized the ring that Nina used to wear on her right hand. A ruby flanked by two diamonds set in pink gold. It had been her great-grandmother's. Her wedding set was in the group, too. She'd stopped wearing rings because her knuckles were too arthritic to get them on anymore. Several pieces I didn't recognize. However, the Victorian gold bangle she always wears was in the group. I picked it up and read the inscription. "To my darling Lulu—April 23, 1892."

"Ah. I see you appreciate fine vintage jewelry," said Cornelius.

"Yes, I do." I hesitated, trying to work up the courage to continue. "Mr. Hembry?"

"Tut, tut. Please call me Cornelius. We're old friends."

I smiled, wondering if he'd feel that way after what I was about to say. "Cornelius. I have not been entirely up front with you. The woman who left these pieces may not be on the up-and-up."

I was treading on thin ice, but I felt I'd be doing a disservice to the kind gentleman, if I didn't tell him what I suspected. "That woman, Donna Baxter, is staying at my dear friend's house. My friend, Nina Lowen, is her aunt. She's in her late eighties, and I think Donna is taking advantage of her. I do not believe for one minute that Nina would give her niece permission to pawn her jewelry." I picked up the bangle. "Nina wears this every day." I did not get into my suspicions that Donna is drugging Nina to keep her sleeping all the time. I probably would have sounded like a nut case.

Cornelius frowned, looking disturbed. "Oh, dear. That is distressing." He pulled the black velvet closer and began to fold the jewelry into it.

"I'm sorry to be so blunt. I can understand how crazy I sound."

He shook his head. "I have no reason to doubt what you say."

"May I take some photos and show them to my friend? You know, to make sure Nina is good with this." I set my hand on his. "I also ask that you do not sell them until I get back to you."

"Absolutely. I have no wish to deal with someone who may have untoward motives. Like your dear friend, I too am in my eighties. There are those who think that simply because someone is in their elder years, they are easy prey for a swindle. I will have you know all my brain cells are intact."

Back in my car, I was at a loss about what to do next. I'd told Cornelius I would show the photos to Nina. But in reality, how was that going to happen, given the way things were going? Then I thought of Angela Yaeger. Our police chief and my friend. The station was two blocks away. I pumped more money into the parking meter and headed there, hoping she would have time to see me.

———

Angela greeted me with open arms at her office doorway. "Katy! It's been too long!"

I embraced her, thinking how fortunate our city is to have her. A while back, the lovely silver-haired black woman tried to talk me into joining the force. I gave it serious thought and concluded I'd make a lousy cop.

"I heard about your adventures in England. Good grief, Katy! How do you always manage to find trouble?"

"To quote I don't know who—*I don't go looking for trouble. Trouble has a way of finding me.*"

"Ha! You sound like a gumshoe in an old film noir mystery. Trouble keeps finding you because you're such a good, caring person."

"Thank you, Angela. Your opinion means a lot to me. Although, I spend most of my days feeling like a total idiot."

She laughed. "That just means you're getting older."

"How do you mean?"

"When we're younger, we think we know everything. As we

143

mature, we learn otherwise. Wait'll you're my age. Every day I keep learning just how much I don't know. Especially the last few years. Just when you think things can't get any crazier, they do." She shook her head, looking peeved. "It's wearing me down, let me tell you."

"You're not thinking about quitting, are you?"

Angela shook her head. "No. I'm in it until they retire me. It's people like you who keep me going. But the load gets heavier every year. In my early years, I lost two partners to domestic abuse calls." She held up two fingers. "Two. Both shot when the door opened."

"My dad had to retire after a domestic abuse call. Shot in the knee and permanently disabled."

"It was a big loss for the department," she said. "Kurt Melby was a good cop. One of the best."

"Thank goodness he survived and went on to open his fix-it shop and enjoy life. Every day, I thank my lucky stars that he is my stepfather."

"I dropped off my ancient Vitamix blender the other day and we had a nice chat. Most of it about you. Go figure." Angela offered me a cup of coffee, and we sat on the saggy, brown leather couch that has held many police chiefs through the years.

"So, what brings you here today?" She cocked her head, looking mischievous. "Any wedding plans with that gorgeous boyfriend of yours? If you need an officiant, I am available, you know."

I sighed. "I wish."

"That doesn't sound good."

I brought her up to speed on the Josh dilemma, and then gave her a synopsis of the Nina situation, however, I didn't mention the part where I entered her home without permission. My big finish were the photos of Nina's jewelry, thinking she'd exclaim, "Let's go arrest that thieving bitch!"

Instead, she calmly said, "Do you have any proof that she stole them from Nina? This woman is her niece, and as you say, her only heir, so perhaps Nina gifted her these heirlooms now."

"And then she turns around and pawns them?"

"If they were a gift, then that's her choice." She waved her hand at me. "Don't give me that look. Of course, I think it's despicable, but people do despicable things every day. Pawning family jewelry is a helluva lot better than murdering family members."

"Can't argue with that."

She arched an eyebrow. "I heard about your little escapade the other day."

I widened my eyes. "Huh?"

"Don't act innocent. I saw the dog door derrière photo. Boy, did that give me a much needed laugh." Her warm brown eyes narrowed, drilling into mine. "You do realize they could have arrested you for that stunt, right?"

"I know, but I was really concerned about her, Angela."

"And now?"

"I *had* decided to quit worrying and leave it to social services. But after seeing the pawned jewelry—and the fact that Donna is getting rid of Nina's clothes." I shook my head. "I'm back to fretting."

She frowned. "How do you know about the clothes?"

"I saw Donna putting cardboard boxes in the car."

"So you were spying on her? Katy, she can get a restraining order. Do you want that on your record?"

"Angela, I wasn't spying. I was walking the dog. Minding my own business. I swear. I can't help what I see."

She shook her head. "I suppose not. However, we can't do anything unless a crime has been committed. We could get sued. As it is, the department has three in the works as we speak. One more, and I might lose my job." She sighed heavily. "I just want to make it to retirement. Five more years and I collect my pension and then my husband and I go on a very long fly-fishing trip."

I hung my head staring at my hands in my lap. "You're basically saying that until something bad happens, there's nothing we can do to *prevent* it from happening."

"This is when I dislike my job. There are a lot of doors in this town that I would dearly love to kick in. But I can't." She reached for my hands and clasped them firmly. "Tell you what. I'll call Adult Protective Services right now and see if anyone followed up on your report." Angela sat at her desk and made the call. After a couple minutes, she hung up and returned to the couch. "I'm sure you got the gist of the conversation."

I nodded. "Doesn't sound like they're concerned."

"They did a home visit a couple days after your call. The woman said she would send me a copy of the report. She said they saw no signs of neglect—such as malnutrition or personal hygiene. Nor physical injury or signs of constraint or assault. They advised the niece to make sure that during the remodel, Mrs. Lowen was able to safely navigate the house."

"Did they talk to Nina?"

"I would assume so," she said. "The bottom line is, they saw no reason to remove Mrs. Lowen from the home."

I shook my head. "I know I'm right about this. I can feel it in my bones. But I guess that's that."

Angela nodded, looking serious. "It is, Katy.

———

I parked in my driveway and was gathering my things when Randy ran over. "You missed the fireworks!"

"It's a little early for fireworks."

"Not that kind of fireworks, Katy. It was Donna. She went totally ape-shit." His eyes widened. "Sorry about the language."

"I'm not offended by anything nasty you say about her. Tell me what happened."

We strolled towards Nina's as Randy told his story. "We were in the back yard when Donna started screaming, so we ran out thinking someone needed help. She was throwing dirt clods at the workers and calling them losers who don't have a clue what they're doing. The foreman dude said he was going to sue her for breach of contract. Then she said, 'Not before I sue you first.'" We stopped on the sidewalk in front of the house.

"Darn it! I would've loved to have seen that," I said.

"Yeah. It was intense. Then the guys packed up their gear and the porta-potty, and left."

"I see the old toilet is still in the yard," I said. "Good thing the house has two bathrooms."

Donna came out on the porch and yelled, "What're you two gawking at?"

I grinned and waved. "Just admiring the yard décor. I've always been a fan of recycling old toilets into garden art. Have a nice day, Donna!"

CHAPTER TWENTY-SIX

THURSDAY • JULY 2

Posted by Katy McKenna

Josh called late last night.

The thing that I feared might happen has happened. Nicole proposed to Josh.

He told me she's not responding as well as hoped to treatment, so she has decided to stop the chemo and enjoy life. How could he say no?

Josh will give her the happy ending she deserves. He's buying an RV, and they plan to visit National Parks across the country. It'll be their home on wheels. They're even getting a little dog to share the adventure with them. A happy family.

I think there's a good chance that Nicole will beat this. Happiness can be potent medicine.

But for me? It's officially time to move on. And I will. Just not today.

CHAPTER TWENTY-SEVEN

FRIDAY • JULY 3
Posted by Katy McKenna

"Katy!" yelled Sam. "We know you're in there."

"Get your butt out of bed and open this damned door," shouted Ruby. "Do you hear me, missy? You're upsetting your mother."

"Please, Katy?" said Mom. "We love you. Things will get better, I promise."

"Geez, Louise. This feels like déjà vu," said Ruby. "Seems like it was only last week that we were standing in this very spot banging on the door and begging her to let us in."

"I don't remember that," said Sam.

"It was Marybeth and me. Katy had just found out that Chad-the-Cad was getting remarried."

Their conversation was recording on my doorbell camera. While they pounded on the front door, I was in the back yard cleaning my shed office. When I finally got weary of Daisy's barking, I checked the app on my phone and heard my loved ones disturbing the peace on the porch.

As I approached the front entry, I clicked the phone's microphone icon and wailed, "I'm never getting out of bed again!" Then opened the door and hollered, "And you can't make me!"

The three of them froze, gawking at me.

"You're dressed," said Sam. "You have makeup on."

"You're having a good hair day," grumbled Ruby.

"My baby," cried my teary-eyed mother, flinging her arms around me. "I hate Josh. He hurt my baby."

"Don't hate him for doing the right thing." I gently disengaged from her viselike grip. "There's coffee in the kitchen and homemade cookies on the counter."

Ruby led the way into the kitchen. "Who brought you the cookies?"

"No one. I made them." I fluttered my hands. "With my own two little hands. I also baked bread and lemon bars." I set the plate of bars next to the cookies. "Grab a few, and let's sit on the patio. It's such a lovely day outside."

I caught Ruby arching a skeptical eyebrow at Mom.

"No, Grandma. I'm not unhinged. I had my cry, and it was long and bitter." I patted my dog's head. "Poor Daisy really had her work cut out, taking care of her hysterical momma. After that, I had a craving for goodies, so I started baking. Cleaning, too. Been wearing my FitTrim, and you'd be shocked how many steps you rack up in a day of serious house cleaning. I even rearranged a few things in the living room. Go look, Mom. Grandma."

"I take it that's our cue to give you a moment with Sam," said Mom, as she guided Ruby out of the kitchen.

Sam took my hand and inspected my chewed-up nails. "Are you sure you're okay? They wanted to come over yesterday, and I told you needed to be alone."

"Good call. Thank you."

She pulled me close, patting my back like a momma. "It'll be okay."

"I know. It's not like I didn't see this coming." I shrugged, swiping away a fresh drizzle of tears.

"True. But it still hurts."

"It hurts like hell. Some good has come from it, too." I cleared the lump in my throat. "I now know what I'm looking for in a man. Josh ticked off all the right boxes, and then some. However, the next one must be a totally unencumbered man."

"At our age, everyone is encumbered. Would you consider someone who has a kid?"

"Yes. Definitely." I thought about that a moment, and cracked a smile. "But only if he's a widower."

CHAPTER TWENTY-EIGHT

MONDAY · JULY 6

Posted by Katy McKenna

My folks invited me over for a BBQ on the fourth, but I wasn't up to it. While channel surfing, I discovered an all-day *Twilight Zone* marathon on the SYFY channel. I spent a therapeutic lazy day on the couch, noshing on snack food and residing in the "zone."

This Afternoon

I ventured outside my bubble to see what's going on in the world. As I passed by the next-door neighbor's house, a humming-bird hovered inches from my face for a few magical seconds. Barely breathing, I felt a breeze from his beating wings while he decided if my orange shirt was a flower. He spun away and slammed into a solar panel in the lawn.

Heartbroken, I cradled the bird's tiny limp body in my hands and marched to the front door. I pressed the doorbell-video camera. No answer. I punched the bell again. And again.

"What?" shouted a cranky, tinny, masculine voice from the doorbell.

I leaned towards it, knowing he'd get a fisheye view of me. "I'm your next-door neighbor. Katy McKenna."

"Hello, Katy McKenna. I'm your next-door neighbor, Simon Prichard. What do you want?"

I held out my open palm so he could see the hummingbird.

"Why are you showing me a dead bird?"

"Because you killed him with your damned solar panels."

"Well, excuse me for trying to save the planet. Do you have any idea how many birds collide with power lines and die every year? Twenty-five million. Twenty-two million die from crashing into house windows. Do you have any windows, Katy McKinnie?"

I gritted my teeth. "It's McKenna. And, of course, I have windows."

"Then you're a bird killer. Buh-bye."

CHAPTER TWENTY-NINE

TUESDAY · JULY 7
Posted by Katy McKenna

Last Night

Stayed up late, reading Donna's book. Not because I love it. Far from it. They say writers write what they know. So, you never know what I might learn.

Patsy opened a new bottle of berry-flavored sleep aid and poured the contents into a crystal syrup pitcher. Then she added liquid melatonin and topped it off with blueberry syrup. She stirred the concoction.

"Ooo. Something sure smells good," called Larry from his leather recliner in the living room.

"Blueberry buttermilk waffles. I picked the berries this morning," said Patsy as she dipped a spoon into the pitcher and stirred the concoction. "And I made your favorite homemade blueberry syrup."

"You're killing me. But, sorry, no can do," he said.

"Tummy still on the fritz?"

"Actually, I feel much better." Larry walked into the kitchen and snapped his waistband. "Even lost a few pounds."

"I'll take a pass on your diet methods."

Larry glanced at the waffle makings on the counter. "Two kinds?"

"I know that blueberry is your favorite. But you know me, I'm old-school and stick with buttermilk and maple syrup. Never been a big berry fan."

"I do love blueberries." He poured a glass of milk and sat at the kitchen table. "Anyway, I think I'm up to going to Anchorage for the Rotary meeting, after all."

Patsy frowned. "Oh, honey. Are you sure? It's nearly a five-hour flight. Do you really want to risk being sick on the plane?"

He nodded. "This meeting is very important, and to tell you the truth, my stomach is so empty that I don't see how I could possibly get sick again at this point."

Patsy forked a hot buttermilk waffle from the waffle iron onto a plate. "You know what? On second thought, I think I'll have a blueberry one, too," she said very slyly.

She poured the batter into the waffle maker and very gently set the top down. Then she sat at the table, spread a few tablespoons of butter on her waffle, and drowned it with Log Cabin syrup.

Larry grimaced. "I don't get how you like that syrup better than your own homemade blueberry syrup. It's not even real maple."

"Takes me back to my childhood." Patsy set down the syrup bottle and shoveled a big bite of dripping waffle into her mouth. She rolled her eyes. "Mmmm." She dabbed her sticky chin, and then leaned back in her chair with a long, satisfied sigh. "So good. Too bad you can't have any. Maybe on my blueberry waffle, I'll have the blueberry syrup. I will enjoy it in honor of you." She hopped up from her seat and went to the steaming waffle iron. "Done and all mine."

Patsy set the blueberry waffle on a plate and set the plate in the center of the table, and liberally buttered it. "This is that fancy French butter you love." Then she drenched it with the blueberry syrup. "I'll let it get a little mushy while I finish my first waffle." She suppressed a little giggle as she watched her husband staring longingly at the heavenly smelling blueberry syruped blueberry waffle. He dipped a finger into the syrup and licked his finger.

"Mmm. So good." He crinkled his brow. "The syrup tastes a little different. Even better than usual. What did you do? Add more sugar?"

"It's the blueberries. I think they're sweeter and juicier this year from that very hot heatwave we had."

Larry took another taste. "Yeah, that must be it."

"You sure you don't want a few bites? I don't want you getting faint from lack of food."

"I don't want to take your waffle away from you," he said.

"No worries. I'm feeling full, anyway. There's plenty more batter if I want one."

"Well, okay." He dragged the plate over. "A few bites can't hurt."

"Larry. Don't eat it! It's drugged!" I shouted at my Kindle. He ignored me and ate the waffle. What a dope!

"I'm so stuffed I might explode. I didn't intend to eat three waffles," said Larry, patting his belly. He glanced at his watch. "Yikes. I gotta get going, or I'll miss my flight!"

Patsy smiled sweetly. "Need any help packing?"

"Nope. All done." He belched, then stood and pecked her on the cheek. "Have fun while I'm gone."

"Oh, I plan to." She reached up and pulled his lips to hers. "Drive carefully to the airport. It's raining cats and dogs out there. I wouldn't want anything to happen to you."

He chuckled. "No worries. I could drive that road—" he paused for a long yawn, "blind-folded."

I stopped reading, distracted by thoughts of Nina and the cold medicine on her night stand. That stuff really knocks me out, so I never take it during the day, unless I'm really miserable and just want to sleep.

Could that be what's going on with Nina? She feels lousy and wants to sleep through the days? Donna was really getting on her nerves, so that could be another reason to want to escape into dreamland. Or, am I grasping at straws here to justify staying out of it?

Today
Late afternoon

I sat on the couch with my laptop to reread the story about Donna's husband's car crash. That story had included an account of her father and sister's tragic deaths. After a few sips of coffee, I set it on the side table and opened the computer.

The first time I read about the plane crash, I felt so sorry for Donna. She had been just a kid when she lost her father and little sister in the plane crash in Ketchikan.

I still feel sorry for her; however, reading Donna's book has got me wondering about her husband's death. "Not a good idea to drink and drive," is what she said to me. If drunk driving caused the accident, you'd think the newspaper story would have said so.

From everything Donna and Nina said about him, the guy was

a rat. He even gambled away their retirement. Thank goodness she got the house, the bakery business, and his life insurance.

I was curious about what Donna's house looks like, so I googled Donna Baxter in Ketchikan, Alaska white pages. I got a big surprise. Her current address is in Lahaina, Maui, Hawaii. It listed Ketchikan as a previous location!

My hands were shaking as I typed in the Maui address. I found it on that popular real estate site—twillow.com.

Currently off-market. Kaanapali condo home that contains 1,545 sq. ft. and was built in 1972. 3 bedrooms, 2.5 bathrooms. The estimate for this house is $1,259,000, which has decreased by $52,078 in the last thirty days.

It was pushing five-thirty, time to trade in my coffee for a glass of wine. Next, I did a Google Earth drive-by. I couldn't see the condo, but the complex was lush with mature landscaping and close to the water. I leaned back, pondering this crazy development. "I need to talk to someone." My puppy nuzzled my leg, gazing soulfully at me, ready to listen to whatever I had to say, but I FaceTimed Sam instead, and Daisy eavesdropped.

When she answered, I said, "I know you're probably busy getting the kids fed, but I have to talk to you now. If I have to wait until Casey is tucked in, I will burst a blood vessel."

"Hold on. CHELSEA! I have an urgent call from Katy. Please come dish up dinner for you and your brother. I'll eat later."

I heard Chelsea yell, "Coming!"

"Sam, get a glass of wine. You're gonna need it."

"I can't drink wine, remember? Pregnant?"

"I meant that non-alcoholic cabernet crap you have."

"It's actually pretty good, but I can't wait for a glass of the real thing." I watched her pour a glass in the kitchen and then go into the living room. She settled on the sofa, and wedged a pillow behind her lower lumbar. "Okay. I'm all ears. Spill."

After I told her what I'd learned, she said, "That explains the hideous muumuus."

"Oh, my gosh! You're right!" I said. "The big question is, why she didn't tell Nina? She thinks Donna still lives in Ketchikan."

"Yeah, that's weird. Why keep it a secret?"

"Who knows? One thing I do know is, the condo on Maui had to have cost a fortune. At least over a million when she bought it. Where did she get that kind of money?"

Chelsea leaned over Sam's shoulder from behind the couch. "Hi, Aunt Katy. When's my next driving lesson?"

"We'll schedule a lesson soon, honey. I promise."

She blew me a kiss and left the room.

"Where was I?" I said. "Oh, got it. The Maui condo and how could she afford it."

"She probably made a down payment and has a huge mortgage."

"Duh. You're right."

"I wonder if she's running out of money," said Sam. "You said the workers have walked off the job more than once for not getting paid. Although I would assume that Nina is the one paying for the work, wouldn't you?"

"I would, but maybe not. Maybe the deal is that Donna will be reimbursed when the house sells. Nina is on a fixed income, so she may not have the extra cash available for all this so-called remodeling."

"I bet that's the deal," Sam said. "Donna's books are really popular on Amazon, so she must be making good money on them."

"Yeah, but it's not like she's a big time writer like James Patterson or Nora Roberts."

"True."

"Plus, the Maui condo payments are probably three to four thousand a month, depending on what her down payment was." I sipped my wine and thought about the bag of Doritos in the cupboard. "And then all the typical monthly expenses, too. I bet there is a high HOA payment." I got up and went to the kitchen.

"What are you doing?" she asked.

"I'm getting some taco chips." I got the bag and returned to the couch. "When Donna's husband bit the dust, she got the house and business. When her mother passed, she inherited the house and whatever else. Maybe life insurance and a pension. She's Nina's only heir, and even in its current state, that house is worth a lot. Plus, her jewelry, and whatever money is left in her IRA or 401K."

"If Donna is going broke, then she needs that money now."

"Are you thinking what I'm thinking?"

"I think I am," said Sam. "I think Nina is worth a lot more dead than alive."

CHAPTER THIRTY

WEDNESDAY • JULY 8
Posted by Katy McKenna

Daisy had her nose glued to the ground, pausing to savor every shrub or weed. Simon Prichard's mailbox must have smelled especially delicious because no matter how hard I tugged her leash, she would not budge.

While she savored the dandelions popping up around the mailbox, I spotted a hawk flopping in the dead grass behind one of Prichard's solar panels. His wing was bent at a grotesque angle. I tied the leash to the mailbox post and crept towards the bird. He stopped fluttering and fixed his beady eyes on me.

"I've had enough!" I rang Prichard's doorbell, over and over, until he finally answered.

"What is your problem?" he grumbled.

"There's an injured hawk in your yard. Clearly another victim of your damned solar panels."

"What do you expect me to do about it? I'm out of town."

Geez. This guy is a heartless creep. "I don't expect you to do anything. I'm merely informing you that I'm calling the wildlife rescue people now. Are you aware that red-tailed hawks are on the endangered species list in California and are protected by law? You could wind up doing serious prison time for this, buddy."

I sat on the porch step and searched for the local wildlife bird rescue people on my phone. Just when I found it, the front door opened. A tall, slim man with a dark blond manbun and a brown bushy beard stood in the doorframe.

"I take it you're," I finger-quoted, "out-of-town-Simon-Prichard."

"Yup. Just got back. And you're my annoying neighbor, Karen—"

"Oh, come on! My name is Katy!"

He stepped off the porch onto the lawn, moving towards the wary bird. I jumped to my feet and blocked him. "What are you planning to do?"

"Put him out of his misery. What were *you* planning to do? Let him suffer?"

"I'm calling the bird rescue people. They can decide what's best for him." He took another step, and I screamed, "Don't you dare!"

Daisy growled menacingly, her leash stretched taut from the mailbox post, and her eyes pinned on Simon.

"If I were you, I would back off. She'll rip your throat out if she thinks you might hurt me. Believe me, she's done it before. You better pray her leash holds."

The man looked at me like I was bonkers. "She's a *Labrador*."

"I'm serious. Daisy saved my life, and my attacker died. Labradors are extremely protective."

He backed a few feet away. "Hey, Daisy. I only want to help the birdie."

"Yeah, by slaughtering it." I pressed the phone icon for the bird rescuer, and seconds later a man answered. "Hi. I found an injured hawk." I listened for a moment. "No, I can't pick it up. I might hurt him more. I think his wing is broken. Can someone with experience in this sort of thing come here?"

I gave the man the address and told him I would stay with the bird until their volunteer arrived.

Simon gave me a lopsided grin. "You think they'll arrest me?"

"No, since you didn't kill it."

"Not to mention that red-tailed hawks are one of the most common members within the genus of Buteo in North America and are definitely not on the endangered list." He winked. "Nice try, though."

"God, I miss the Millers," I muttered.

Dinner Time

I needed advice, and nothing looked good in my fridge, so I called the folks to wrangle a dinner invite.

Pop chuckled. "Interesting how you call just as we're sitting down to eat."

"Golly. I didn't realize what time it is. What're you having?"

"Meat and lots of it. Piles and piles of meat. Really bloody rare, too. Moooo!"

"Kurt," said Mom. "Give me your phone."

"Yes, dear."

"Honey? Why don't you come over? We have scalloped potatoes, salad, and green beans."

"You had me at scalloped potatoes, Mom."

———

When I arrived, she had already set a full plate for me on the kitchen table.

"Looks good, Mom."

She put her hands on my shoulders. "I'm worried that you don't get enough protein on your pescatarian diet. Do you want me to open a can of tuna?"

"Do I look like I'm not getting enough protein?"

"No. You're the picture of health."

"Then don't worry, Mom." I turned my gaze to the table. "Dinner looks delicious."

After a few bites and a quick catch-up, Pop set down his fork and asked my real reason for being there.

"Can't a girl want to spend quality time with her folks?"

"Yes, dear." Mom patted my hand. "Now spill."

"Okay. It's about my neighbor, Nina."

"I thought you'd moved past that," said Pop.

"I tried. I really did."

"I read your blog about the Maui condo," said Mom. "That sure was a shocker."

"I know. Right?"

"What Maui condo?" asked Pop.

"Kurt, she's posted everything on her blog," said Mom. "I've told you all about it."

"Well, I'd like to hear it straight from the horse's mouth," he said.

Mother arched a cranky brow at him. "In other words, you don't listen to me, do you? Go on, Katy."

"Well, as Mom already knows, I suspected that Nina's niece has been keeping her doped up with cold medicine, and then the other—"

"Why do you think that?" asked Pop.

Oops. Mom and Pop don't know about the con job. I kept that post private.

"I said I *suspected*."

"Why?" he said.

Mom saved me. "Kurt, I already told you all of this."

"I think maybe she's keeping her doped up so she can take

advantage of her." I told them about Donna taking the jewelry to the pawnshop. When I finished, Mom said, "Yup. Read that post and told your dad."

"And I remember you telling me, honey. However, it helps to hear it again firsthand from Katy. It's lucky that you just happened to be in the right place at the right time to see her leaving the pawn shop. Were you following her?"

"No. Like I said, I was running errands and it just happened. And yes. I agree. It was lucky. A lucky coincidence."

He harrumphed, and Mom said, "If she says it was a coincidence, then that's what it was, Kurt."

"I swear it was. And now I need some expert criminal advice."

Mom frowned. "Oh, boy. What have you done? Have you broken into the house again?"

"I haven't done anything. Yet. But I may have to. Would you pass me the salt?"

"I salted everything when I cooked it. What needs more salt?" Looking like I'd stabbed her in the back, she handed me the shaker. "Excuse me for trying to cook heart-healthy for your father."

"The dinner is wonderful, honey," said Pop, shoveling a forkful of green beans that I know he detests into his mouth. "Delicious."

I nodded. "Everything is super good, but I just need a smidge more salt on the potatoes."

Pop poured a little more wine into my glass. "That's all you get since you're driving. Now, why do you need criminal advice?"

Ten minutes later, I ended with Angela's call to Social Services, and Mom ended with, "Yes, I read all that on your blog."

I continued, "According to them everything was hunky-dory."

Mom smirked. "Hunky-dory? You need to get a younger peer group."

I laughed. "Heavens to Betsy, why would you say that? The thing is, I've tried to quit worrying about Nina, but now I truly think she's being taken advantage of. I don't believe for one minute she would choose to be sleeping all the time. That's why I think Donna is forcing her to take cold medicine. However, it's not like Donna is giving her arsenic, so I doubt this qualifies as a crime."

"*If* Donna is giving her cold medicine. You *suspect* it, but you don't really know that," said Mom. "Kurt. Isn't there anything you can do? This really sounds like elder abuse, no matter what the social service report said."

"Pop? There's something else, too," I said.

He scooped a second helping of the scalloped potatoes onto his plate. "What?"

"Okay, don't laugh. I'm wondering about Donna's husband's death in Ketchikan." I told him that she'd said he was drunk while driving and slid off the road. "But, now I'm wondering about that. Was he drunk?" I paused. "Or did Donna drug him with nighttime cold medicine? You know, like in her book."

"In her book?"

"The main character in her first book drugged her husband with cold medicine and then he crashed the car."

"Let me get this straight. You think Donna drugged her husband with cold medicine. Plus you suspect that she's keeping her aunt doped up—all because of what a character did in a book she wrote," said Pop.

Yes—and also because I saw the medicine on Nina's night stand. But I can't tell you that.

Pop got a beer out of the refrigerator and leaned against the counter. "It seems pretty far-fetched, Katy. Her book is fiction, and this is real life. Just because she writes about murder does not mean she *commits* murder. Tell you what, Katydid. Tomorrow, first thing, I'll get on the horn and make some calls. Email me the full names of everyone. Nina, Donna, her husband. If you can find that article about the car crash again, send me the link."

I leaped out of my seat and threw my arms around him. "Thank you! Thank you!"

"Hey, hey. Don't get your hopes up. I can't promise anything, but I'll try."

"That's good enough for me."

CHAPTER THIRTY-ONE

THURSDAY· JULY 9
Posted by Katy McKenna

8:45 A.M. I'm on hold until I hear from Pop. It's going to be a long morning. I've already cleaned my closet and have three bags ready for the Salvation Army.

1:00 P.M. There are no weeds in my back yard now.

2:15 p.m. Ditto for the front yard.

I went inside and brewed a cup of coffee. Too antsy to use my percolator, I did a pour-over instead. I scrounged in the cupboard and found the last two Oreos in a bag behind the stale Raisin Bran.

2:33 P.M. Finally, he called.

"Hey, Pop! What did you find out?"

He laughed. "Well, nobody can ever accuse you of beating around the bush."

"Sorry."

"I spoke to the chief of police in Ketchikan and he remembered the car accident very well because he was the first responding officer at the scene."

"What did he say?" I said.

"It had been raining hard. Morgan lost control and slid off the road. He could have been trying to avoid a moose. There were droppings on the pavement."

I slumped low in my chair and stretched my legs out. "Had he been drinking?"

"I asked, and the chief said there were no indications of drunk driving."

"Did they do an autopsy?"

"No. There wasn't anything suspicious about his death. He drowned. I've got a call into social services, but doubt I'll get any further than the chief did."

I sighed huffily. "Oh, well. Thank you for trying, Pop."

"I'm sorry I couldn't do more, Katydid."

I sat staring blankly out the window, sifting through everything that had happened since Donna arrived. I kept coming back to: Why did Donna say her husband was drunk? Is Nina really okay? Yes, I know I saw her sleeping, but is she *really* all right? I won't be satisfied until she tells me she is.

Obviously knocking on the door has been a dead end, but maybe there is another way.

After Dark

Sunset was at eight-fifteen. I waited another hour until it was pitch dark, before setting out on my reconnaissance mission.

Passing by my new neighbor's house, I glanced up at an illuminated second floor window. The curtains were open. Sitting side-by-side on a table fronting the window, three large desktop monitors cast cold blue light on Simon's intense face.

I surveyed Nina's yard and porch at the property's edge wishing I could use a flashlight. The plan was to sneak around the house, peeping in windows, hoping to see what was going on inside. Being outside in the dark meant Donna wouldn't see me, but with the house lights on, I'd see her. She'd made it easy for me because she'd removed most of the window coverings in the main part of the house. I guess they were too "dated" for her exquisite taste.

I stumbled my way to the right side of the house and peeked into the first window—the kitchen. My heart sank when I saw the blank, dusty space where the old stove had been. The vintage O'Keefe and Merritt that Nina had planned to give me when she moved.

A folding table held a toaster oven, a microwave, a hot plate, and dishes. The cabinets had been ripped off the walls, and the wall separating the kitchen and dining room had been removed. Considering how messy my kitchen usually is, I'm not a fan of the "open concept" trend.

I crept to the dining room window. The vintage Arts and Crafts mahogany table that had fit the home's character was gone. No surprise since Donna was hell-bent on ruining the house's charm with typical twenty-first-century-whatever-is-the-current-trend-this-year.

On to the living room. The sofa, recliner, and end table were still there. Dirty dishes were stacked on the table. The dog was standing on the leather recliner, stretching over the table, sniffing the plates. No sign of Donna or Nina. I worked my way to the back of the house, stepped over the orange mesh temporary potty area fence, and was near the slider when Donna shouted, "STOP!"

Startled, I scuttled backward and tripped over the fence. My foot snagged in the mesh, and the entire flimsy enclosure toppled over.

"I said STOP!" shouted Donna.

Baby Girl squealed in pain.

"Dammit! When I say stop, I mean it! I did not give you permission to lick that plate, you stupid moron."

I dashed to the next window on the left side of the house. That room was dark. I remembered it was Donna's. The next window would be Nina's. Her window was still up about a couple inches with the old towel stuffed in the crack, like the last time I visited. The drapes were open, the bedside lamp was on, and Nina was propped up on pillows. She looked gaunt and ancient. Her eyes were closed, and her mouth hung open, slack-jawed. A full bottle of cold medicine sat next to an empty one on the table.

As I raised my phone to take a photo, the bedroom door opened, and I ducked. Donna entered, dressed in a blue, knee-length flannel teddy-bear print nightgown.

"Aunt Nina. Time for a drinkie-poo."

I raised my head until my eyes were level with the sill. Even though Donna's back was to me, I could see her pouring the cold medicine into a glass already half-full of a red beverage.

Yup. Just as I suspected.

She plunked a straw into the drink and stuck it in Nina's mouth. "Aunt Nina! Wake up and drink this. It's cranberry juice mixed with your liquid vitamins and your sleepy-time medicine. It tastes yummy."

I have to get a photo of this.

"Wake up. You need your vitamins so you can get strong and move to Shady Acres. Won't that be wonderful?"

Nina's eyes popped open, and she spat out the straw. "No. Don't want it." She turned her head towards the window, and I could swear she was looking straight at me. I waved, but her face did not register acknowledgment. Probably all she saw was the reflection of her bedroom.

"Dammit, old lady! Drink it or else."

Or else what?

Donna plugged Nina's nose and jammed the straw between her lips. "Quit being a brat and drink your damned medicine. I've got better things to do than molly-coddle you. I'm worn out."

Nina shook her head, swatting at Donna, trying to get free.

I had to do something. I dashed to Donna's window and

rapped on it, hoping to get Baby Girl's attention. It worked! She tore through the house yipping. I rushed to the back of the house and tapped a living room window. The dog scrambled for that room, barking hysterically.

"Shut up!" screamed Donna.

I returned to Nina's window in time to see Donna slam the drink on the nightstand and stomp out of the room. "Shut up, you damned dog, or I'll give you something to bark about!"

I watched Nina, trying to think of some way to help her. I held up my phone and snapped a few photos. She raised her arm and wavered it in the air over the nightstand, connecting with the glass and tipping it over. A tiny smile of victory lit her face.

"What the hell are you barking about?" shouted Donna from the living room. "There's nothing in here."

I hurried to the corner of the house and threw a couple rocks at the back fence. Baby Girl heard the noise and zipped to the patio slider window, continuing to bark.

Seconds later, the back yard light flicked on. The slider screeched open and Donna yelled, "Who's out there? What the hell happened to the fence?" The dog slipped through the open window. "Get back in here, Baby Girl!"

Donna stepped out, forgetting there's over a two-foot drop from the slider to the ground since she removed the steps and patio. With a shriek, she landed in a heap in the dirt, blubbering and moaning like a sick cow. "My ankle! My ankle!"

Her accident had bought me some time. However, what to do with it, I did not know. It weren't as though I could climb into Nina's room, hoist her over my shoulder, and run home. I scurried back to her room and tried to push up the window, but I failed to open it just like the last time I had tried.

"Nina!" I whispered through the crack. "Nina!" She turned her head towards the window. "Nina! It's Katy. I will figure out how to help you. I promise!"

Baby Girl poked my calf, whining and wagging her tail.

"Go 'way," I whispered.

She shimmied around until she was between me and the exterior house wall.

"Go. Away."

She licked my shoe, then gazed up at me like I should do something. So I did. I scooped her up into my arms. She's heavier than I expected—around twenty pounds. I looked at Nina again. Her eyes were closed. I listened for a long, satisfying moment to Donna wailing about her ankle and then sneaked out of the yard.

When I got home, Daisy went bonkers over Baby Girl. The little dog rolled on her back and submitted herself for approval. With her tail thumping the floor, she continued to lie still while Mr. Snickers and Tabitha checked her out.

Even though she was being good, I wagged a finger at her. "Do not even *think* about chasing the cats. You got that?"

I gave everyone a small meal, then it hit me what I'd done. I'd stolen a dog, and her owner would hear her barking in my yard. What was I going to do?

———

While brushing my teeth before bed, I wondered if I should've called an ambulance for Donna. She might have been seriously injured. I may be a pet-napper, serial trespasser, and creepy window peeper, but I couldn't go to bed without knowing if she was all right.

With great reluctance, I went back over to her house to take a look in the back yard. If she was still out there, I'd call an ambulance.

As I made my way along the side of the house, I glanced in the living room window and saw Donna sitting in the recliner with an ice pack on her ankle.

With a long, grateful sigh of relief, I went home.

CHAPTER THIRTY-TWO

FRIDAY • JULY 10
Posted by Katy McKenna

Mom called this morning to talk about my spy mission last night. "Katy, I know you're trying to do the right thing, but sneaking around peeping into windows could land you in jail."

Darn it! I should have made that post private. "You're right, Mom, but have you got any better ideas?"

"No. Just please be careful. I'm not going to tell your father about this, although half the time he never hears me anyway."

"Mom? Are you guys all right?"

"Yes. Of course. Why do you ask?"

"No reason. Hey, do you think Ruby would take care of the dog until Donna leaves?"

"About that. I am glad you took the dog. Clearly she wanted to go with you. I'm sure Mom would be glad to take care of her. Do you want me to talk to her?"

"No. I'll handle it. Please don't say anything."

I fretted all morning about Donna's ankle. Was she able to walk and properly take care of herself and Nina? If I hadn't been so caught up in my "one woman neighborhood vigilante crusade," I wouldn't have knocked down that plastic fence, and Donna wouldn't have taken a tumble.

Although, on the upside, it did give me the opportunity to save BeeGee—formerly known as Baby Girl. Plus, I took photos that prove that Donna has been forcing Nina to drink cold medicine. Photos that I can't show the police, because I was trespassing.

I looked up my "crime" on the Santa Lucia Police website:

It is a misdemeanor to spy on—or take pictures of someone—in a private place without that person's consent. Punishment can include:

- *Up to six (6) months in jail; and/or*
- *A fine of up to $1,000*

I could wind up in jail for trying to be a good neighbor, and I bet my photos wouldn't be admissible in court because I was technically breaking the law. Plus, it was over-the-counter cold medicine that Donna was forcing Nina to drink. Not poison.

———

After pressing Nina's doorbell several times, I yelled, "Hey, Donna. I thought I heard some commotion over here last night. Everything all right? I'm worried about you!"

"Go away!" she screamed.

"Show me you're okay, and I will."

"I hurt my ankle, not that it's any of your business."

"Do you need help? A ride to the ER? An ambulance?"

If I call an ambulance, they'll go in, and then they'll find Nina! Problem solved. I was about to call for help when the door opened.

Donna looked like hell. Frazzled hair, swollen ankle, red puffy

PAMELA FROST DENNIS

eyes, and still in the blue nightgown. "I do not need an ambulance. Why can't you mind your own business?"

"Because I'm a caring neighbor. It's what neighbors do."

"More like neighborhood busybody," she grumbled.

"Somebody's gotta do it. Might as well be me." I gave her the once-over. "Obviously, you need help." Then, without waiting for an invitation, I shouldered past her into the foyer. "Let me help you to a chair." I steered the limping woman to the living room recliner, eased her down, then raised the footrest. "You need to keep that ankle elevated." I glanced around the room. "Love what you've done to the place."

"Hilarious," she snarled. "When it's all done, you'll be shocked at the transformation."

"I'm pretty shocked now. Haven't seen the contractors over here in days. What gives?"

"They're on vacation. It's a family business."

Yeah, right. You're out of money. "How annoying for you. May I make you and Nina a cup of tea?"

"Coffee would be nice," she said. "All we have is instant. None for Aunt Nina, though. She's asleep."

"No surprise there. Would you like something to eat?"

"Maybe some toast?"

"You got it," I said. "What do you take in your coffee?"

"Black is fine. There's jam in the refrigerator."

From the kitchen, I hollered, "Where's the stove?"

"I got rid of that old heap of junk. I ordered a six-burner stainless steel model, but I got a notice telling me it's on back order, so I don't know when it will arrive. What a pain! You can boil water in the microwave."

While the toast got toasty, I bundled some ice in a plastic bag, and wrapped a kitchen towel around it. "Let's get some ice on your swollen ankle. Are you sure you don't want to see a doctor?"

"Thank you for the ice and, yes, I'm sure about the doctor."

"Okay, but if you change your mind." The toaster oven dinged.

176

"Be right back." In the kitchen, I yelled, "Too bad about that stove. Hope you got a good price for it."

"Who would buy that old out-of-date thing? I had it hauled to the dump."

I returned to the living room. "Donna, that old stove was worth at least five thousand dollars."

Her eyes widened, and I saw her swallow. "Five thousand?"

"Probably more. There's a big demand for them nowadays. What a shame. Hopefully, someone at the dumped snagged it. Anyway, here's your snack. Toast with blackberry jam and black coffee. Do you need any ibuprofen?"

Looking sick, she nodded. "Why are you being so nice to me?"

"My parents raised me to care about my neighbors." I squatted by the chair. "It can't be easy caring for an elderly person and fixing up the house for her. I'm sure you would love to go home to Ketchikan." I paused, watching her face, but her expression didn't change at the mention of her former hometown. "You know, get back to your own life in *Alaska*. Yet, here you are. Doing the right thing." I was laying it on thick, wasn't I? "Now, how about that ibuprofen? Or acetaminophen? Aspirin?"

"There's ibuprofen in the bathroom, by the sink."

I patted her hand and stood. "Be right back."

On my way to the bathroom, I took a quick peek into Nina's room. She was asleep, of course. In the bathroom that had so far escaped Donna's demolition derby, I poured a glass of water and returned to her. "I've heard that four equals prescription strength." I dumped the pills in her hand and set the bottle on the side table.

After she'd eaten half the toast, I made a big show of glancing around the room. "Where's Baby Girl? Outside? Do you want me to feed her?"

"I," her voice choked, "I...don't know where she is. Last night her fence fell over and she ran off." A tear trickled down her ruddy cheek, and I felt a tiny twinge of guilt.

"I'm sorry." I shook my head, looking so sorrowful I could have won an Oscar. "Boy, this family has the worst luck for pets vanishing. First Mr. Snickers and now your sweet doggie."

She swiped her eyes with her hand and sniffed. "I wasn't very nice to you when you asked for a picture of the cat."

"No, you weren't, Donna. It surprised me since you obviously are an animal lover."

"I didn't know how awful it feels to lose a pet. I'm thankful that Nina doesn't realize her cat is missing."

Because you're keeping her doped up. "You're kidding. How could Nina not know her beloved cat is gone?"

"Because lately she's been, uh, out of it."

"Every time I ask to see her you tell me she's asleep. Maybe there's something seriously wrong with her. Has she seen a doctor? You know, to be evaluated."

"No. Not yet. I guess I should schedule an appointment soon."

Soon as in never. "As far as your dog goes, I'm sure you'll get her back, Donna. She had a collar on, right? And I'm thinking you had her microchipped. So even if she lost her collar, a vet could still identify her."

She hung her head, shaking it slowly. "She didn't have her collar on. I only put it on when we're going somewhere. And she's not microchipped."

Thank goodness! But I'll have her microchipped. "Tell you what? I'll make flyers and tack them up around the neighborhood, and you can post about her on Facebook in one of those local lost pets groups."

"I don't do Facebook or any of that social media stuff. I hate it."

"What about for your books?"

"I have a media company that takes care of that stuff. You know, Twitter, Facebook, Instagram, and whatever."

"No problem. I'll take care of it for you. Let me put my number in your phone so you can text me a photo of her."

"You're an angel."

———

"Hey, Grammy! Whatcha doin'?"

"I'm talking on the phone with you," she said flatly. "What are *you* doing?"

"Ha! Ha! Same thing. Hey! How about I run over for a cup of coffee?"

"You're up to something, but come on over."

Click.

BeeGee was at my feet staring adoringly up at me. "Hey, kiddo. Let's go visit your new grandma."

The word "grandma" prompted Daisy to do her happy dance routine until I told her she had to stay home. The expression on her mug was sheer misery while she watched me put her halter and leash on BeeGee. I had to tighten up the straps quite a bit, but it worked.

At Ruby's, I left the dog in the car, parked under a tree with all the windows cracked. Talking my grandmother into taking care of her might take some finesse even though Mom was sure she'd be fine with it.

The front door was unlocked. "Hey, Grams. I'm here."

"In the bathroom. Hold on." The toilet flushed, and she joined me in the kitchen.

"I got fresh, warm donuts at the drive-thru donut shop." I open the pink box. "Look, your favorites."

She peeked in the box, raised a suspicious brow at me, and selected a buttermilk donut. "Pour yourself some coffee."

I doctored a cup with half-and-half and sugar and got the usual remark from Ruby. "Want some coffee with your cream and sugar?"

I took a sip and added more sugar. "Ah. Perfect." I set my mug on the counter. "Oh my gosh, I nearly forgot. I brought a friend with me."

She made a big deal of looking around the kitchen. "Is it by any chance your old imaginary friend you had when you were in kindergarten? George Washington McKenna?"

"*Nooo.* She's real. Be right back."

When I left the room, she muttered, "This should be good."

I opened the car backseat door to a delighted dog. "I didn't forget about you. Let's go meet your grandma." I picked her up and hugged her. "You're a sweet girl, you know that?"

I set her down and she trotted to the porch with me.

"And who do we have here?" Ruby stood in the doorway, arms crossed, looking grouchy.

"This is my friend, BeeGee. Formally known as Baby Girl."

"Oh, no. Nuh-uh." She shook her head, waving her hands. "Tell me you didn't."

"It's a funny story. You'll laugh."

"I doubt that." She glared at me for a long moment. "Are her feet clean? You know I have beige carpeting."

I lifted a paw. "Looks clean to me."

"Wait here." She returned and gave me a hand towel. "I have heartburn today, so I can't bend over without urping."

"You get heartburn every time you go to Martini Piano Bar Night."

"I know. And still, I go."

After I made a big show of wiping BeeGee's paws, we sat in the living room.

"Did you by any chance read my blog this morning?" I asked.

"No, I'm a few days behind. Why?"

I cuddled the pup on my lap while I related last night's events. When I finished, she jumped down as if on cue, and approached Ruby while wagging her feathery tail.

"Oh, brother. Did you two rehearse that move?"

"No, but you gotta admit, she's pretty cute. I only need you to take care of her until Donna goes home. Then BeeGee can live with me."

"*If* that woman *ever* goes home." She cracked a smile and petted the pup. "Much as I hate to admit it, you did the right thing." She leaned down to the dog's muzzle. "Didn't she?"

BeeGee licked her chin. And that was that. Ruby was on board.

"Here's the deal, Katy. I'll give her a trial run. If she minds her p's and q's, she stays permanently. I don't want to get attached, and then you take her back and break my heart."

BeeGee decided it was time to jump on the couch and cuddle up to Ruby. She was really selling it.

"What are the p's and q's?" I said.

Ruby stroked the girl's silky black fur. "She can't be barking all the time because the neighbors will complain, and the HOA board will kick her out."

"What else?"

"I assume she's potty trained?"

"Yes, but she's used to a dog door. I'll go to the pet store today and get one to fit in your slider. I'll also get a collar and tag, and a harness and leash."

"All right." She paused, thinking. "She needs a couple toys, too. Oh, and dog food."

I high-fived her. "Deal." Then I snuggled BeeGee. "No one will ever hit you again, sweetheart."

"Damned straight about that," said Ruby.

CHAPTER THIRTY-THREE

SATURDAY · JULY 11

Posted by Katy McKenna

This Morning

I created a phony missing dog flyer and printed out a few to hang around the neighborhood. I doubt Donna does much walking even when she doesn't have a sore ankle, but if she does take a stroll she will see them on the lamp posts in our vicinity. I also posted in the Facebook "Lost Pets of Santa Lucia" group.

I warned Ruby not to walk the dog until I remove the Facebook post—which will happen right after I show it to Donna. Ruby's dog groomer friend, Celeste, is coming over to give BeeGee a stylish haircut today. It's unlikely that anyone seeing BeeGee would have a clue who she belonged to, but a short, new "do" will give Ruby peace of mind. Me, too.

———

I rang Donna's doorbell, hollering, "Hey, Donna! I have those flyers I said I'd make. I want your approval before I put them up around the neighborhood."

She opened the door, looking worse than yesterday. She was still in the flannel nightgown, which concerned me because I'm the reason she injured her ankle.

I glanced at her foot. "You better sit down. That ankle is still pretty swollen. Then I'll show you the flyer and the Facebook post I did."

After she was settled, I handed her a flyer.

"Wow, that's nice. Look how cute Baby Girl looks." Her chin trembled and she sniffed. "Oh, God. I hope she's all right."

"I bet someone nice has found her and is taking good care of her. Did you call the SPCA and report her missing?" She nodded. "Then I'm sure you'll have her back soon." I drew my phone from my pocket. "I posted a picture of her in a local lost pets group on Facebook." I scrolled for a moment. "Here it is."

Donna stared at the post with tears welling in her eyes. "There are several comments already." She read one aloud, sounding choked up. "Did the dog have a tag on? Microchipped?" She gazed at me. "I appreciate you doing this. Thank you." She pointed at a cardboard box on the floor. "There's a framed photo of Mr. Snickers in there. Would you take it and make a flyer for him, too?"

"Sure thing. I'm worried about you. Are you sure you don't want me to drive you to the ER?"

She appeared to consider it, then shook her head. "No, it'll be fine in a few days. The black and blue bruises make it look worse than it is."

"Then I'm going to go. I'll make a flyer for the cat and put them both up around the area."

"You'll post it on Facebook, too?"

"Sure will." I started towards the hallway. "I want to pop into Nina's room and say hi, real quick."

"She's sleeping. She had a rough night, and I don't want her to wake until she's fully rested."

I was halfway down the hall. "I'll just take a little peek in case she needs something, so you don't have to get up."

"No. Don't!"

Nina was snoring like a hibernating grizzly. I tiptoed around her bed to the stuck window to see if I could hoist it up. I thought that being inside at a higher level than outside might give me the leverage to do it. Sure enough, my third tug loosened it. I left it halfway up and drew the drapes together. I don't know that I'm ever going to sneak in the house that way, but at least I have the option, if needed. With hope, Donna won't notice. The bedroom was stinky, so, if she confronts me about it, I can always say I opened it to air out the room.

On my way to the front door, I said to Donna, "Nina is sleeping like a log. Maybe you can get some rest, too." I started to leave, then stopped. "Donna? Don't you think you'd feel better if you got out of that nightgown? Whenever I feel lousy, I'm always amazed what a quick shower and fresh clothes does for me."

"It's not the ankle that's got me down. It's my dog. I was mean to her right before she ran off. It's my fault she's gone."

Partly your fault. Mainly mine.

"But you're right. A shower would do me good. I probably stink." She lifted an arm and took a whiff. "Yup."

———

I started reading the next book in Donna's series—*The Ketchikan Kulinary Mysteries*. Patsy got away with murdering her husband in the first one. I'm curious to see what she's up to now.

In the second book, she has hired a senior woman to run the bakery counter and a hot, young mysterious guy named Brandon to do deliveries. Business is booming, and she's got her eye on the delivery boy's bulging biceps.

CHAPTER THIRTY-FOUR

SUNDAY · JULY 12
Part One
Posted by Katy McKenna

While rinsing dishes at the kitchen sink this morning, I noticed through the window, a squad car slowing in front of my house. The driver's side window was down and I recognized her as the same officer who'd warned me about trespassing at Nina's house.

She decelerated to a crawl, flicking a glance at my house but not stopping. Relieved she wasn't after me, I set the last dirty plate in the dishwasher and turned it on. Then I got curious and walked over to peek through the bushes lining the border between Prichard's and Nina's properties.

Simon strode across the yard. "Spying on the neighbors again?"

"Yes, and I'm trespassing on your property, too." I gave his mud-stained jeans a once-over. "Doing some yard work?"

"You're very astute." He pointed at a rototiller sitting near the porch. "I'm going to plant vegetables after I turn over the soil."

"Out here? In the front yard? What about the solar panels?"

"They're only on one side of the yard. I can plant on this side, plus the dirt under the panels can be planted, too. I've already got corn, beans, potatoes, carrots, and onions growing in the back."

"What are you planning to do—open a neighborhood farm stand?"

"I'm putting my land to good use. I see no reason to be watering useless ornamental grass when I can grow food." He peered through the leafy evergreen shrubbery. "What're the police doing over there?"

"That's what I'm trying to find out. I hope nothing bad has happened."

"If that were the case, there'd be an ambulance and a fire truck here, too."

Randy and Earl joined us. "Is everything okay?" asked Earl.

Randy poked his arm. "If everything were okay, the cops wouldn't be there, bro."

"Why don't we stand out front on the sidewalk?" I said. "Maybe we'll hear something."

"You mean loiter like a bunch of nosey neighbors," said Simon.

"I mean loiter like *concerned* neighbors."

We shuffled to the sidewalk just as Donna stepped onto the porch, leaning on a cane. "Thank you, officers, for coming so quickly. My auntie is missing and I'm very worried."

Stunned, I glanced at my neighbors to see their reaction. Simon whispered, "This is an unexpected development. Where would she have gone?"

"And how?" said Randy.

"And why?" said Earl.

"Maybe because she'd had enough of her niece," said Simon.

I said, "I managed to get a quick peek of her yesterday. She was dead to the world."

Earl drew in a sharp breath. "She was *dead?*"

Randy bonked him on the head. "It's an expression, dude."

"I meant she was sleeping. Snoring. It's hard to believe she got up and left."

The four of us edged our way into the yard to better hear the conversation.

Donna glanced at us and continued talking to the cops. "I went into her room to give her breakfast and the bed was empty. Her window was open. I can't imagine her climbing out, though. But what else can I think?"

Not realizing it, I grabbed Simon's forearm.

"Ow. You got a mean grip, lady," he said.

I released my claw. "Sorry." *Oh, my God. I opened the window. Did she climb out? No, she was too feeble. I can't imagine her doing that—ever. I can't imagine me doing it, either.*

"She most likely walked out the front door," said the brunette officer. "When did you last see your aunt?"

"I guess it was around eight o'clock last night. I helped her to the bathroom and then tucked her in."

"You guess?" she said. "Did you or did you not see her last night?"

"Yes, of course, I did. I'm just not sure of the exact time. I don't check my watch every time I do something. Do you?"

The stony-faced officer ignored Donna's sarcasm. "Have you searched the entire house and yard?"

"The house, yes. The yard, no." Donna joggled her cane. "I had a little accident. Go in and search for yourselves."

The officer turned to her partner. "Check the yard, then meet me inside."

The young, brawny cop asked us to step back onto the sidewalk while he searched the bushes. By now, several neighbors had joined us.

"What do you think happened, Katy?" whispered Earl.

"I don't know. People don't just disappear from their home. Especially an elderly person."

"It happens more often than you'd think," said Simon. "My

grandfather went for a stroll in the garden and vanished. He was found dead in a vacant lot several days later."

"That's awful. I'm so sorry," I said.

"He had Alzheimer's and didn't know who any of us were anymore. However, he could still name every plant in the yard with its common and Latin name. After he died, I dropped out of college to work on a GPS tracking system app for people like him. There was nothing on the market that would track further than five hundred feet, and those were sketchy at best."

"I'm impressed," I said.

"I couldn't save my grandpa, but the device has helped many people."

"What's your company called?"

"Wandering Angels. However, it's not my company anymore. I sold it a couple years ago."

The front door was wide open, and we heard Donna shout, "Stop questioning me like I'm guilty. You have to find her before something terrible happens to the poor thing. She's demented—"

"She is not demented," I whispered to my neighbors.

"—and has heart trouble—"

I shook my head. "She has never mentioned heart problems to me."

"—and a history of strokes. For God's sake, she could be out there somewhere having another stroke this very minute while you two are wasting time grilling me. Me! An innocent disabled senior citizen."

Randy scrunched his face. "Disabled? Since when?"

"She twisted her ankle," I said.

The cops came out of the house and motioned us into the yard. The attractive brunette glanced at me and nodded, then said, "I'm Officer Rodriguez and this is my partner, Officer Dawson."

"Did anyone see or hear anything suspicious during the night?" asked Dawson, staring at me as if he'd read my mind. "Shouting? Cries for help?"

Everyone shook their heads, murmuring, "No."

Earl said, "Violet—she's our dog—started barking around two in the morning. Maybe she heard something."

"That's right," I said. "Daisy was barking, too. It made me nervous, so I got up and checked the doors. By then, she'd settled down, so I didn't worry about it."

"Your dogs may have been barking at my son, Ethan," said a striking, curvy blond standing on the fringe of the group. She glared at the cute pimply, gawky boy standing beside her, "…who came home hours past his curfew."

"*Mommm*," he whined. "I told you Jack's car broke down."

Mom waved her phone at him. "See this thing? It's called a phone. All you had to do last night was take your phone out of your pocket and answer one of my umpteen calls."

"Mom. You're embarrassing me."

"Well, too bad." Then she said to the rest of us, who were probably all experiencing painful flashbacks to our teen years, "I'm sorry if my grounded-for-life son woke up the neighborhood. I assure you it won't be happening again."

Dawson said, "Ethan, did you notice anything suspicious when you got home?"

The kid jammed his hands into his pockets. "Like what?"

"People out walking. That would be unusual that late at night."

"You mean morning, right?" said Mom.

The officer nodded. "Yes, ma'am. I'm giving everyone our business cards. If you think of anything, call us. Even if it seems trivial, we want to hear it. We need to get this lady home."

Officer Rodriguez said, "Does anyone happen to have a recent photo of Nina Lowen? It seems everything in the house has been packed up and put in storage."

I raised my hand. "I do."

———

I posted the photo that I gave to the police on Facebook. Afterwards, I packed a water bottle and a plastic dish in my backpack, leashed my dog, and set out to search the neighborhood for Nina.

Daisy sensed that our walk had a purpose and trotted beside me, looking vigilant.

"We have to find our friend," I said. "Mr. Snicker's mama."

As if on cue, Daisy put her nose to the ground and began following its lead.

Then an idea hit me.

———

"A shirt. Or a scarf. You know, something that hasn't been washed since Nina wore it."

Donna frowned. "You want something with Aunt Nina's scent on it because you think Daisy is a bloodhound?"

Daisy's tail wagged when she heard her name.

"She may not be a bloodhound, but she knows Nina and has a very sensitive nose. I thought if she got a whiff of Nina, she might pick up her scent while we're walking and, you know, start wagging her tail or something." I shrugged. "It's worth a try."

Donna sighed. "You're right. Hold on."

She closed the front door. My "bloodhound" yawned and sat down to give her crotch some unladylike attention.

The door opened again. "How about this?" She dangled a red blouse. "It was at the bottom of her hamper. I'm behind on the laundry, so it's been in there for a while."

I took the wrinkled shirt and resisted giving it a sniff test. "This is great. Thank you."

"I wish I could go with you, but I'm stuck here with this bum ankle." Donna tapped her metal cane on the floor. "Between losing the cat, my precious dog, and now Aunt Nina, it's all too much." She sniffed and clamped her hand over her mouth.

I shook off a pang of guilt about her dog. "I have a nice photo of Nina that I took recently. We were sitting on my porch swing having coffee. I gave it to the police and posted it in several local Facebook groups, so maybe someone will see her."

"That was a good idea. Thank you." She snickered bitterly. "We have the missing cat, Baby Girl, and now Aunt Nina on Facebook. People are going to wonder."

"Don't worry. They're in different groups, so it's doubtful anyone will notice."

Plus, the fact that the only real post on Facebook is about Nina, I thought. "By the way—where did you get the cane? I didn't think you went to the doctor's."

"I found it in the hall closet. Lucky find for me."

"Yes, it sure was. How does your ankle feel?"

"It's improving each day," she said.

"I should get going. With any luck, Nina will be back by dinnertime."

"From your mouth to God's ears." She swiped an invisible tear and shut the door.

"Okay, Daisy. Take a big whiff." I jammed the shirt against her nose. She grabbed it with her teeth and yanked it with a playful growl. "No. We're not playing tug-of-war. Let go!"

We checked empty lots, skulked around vacant houses, showed Nina's photo to everyone we saw, and came up with zilch. According to my FitTrim, we had walked over four miles when I finally gave up.

"My stomach's growling. Let's go home, Daisy, and have a snack. Then we can drive around and look for Nina."

Daisy cocked her head at the word "snack," gave me a woof of approval, and dragged me home.

———

We spent the next several hours cruising through nearby neighborhoods. Whenever I saw someone, I'd pull over, show them a letter-sized photo of Nina that I'd printed, and ask if they'd seen her. A few people acted like I was a crackpot and ignored me. Then Daisy would stick her head out the back window, and I would get instant approval.

At six-twenty, Ruby called. She'd watched a story on the local news about Nina's disappearance.

By eight-thirty, it was getting dark, and I was down to fumes in my gas tank. After a fill-up, I headed home feeling like a failure. I rummaged in the fridge for something tantalizing to cheer me up. Nothing in there was going to cheer me up, so I settled for cheese puffs and a glass of wine.

I dragged the comforter off my bed and got cozy on the couch to watch the local news that I have set to record every evening at six. I wanted to see the story about Nina that Ruby had told me about, so I fast-forwarded to it. When I saw her name on the screen, I paused, staring at it for a long minute, my thoughts wandering.

Suddenly, I felt compelled to go over to Nina's. Who knows? Maybe she was home by now and I could stop fretting. I stood for a few minutes in the dark staring at the well-lit house, then picked my way through the yard to the living room window and took a peek. I'm becoming an expert peeping snooper.

Donna was sitting on the green sofa chowing down on delivery pizza. She picked up the TV remote and paused the show she was watching—an old *Big Bang Theory* episode. Then she glanced over her shoulder towards the hallway and hollered, "Hey! You're missing the show!"

CHAPTER THIRTY-FIVE

SUNDAY · JULY 12
Part Two
Posted by Katy McKenna

"What's taking you so long?" yelled Donna.

Oh, my God! Is Nina back?

The plumbing groaned and rattled. A few moments later a stranger appeared. Scrawny frame. Short, curly mousy-brown hair. Late sixties-early seventies—or too many years worshipping the sun back in her youth.

"I was in the bathroom. My colitis is really kicking up."

"I'm sorry, honey. It's got to be the hotel food. You know how you get when you're off your regular diet." Donna patted the couch. "Come sit. A good laugh will make you feel better."

Who is this person and why is she here?

"I'm not a big fan of that show. It's too weird for me. I like old shows like *Cheers, Frasier, M*A*S*H*, The Mary Tyler Moore Show.* Those are funny, timeless shows."

"Honey. Keep up with the times or you'll get old," said Donna.

The woman scooted closer to Donna and flung her bony,

sleeveless arm around her. "I am old. So are you, sweetybabe." She rested her head on Donna's broad shoulder. "You were right about the weather, though. I've been here for nearly two weeks and my achy old bones feel so much better." She extended her arm. "Get a load of my gorgeous tan from laying by the pool at the hotel. Can't get a tan like that in Ketchikan."

Who is she?

Donna slowly and delicately ran her fingers down the woman's arm. "You got a lot of cute freckles, too."

That's pretty intimate. Are they a couple?

Donna turned over her hand. "Those are nasty blisters. How'd you get them?"

"I've been using the rowing machine in the exercise room. Trying to get in better shape."

"I better give them a kiss."

Okay. They are definitely a couple, but who is the woman?

Donna went on. "I wish I'd known you were coming, though."

"I thought it would be fun to surprise you—but if it's too much having me here, I can go back to the Ramada. Or maybe I should go home."

"No, I want you here, Michelle," said Donna.

Oh, my God! That's her best friend, Michelle.

Donna went on. "I should've had you stay at the house as soon as you arrived. But I didn't know how she'd feel about us sharing a bed. Now that I think about it, I could've slept on the couch and given you my room."

"We could've had clandestine midnight sex," said Michelle. "Your aunt never would've suspected we're more than best friends."

Donna playfully slapped Michelle's arm. "Aren't you a naughty girl! When Aunt Nina is found—"

"And she will be. Very soon. I can feel it in my bones."

"From your mouth to God's ears. When she's safely home, I

promise I will tell her about us." Donna kissed Michelle tenderly. "I should've years ago, and I'm so sorry."

"It's okay. She comes from a generation that frowns upon gay relationships," said Michelle. "And it's not like we live close by. There really was no reason to tell her."

"I still should have. You know, I think she'll be okay with it. She never liked Gary."

"No one liked Gary, except for his floozie girlfriend, Tami." Michelle slid off the couch onto her knees with a groan, holding the couch arm for support.

"What's wrong?" asked Donna.

"I pulled a muscle in my back, and this knee replacement is not meant for kneeling." Michelle adjusted her position, then let go of the sofa and took Donna's hands in hers.

"Shelly? What're you doing? You're hurting your knee."

"Screw my knee." She kissed Donna's hand. "Sweetheart? Love of my life?"

Donna shrieked like a giddy schoolgirl. "Oh, my God!"

"Will you do me the honor of being my wife 'til death do us part?"

"Yes, yes, yes!"

Things proceeded to get hot and heavy, and it was time to leave. I may be the neighborhood Peeping-Katy; however, I do have certain standards.

But I had to tell someone! As soon as I got in my house, I Face-Timed Ruby and Sam, my partners in crime.

CHAPTER THIRTY-SIX

MONDAY · JULY 13
Posted by Katy McKenna

Nina has lived here for eons, so she's bound to have a few friends around town that may know where she might be. Perhaps she called someone, and they came and sneaked her out of the house.

However, if they watch the local news, then they'd know the police are looking for her. So you'd think they would tell the cops where she is.

Unless they believe Nina's life is in danger. If this was Samantha, and she asked me not to tell anyone, I wouldn't. Friends protect friends.

So, who are Nina's friends? I'm thinking she's not on Facebook, but you never know. I shouldn't presume that because she's older, she wouldn't use it.

Nina has a profile! However, she hasn't posted in a couple years. She didn't set her privacy settings, so I can see her friends list. I concentrated on the local ones.

• *Ruth Bennett:* Four kids, seven grandkids, three great-grandkids. She lives on Cedar Court. That's about a mile from my house.

• *Bev Rowan:* A very active political poster. Despises the president, the governor, the senators, etc. Pretty much everyone on both sides of the aisle, and thinks everything is a conspiracy. She types all her posts in capital letters and uses a lot of angry faces and fire emojis. A real hothead that I doubt Nina would go to for help.

• *Phyllis Yinn:* Lives in assisted care, so that's a no.

• *Gail Kemp:* Not as old as Nina's other friends. Looks like she's in her early sixties. She makes and sells kettle corn. I love kettle corn, so I will definitely pay her a visit.

• *Janey Whitaker:* She and her husband Wilson teach ballroom dancing and Zumba at the senior center and are foster parents for the humane society.

There are a few others, but this will be enough to start. I messaged Ruth, Gail, and Janey.

Hi. I'm a concerned neighbor of Nina Lowen. Have you heard from her? I thought she might be staying with a friend.

———

An hour later, Janey Whitaker responded to my message.

Sorry. Haven't heard from Nina in a few months. I'm worried, too. I can't imagine her just walking away. The reporter made her sound demented, but she was sharp as a tack last time I saw her.

I hadn't received a response from Gail and Ruth. That didn't surprise me since it had only been an hour since I messaged them, plus we're not Facebook friends. I found their addresses online and decided to drive by their houses.

First up—Ruth Bennett on Cedar Court. There was a For Sale sign planted in the lawn, with "Sold" attached. The house looked unoccupied. Window coverings were closed, and a plastic-bagged phone book sat on the front walk.

Next up was Gail Kemp, the kettle corn lady. Her house is a sprawling rancher. Black metal roof, white board and batten siding with a cheery yellow farmhouse-style front door. I parked across the street under a shady old oak and watched the house for a while. At some point I dozed off, and a sharp tap on the car roof startled me awake.

"You all right?"

I sat up straight with a sheepish smile, and looked up at a older strawberry blond peering at me through horn rims balanced on the end of her nose. "Yes, I'm fine. Just waiting for someone."

"Who? If you don't mind me asking."

"No, that's fine. I probably look a little suspicious sitting here in my car."

She grinned. "Maybe a little. But I doubt many criminals are driving old orange Volvo wagons. You kind of stand out in the crowd."

I got out of the car. "I'm looking for Gail Kemp. Are you her by any chance?"

She stepped back, crossing her arms. "Are you going to serve me a subpoena or something?"

I laughed. "No. Actually, I'm a friend of Nina Lowen's."

"Oh, dear. I saw she went missing on the news."

"So, you haven't heard from her?"

"No, why would you think that?"

"I live a couple houses down from her on Sycamore Lane, and I thought she might be at a friend's house and not want anyone to know. I found you in her Facebook friends list."

She brushed aside her long bangs and they immediately flopped back. "I'm sorry. I wish I could help."

"Oh, well." I shrugged, and opened the car door. "It was worth a try."

"Wait. Give me your number. In case I hear from her," she said. "You never know."

———

There were no updates about Nina on the evening news. My Facebook post hasn't gathered any helpful information either, just a bunch of prayer and teary emojis, and one nasty troll who wants to be my friend. Gail called and said she'd talked to a few of her mom's old friends, but no one had any knowledge about Nina's whereabouts.

How does an elderly person just up and disappear in the middle of the night? My last visit to her house had been quite a shocker. While it didn't solve the mystery of Nina's disappearance, Donna's girlfriend certainly added a whole new dimension to the story.

With no fresh ideas, I guess it's time to pay another snoop visit. Who knows what new things I might learn? This time I'm ramping up my investigation by documenting it with a video.

———

Feeling like a creepy criminal, I stood on the right side of the living room window holding my phone near the bottom corner. The evening was warm, and the window was wide open. With a little luck, I would get a good recording.

Donna's fiancée Michelle sat on the couch pawing through a red velvet jewelry box. She held up a bracelet, inspecting it under the lamp, then slipped it on and held out her scrawny arm to admire it. "Sure wish you hadn't pawned her wedding rings, sweetybabe. They would have been perfect for me."

"I don't know what I was thinking," yelled Donna from another room. "The ring wasn't mine to pawn, or give to you for that matter."

"You were thinking you needed money to finish the remodel, and she never wore her rings anymore, so she'd never miss them." She dipped into a big bowl of potato chips sitting on the couch next to her and stuffed a handful in her mouth.

Donna lumbered into the room still leaning on a cane. "I had no business doing that. The jewelry hasn't sold yet, so maybe I should go back and get them."

Michelle held up the chip bowl and Donna shook her head.

"I don't think you should. But it's not my call." Michelle set the bowl on the floor and plucked a ring out of the box. "Here's something nice." She slipped it on her left ring finger. "This could work. Come see."

Donna collapsed beside her with a loud groan. "That emerald ring was my great-grandmother's."

"It would have to be sized. It's too loose." Michelle held out her hand, wiggling her finger. "But it's lovely. Two emeralds entwined in a circle eight of gold. A symbol of our neverending love." She pecked Donna's cheek, and dropped the ring back in the jewelry box. "Now, let's find something for you."

"You know, I still have my wedding ring." Donna closed the box and set it on the end table.

"Why on earth would you still have it?"

Donna sighed. "It's a family heirloom, so it's not like Gary bought it for me. When he died, I threw it in the jewelry box and forgot about it until now." She put the chip bowl on her lap. "Potato chips are my downfall." She delicately bit into one, and then jammed it in her mouth. "Mmm. So good."

"If you ask me, it all worked out perfectly. Gary died; you got everything, plus all that life insurance. Justice prevailed."

"I'm glad you talked me into getting those life insurance policies," said Donna. "Although, I never, in my wildest dreams, thought I would be the one collecting it."

Michelle embraced her, and the chip bowl spilled onto the

floor. She pulled back, laughing. "We're truly a couple, now. Soon to be married. Finally."

Donna touched Michelle's cheek. "We've wasted so much precious time hiding in the shadows—worrying about what everyone else thinks." She dabbed her eyes with the hem of her knee-length lime green muumuu. "But we can't do anything until we get Aunt Nina safely back home. Then you and I will go back to Ketchikan and get married."

Whoa! Wait a sec! I thought Donna sold her Ketchikan house and moved to Hawaii.

Michelle placed a hand on Donna's shoulder. "Sweetie? Do you really want to go back to Ketchikan? It's like paradise here. Ketchikan, well, sure it's beautiful, but you've said you're sick of all the rain. You know what? You need to take a ride in my snazzy rental. That'll change your mind. We couldn't have a Mustang convertible in Ketchikan."

"Sure we could. But it wouldn't be very practical."

"I am so tired of living a *practical* life. Aren't you?"

"We can't afford to live here."

"If your aunt is deceased..."

Donna started sputtering protests, and Michelle set a hand on her knee. "If Nina is… God forbid…gone. Then this house is yours."

"I suppose you're right."

Michelle moved away from Donna, facing her square. "This house is worth over a million, you know."

"I know that." Donna nodded. "That's why I figured if Aunt Nina put fifty to seventy-five thousand into it to bring it up to date, she could get at least 1.5 million. At first, she was on board with the remodeling idea, but then she got that bug before we even got the job started, and the chaos was too much for her. I told you how ornery she was getting. Rejecting the medicine and her vitamins. It got to where I was forcing her."

"Don't beat yourself up. It was for her own good."

"Was it? Let's face it. Keeping her doped up made life a lot easier for me. Then the other day, when I was yet again, forcing her to take her medicine, she said she wasn't signing any more checks. She told me—" Donna sighed heavily, her voice trembling. "She wanted me to go home. She said she'd seen the yard and hated it. Hated me. I tried to explain that she would love it when I was done. Then she grabbed the medicine and swallowed it, saying she wished she would die and be done with it. I'm sorry I'm venting. You already know all this."

"You thought you were doing a good thing for Nina, so quit beating yourself up."

Donna covered her face with her hands. "I literally drove my aunt out of her own home. I have to fix the mess I've made, but how can I with no money?" She lowered her hands. "I do have one idea."

"What?"

"We take a second mortgage on the vacation condo. It was so stupid to use my inheritance from Mom as a down payment on that place. What a waste of money."

"At the time, we thought having a vacation rental in Maui was an excellent investment," said Michelle. "We'd vacation there a couple times a year and make loads of money."

"Yeah, and then the home owner's association made that new rule prohibiting vacation rentals," said Donna. "Maybe we should sell my house in Ketchikan and move there. Then you'd have your sun and warm weather—and you could tool around in a fun convertible."

Michelle shook her head. "No. It would be like living in Ketchikan."

"How on earth is living in an island paradise even remotely like living in Ketchikan?" asked Donna.

Yeah, how is that? I wondered.

"Island fever. Not being able to take long road trips. I want to see the country before I'm too old to do it."

"You have a valid point. I didn't think of that."

"I do have an idea," said Michelle. "But you may not like it."

"What?"

"Please keep an open mind." She inhaled a big breath. "You forge Nina's signature on a power of attorney and predate it to a couple weeks ago."

"There's no—"

Michelle held up a hand. "Let me finish. If you did that, you could write all the checks you want and wrap up this remodel quickly for Nina, so she can sell it. Or if she's no longer with us, then at least the remodel will be done, and—"

"I already have power of attorney," said Donna. "We did it a couple days after I arrived. She wanted me to have it in case something happened to her. Like a stroke or something. She would need someone to make decisions. "

"That's great!" Michelle looked elated. "Then you can go ahead and write the checks you need to get the job done. But, if Nina is gone, then please, please, please consider *not* selling this house. We can sell your house in Ketchikan and the Maui condo, and live happily ever after right here in our own little paradise."

"What if she's never found?" said Donna. "Then what?"

"Well, I had wondered about that. So I did some research. If she isn't found, we will have to wait five years before she can be legally declared dead."

"So I guess we'd have to go back to Ketchikan."

"I've never heard of relatives being forced out of homes when a family member goes missing."

"Maybe you're right." Donna stared at her lap. "God, I miss Baby Girl."

Michelle draped her arms around Donna. "You know what else I'm right about, sweetybabe? I'm right about not waiting to get married. We've waited long enough!"

HEE-HAW! HEE-HAW!

CHAPTER THIRTY-SEVEN

TUESDAY · JULY 14
Posted by Katy McKenna

Last Night
Continued

HEE-HAW! HEE-HAW!

I jammed my braying phone into my pants to muffle the sound, and scrambled for the street, tripping over rocks and dirt clods. When I reached the sidewalk, Michelle screamed from the front door, "Who's out there?"

Safe on my porch, I clicked recent calls. It was a spam call about my car warranty expiring. My 1976 car.

"What's the big rush?" Simon was coming up the walk.

"Getting some much-needed exercise." I patted my sternum. "Woo! Am I out of shape or what?"

He leaned against the stair rail like he had all the time in the world to listen to whatever fib I would spin. "You know it's not safe to run in the dark all dressed in black." Simon pushed away from the rail and crossed his arms. "I think we have a few things to talk about. Like who owns a donkey in the neighborhood." He gave me a devilish grin. "Are you going to offer me a glass of wine, or—"

"You'll call the cops?"

"I was going to say a cold beer would be good, too."

"Not a nice cup of tea?"

"At this time of night? Should I get a bottle from my house?"

"No. Obviously, you intend to grill me, so come on." I opened the door to Daisy waiting on the other side. I didn't bother to excuse the mess as he followed me past the kitchen sink full of dirty dishes. I removed a bottle from the wine rack on the counter and held it out for him to see the label. "Red okay?"

He nodded. "Mud Lover Syrah. I've heard that's good."

It had been a gift that I was saving for a special occasion, and this certainly was not that. Or maybe it was. I mean, what exactly defines a special occasion?

I've done online research on this guy and learned some interesting facts. And no. Do not go there. Simon is not my type. Even if he were, I would never again cavort with a next-door neighbor.

He made a bazillion selling his "Wandering Angels" business. However, he also comes from a famous "old money" family—the Prichards of Upstate New York. I'd never heard of them, but I travel in different circles. It turns out they're right up there with the Astors, the Rockefellers, and the Vanderbilts. American royalty— la-di-da. That was a surprise, considering he's living next door and planting tomatoes in his front yard. Although, why should I find this surprising? An English duke chauffeured my grandmother and her pals around in a Senior Dial-A-Ride van for several months.

"It's local, and I like blends." I set the bottle on the counter, then rummaged in a drawer for a corkscrew. "Dammit. Where did I put that thing?"

"You mean this thing?" Simon dangled the corkscrew. "It was on the counter beside the rack." He opened the bottle. "Glasses?"

I set two of my best on the counter, and he poured a few ounces in each, and then lifted his glass. "Cheers." He swirled, sniffed, then sipped, looking thoughtful. "We probably should have let it breathe a bit, but this is decent." He sipped again. "Earthy. Plums and a bit peppery. It'll be interesting to see how the second glass tastes."

He thinks he's getting a second glass of my decent, earthy wine?

I led him to the living room and dropped in an easy chair, leaving the sofa for him. And Daisy.

"She seems to like you," I said. "Are you okay with her lying next to you?"

"I grew up with dogs." He scratched her neck, which made the wanton girl roll on her back for a tummy rub. "So, Katy. Why were you running through the neighborhood braying like a donkey? Curious minds want to know."

"That was my phone."

"Really? I could've sworn it was you. Next question. Why were you in the neighbor's yard?"

"How do you know I was?"

"It was pretty obvious."

"If you must know, I was trying to find out what happened to Nina. That's all."

"And did you?"

"I learned a lot, but I don't know where Nina is." I sipped my wine, wondering if I should tell him what I'd done. "If I tell you something, do you promise not to repeat it?"

"It depends. Did you murder someone?"

"No. Of course not."

"Then I won't tell."

"I was standing outside their living room window—"

"Of course, you were."

I didn't respond to his sarcasm. "I was video recording them talking. You know, hoping to learn something that would give me a clue."

"Them?"

I nodded. "Them." I told him about Michelle.

He gave me an approving look. "You are one surprise after another. Maybe you should be a private investigator. So, what did you hear?"

Phone in hand, I sat next to him. "Let's see if I got a good video."

Michelle: "Sure wish you hadn't pawned her wedding ring, sweetybabe. That would have been perfect for you. Or me."

"Turn up the volume, sweetybabe," said Simon.

We watched all the way to "Hee-Haw." I clicked it off before it got to the part where I shoved my phone down my pants.

"Michelle is really something, isn't she?" he said.

"I know." I told him about visiting Nina's Facebook friends earlier.

Simon pointed at my glass. "Looks like you're running low." He went to the kitchen and returned with the wine.

I moved back to the easy chair. He filled my glass, then set the bottle on the coffee table.

"I saw you walking over there earlier," he said. "My desk faces the window."

I know.

"I see a lot from up there."

"Don't suppose you saw Nina walking by the other night when she vanished, did you?"

"No. I checked all my surveillance footage, too. Nothing."

"Surveillance footage?"

"Security cameras," he said.

"Oh, okay. I have a doorbell camera." I tasted my wine. It was a little less peppery now. "I'm dying to know what you're doing here. In this neighborhood. I mean, you're Simon—"

"Prichard?" He continued in a snooty tone. "Of the illustrious Prichards?"

"Well, yeah. I admit I looked you up."

He cocked his head with a sardonic smile. "Maybe I should change my name. Can't keep any secrets these days. I'm conducting an experiment; and an old college friend of mine who lives in the area suggested I might like it here. I want to prove that a person can live off the grid in suburbia. I plan to write a book about the experience and start a company for serious suburban off-gridders."

"Suburban off-gridders? Is that a thing?" I said.

"It will be."

Today

"I'm dying to see that video!" said Sam when we met at Starbucks this morning. "That is too funny about the braying donkey. Have you changed your ring tone?"

"Yes, I did. Now it's a nice twittering bird."

I handed my phone to her, and while she watched the video, I retrieved our coffees and warm goodies at the counter. Sam's coffee looked like 5,000 calories of scrumptiousness, and mine was a plain old dark roast. I set hers on the table, then added calories and cream to my cup. The video ended as I was sitting down.

"That video is really something," said Sam. "The good news is, it doesn't sound like Donna did anything to Nina, other than keep her doped up on cold medicine. This Michelle person is sure a piece of work, though."

"I don't think Nina is going to have a happy ending, and it makes me sick thinking about her. If she's dead or suffering somewhere out there." I sipped my coffee. "I've done all I can. It's time to leave it to the police and move on with my life, before I wind up in jail."

Sam lifted her brows with a mischievous grin. "Move on to Simon, perhaps?"

"Good grief, no. You know what I mean. Get a job. Start a hobby. Maybe I'll take up stamp collecting."

She laughed. "At least that would be a safe hobby. A lot safer than your current one."

"My current one? I don't have any hobbies."

"Yes, you do. Saving the world."

I took a big bite of my pastry and rolled my eyes.

"You and your cheese danishes," she said.

"Hey, Grandma. Enjoy your bran muffin. Looks super yummy."

Sam said in a crackly old lady voice, "At least I'm getting my fiber so my bowels will be regular." That got her dirty looks from the old ladies at a nearby table.

"Ooo. So not P.C.," I whispered.

"Hey! There was an event in my Facebook feed that might be fun for us to do."

"What?"

"A local stable that works with special needs children is doing a fundraiser trail ride and cookout. It's in a few weeks and includes a two-hour ride out at the lake, followed by a barbecue at the ranger station. Could be some cute rangers there."

I laughed at her. "Yes, to the event, and no to the cute rangers. Plus, you're assuming the rangers will all be men. They could just as easily be cute women, you know."

———

I made the mistake of watching the local evening news. They did a follow up story on Nina. The news anchor, standing in front of Nina's house, ended somberly with, "So far the police have no leads in this case."

That made me realize, once again, that I can't give up on Nina. Plus, Simon Prichard said I should be a private investigator. A detective wouldn't give up, and neither will I.

CHAPTER THIRTY-EIGHT

WEDNESDAY • JULY 15
Posted by Katy McKenna

Like a dog with a bone:
Not willing to stop until you have finished dealing with something, especially a worrying problem.

This Morning

Dressed in faded jeans and a red t-shirt from the "Forever Fit" club that I didn't go to anymore, I sat on my porch steps, soaking up the sun—wondering what else I could do to find Nina.

Just two days after Donna's arrival, Nina had told me she was ready for her niece to go home. A couple days ago, I heard Donna tell her fiancée that her aunt had told her to go home. Donna didn't leave, so my idea that Nina is staying with a friend until her niece leaves may still be a possibility.

I always record the local morning news, so I can watch it at my leisure. I thought I'd see if they had anything more to say about Nina, so I went inside and turned it on. After the weather report and a few commercials, they did a story about people protesting our school board's policies in front of the school board president's home. The parent protesters brandished signs that said "Teach the 3 Rs. Not Radical Ideology!"

The president, Scott Williams, came out and said, "These people have been protesting out here for days. They do not have the right to tell the schools what their children should be taught. They all should be investigated and prosecuted under federal anti-terrorism laws and thrown in prison."

The reporter asked a cop at the scene if the folks would be arrested, and she said they weren't breaking any laws as long as they stayed off Mr. William's property.

The story had given me an idea. What if I could make Donna and her fiancée's lives so miserable that they'd give up and leave?

———

I have a mountain of cardboard boxes in the garage from all my online shopping. I broke down a large one and made a sign: *Where's Nina Lowen?* Then filled a water bottle, grabbed a beach chair, and set up camp on the sidewalk in front of Nina's house.

Every time a car rolled by, I stood, waving my sign and yelling, "Where's Nina Lowen? Donna Baxter knows!"

Ten minutes into my vigil, Donna appeared on her porch, cane-less and peeved. "What the hell do you think you're doing, Katy?"

"What does it look like? I want justice for Nina! The cops are getting nowhere, so someone has to do something. If you're not going to, then I will!"

Michelle joined her. "You can't do this! It's harassment."

"Last time I looked, there's no law against protesting on a public sidewalk."

"You're disturbing the peace," Michelle screamed.

"Your—" I caught myself before I referred to Donna as her

fiancée. "I have no idea who you are or what business this is of yours, but Donna was disturbing the peace when she ripped up Nina's yard."

Donna tried to drag her betrothed into the house, but Michelle wasn't having it. Instead, she nimbly picked her way through the yard to the sidewalk. "My fiancée was helping her aunt by making the house beautiful."

I was facing her and didn't realize Randy had joined us until he murmured behind me, "Fiancée?" And then he shouted, "Your *fiancée* destroyed the most serene yard in the neighborhood."

My turn to scream again. "Look at it now. One big torn-up mess. Lumber piles, rock piles, dirt piles, gopher holes, weeds. The place looks like a dump and affects the values of all the houses on the block."

"Yeah! What she said!" shouted Earl, as he came across the street.

"Solidarity," said Randy, then hollered, "Bring Nina home! Bring Nina home!" at a passing city bus. "Bro, go get our signs."

Earl trotted to their porch and brought back two colorful signs covered in peace symbols and Nina's name. "She will come home," he said to me. "I've been meditating, and I'm getting good vibes."

"Oh, good grief!" said Michelle. "Did you hear that, Donna? Mr. Hippie is getting good vibes!"

Donna held the screen door open. "Michelle! Please come back in the house." Michelle was halfway up the wood plank to the porch when she spun around to flip us off and fell off the plank in mid-flip-off.

"Are you all right, honey?" said Donna from the porch.

I dashed over to help Michelle up, and she pushed me away. "I'm fine!"

I backed off, watching her struggle to her feet. When she was mobile, I approached again to help her walk up the plank, but she didn't appreciate my assistance and swatted me away.

Pointing to Michelle hobbling up the plywood plank, I said, "Hey, Donna. Bet ya wish you hadn't removed the brick steps!"

Earl high-fived me. "Good one."

For the next hour, we waved our signs and hollered at every passing car. Josh's cousin, Dillon, cruised by in his Jeep Wrangler and tooted his horn. A few minutes later, he came over carrying a piece of cardboard.

"My great-grandma is about the same age as the lady who's missing. She's the coolest person I know. If something like this happened to her…" He shook his head. "I didn't have any markers, so I printed out a sign and taped it to this piece of cardboard. The letters were supposed to be black, but I'm low on ink."

"Your sign looks great," I said.

He quietly gazed at Nina's house for a long moment. "Sorry, again about, you know, the parties."

"Water under the bridge, and I probably overreacted. I was once your age,

and—"

"You're not that old. I mean, you're still pretty hot."

I tried not to obsess on the "not that old part." I really loved what Randy added. "Bro, she's smokin' hot." Then to me, "I hope that doesn't offend you. If it came off as harassment, I apologize."

"How can I be offended by a nice compliment?"

Ethan's mom (talk about smokin' hot) strolled over from the next house beyond Nina's. "Hey, guys. What's going on?"

"Hi. I'm Katy McKenna." I pointed down the street. "I live a couple houses past Nina's. I remember you and Ethan from the other day when the cops were here."

She winced. "Not my finest hour. I'm Madeline Dubois, but call me Maddie. My son and I live next door in my parents' house. We moved in a couple months ago."

"A multigenerational home. Lots of folks doing that these days," I said.

"Mom and Dad are fulfilling their retirement dream and

exploring the country in their R.V., so most of the time, it'll just be Ethan and me."

Everyone introduced themselves. I wasn't surprised to see that her low-cut tight blue top had Dillon mesmerized.

"How's Ethan doing?" I asked.

"Still grounded."

I laughed. "For life?"

"He'll get time off for good behavior, so maybe he'll be free by the time he's thirty-five."

"Ha! My parents won't allow me to date until I'm thirty-five." I held up three fingers. "Three more years."

"My folks said the same thing. So how's that going for you?" she asked.

I twiddled my left finger. "Divorced. Maybe I should've listened to them. Would've saved me a lot of grief."

"Same here. But I did get a great kid out of it." Maddie glanced down the block. "Here comes the jailbird now."

"What're you guys doing?" asked Ethan.

"We're protesting our neighbor's mysterious disappearance," I said.

He looked at me, his big brown eyes solemn. "Do you think she's dead?"

"Honestly, I don't know what to think. I sure hope not."

A white SUV cruised by, and we yelled and brandished our signs. When they rounded the corner, Maddie said, "It's been days. You would think someone would know something by now."

"Here comes Simon," said Earl. "Namasté, neighbor."

"Be still my heart," muttered Maddie to me. "Man-buns are so sexy. Who's the hunk?"

"Mom!" whined her son. "I can hear you, you know."

"Hello, Katy, Randy, Earl." Simon's gaze swung to Maddie, and I noticed his eyes widen briefly. "Hello."

Feeling flat as a pancake, I said, "Simon? This is our neighbor, Maddie Dubois. Maddie? This is Simon Prichard."

"I remember you." He held out his hand. "You were there with your son when the police were at Nina's."

"I apologize for my behavior that day." She hung onto his hand until he reclaimed it.

"No worries. Not easy, raising kids, I imagine."

Maddie batted her eyelashes. "Especially when you're single. Which I am. Single." She pulled her son close and swung her tan, gym-toned arm over his scrawny shoulders. "This is Ethan. My son —the juvenile delinquent."

Simon shook the kid's hand. "Nice to meet you, Ethan." He turned his attention to me. "What're you up to now, Katy?"

Dillon flipped his sign, and Simon read it aloud. "Where's Nina Lowen? What're you trying to accomplish?"

"Trying to make Donna and her girlfriend feel so unwelcome in the neighborhood that they'll leave, and then if Nina is all right, she can come home," I said. "May I have a word with you? Privately?" I guided him down the sidewalk towards his house. "I don't want anyone to know about that video I showed you."

"Of course. I wouldn't do that. And no matter what happens, those women have got to go. So count me on board."

My phone twittered sweetly in my pocket, and Simon laughed. "No ass?"

Sam's smiling face was on the phone screen. "Hey. What's up?" she said.

I told her, and she asked, "Got room for two more?"

"Come on over. You might want to bring some folding chairs. Better bring snacks, too."

———

You should've seen Ethan's eyes bug out when he saw Chelsea step out of their Ford Escape. At the moment, her shoulder-length straight hair is patriotically streaked red and blue because her All-Star soccer team marched in the Fourth of July parade.

215

Sam opened the backend of the vehicle. As Chelsea tugged a large cooler towards her, I poked Ethan in the arm and whispered, "Go help her." Together, they set it on the sidewalk. Sam thanked him, and introduced her daughter. Ethan said, "Hi," and his gaze slid to his sneakers. My usually bold niece instantly shifted into shoe-staring mode, too.

I announced to the growing crowd, "This is my best friend, Samantha, and her daughter, Chelsea. I'll let you all introduce yourselves."

Sam unfolded her chair and plopped her keister in it—then opened her cooler. "I brought water, soda, and wine, and paper cups. The wine is cheap but tasty."

"I always say cheap wine is better than no wine." After everyone had a beverage of their choice, I raised my cup to the group of people lining the sidewalk. "To our dear friend, Nina. Come home soon."

We all turned to face her house and toasted, "To Nina!"

I watched my wine snob neighbor taste his wine. "How is it, Simon?"

"Not bad." He read the label on the box. "Chablis. Would not have guessed that." He said he'd be right back, and went to his house and returned bearing a few bottles of red.

I ran home and filled a grocery bag with chips and crackers. When I returned, several more neighbors had joined us.

My vigil had turned into a block party.

CHAPTER THIRTY-NINE

THURSDAY · JULY 16
Posted by Katy McKenna

I was back to harassing Donna and Michelle at ten this morning. My vigil didn't turn into another block party, which was fine with me. It was fun meeting new people; however, I'm on a mission to make my neighbors miserable.

Around noon, Michelle came out wearing a floppy sunhat, carrying a shopping bag, and using Donna's cane. Before getting in her shiny, black Ford Mustang convertible, she hollered, "I have a lot of errands to run and Donna is napping, so I'd appreciate if you would keep the noise down."

I yelled, "You should be searching for Nina."

"Like you are?" she jeered, waving the cane at me. "Don't forget to put sunblock on. I'd hate to see you get a nasty burn."

She started the engine and revved the motor a few times, then peeled out. As soon as she rounded the corner, I crossed the street to my house to get some sunblock and a hat. I was punching the code into my front door keypad when Simon called from the sidewalk, "Hey, Katy. We need to up your game. Waving a sign is not getting you any useful information."

"I totally agree, but it's better than doing nothing. What do you have in mind?"

He joined me on the porch. "It's not exactly legal." He gazed at me with a little grin. I raised my eyebrows in anticipation. "I have a little listening device that would enable you to hear what's going on in their house while sitting in the comfort of your own home." He followed me to the kitchen.

"A bug, like they use on the cop shows? Something I would have to stick under a table or in a lamp because that's not happening. I'm done with breaking and entering." I picked up the percolator from the stove. "Coffee? It's this morning's. It's pretty good reheated, and I'm too lazy to make a fresh pot."

"I'll take half a cup. We can stick the device on the house exterior, and it'll pick up everything."

I turned the burner on and set two mugs on the counter. "Won't they notice this thing on the house?"

"Doubt it." Simon held out his open hand to reveal a quarter-sized disk. "We can put it where they won't see it."

I plucked it from his calloused palm and scrutinized it. It was less than a quarter-inch thick and weighed an ounce at the most.

He continued his sales pitch. "It's voice-activated with a battery life of about ten days before needing a recharge."

"Where'd you get it?"

"Let's just say I have friends."

Is he being funny, or should I be worried? I'm going with funny.

"May I see your phone?"

I couldn't resist holding it up and saying, "See?"

He shook his head at my hilarity, took the phone, and asked for my passcode.

"1969."

Simon nodded. "Ah. Your birth year. That's always easy to remember."

"Very funny. It was the summer of love. You know, hippies, Woodstock."

A minute later, he said, "I installed an app. You can listen live, although everything is recorded, so you don't have to be glued to the phone day and night."

"I don't want to break the law. Been there and done that." I divided the reheated coffee between the cups. "I also don't want to get sued."

"You standing outside their window filming them is a lot more risky than this little bug. You can't get sued if they don't know about it." He sipped the strong coffee. "Not bad."

I opened a cabinet and waved a box of cookies at him. "Want some?"

"No, thank you. I'm Keto—more or less."

"One more reason not to be Keto." I put the cookies back in the cabinet, and we sat at the kitchen table. "What did you think of Maddie Dubois? You know, the woman with the…(I almost said big boobs)… teenager?"

"She's something." Simon grinned. "However, I have a strict rule not to date anyone I live near or work with. Also, not ready for someone else's kids and exes." He set the bug on the table.

"Yeah. Me too. All of that. Way too complicated. Been there and done that—except for the kid thing." I tapped the listening device. "Is this thing all charged up?"

He nodded. "It's ready to go. How about we do the deed tonight?"

Sex? No, idiot, he means to set up the bug. "You're okay with getting involved?" I hesitated. "I mean, it is illegal and I don't want to be responsible for you getting into trouble."

"No worries. Let's meet in front of my house at nine-thirty tonight."

———

9:30 p.m.

"Any ideas where to put the spy thingie?" I asked.

We were standing on the edge of Nina's property, and I had butterflies dive-bombing in my stomach. I am not cut out for a life of crime.

"I was thinking under the living room window. You got a good recording from that location until your phone…" I couldn't clearly see Simon's face in the dark, but I heard the little giggle bubbling in his voice. "Hee-Hawed. Still can't stop laughing about that. Sure wish I could've seen your face when it happened." He set a hand on my shoulder. "Is your phone off?"

"I left it at home."

We sneaked to the living room window and flattened our bodies against the side of the house. I felt like I was in a *Mission Impossible* movie.

"Where are we putting it?" I asked. "The window frame?"

"No. Too risky," he whispered. "Someone might notice a black disk against the white paint. "I'm sticking it underneath."

"Won't it fall off?"

"I'm using double-back industrial-strength tape. "We'll be lucky if we can pry it off once it's stuck on." He peeked in the window. "They're watching TV."

My eyes had adjusted to the dark, and I watched him press the disk firmly against the wall.

"That should do it," he said. "Let's go."

Back on the sidewalk in front of his house, Simon said, "Any questions on how to use the app?"

"I'm sure I can figure it out."

"Good. Call me if you have any problems. I put my number in your phone." He started up the walk to his front door. "Good luck!"

I zipped home, poured a glass of wine, and settled on the couch to listen to the Donna and Michelle show. The first thing I heard was a loud yawn that sent me into a fit of yawns.

Michelle: "I think it's my bedtime, sweetybabe. I'm really pooped. Busy day."

Donna: "Me, too. We're getting too old for all that heavy lifting."

Michelle: "I'm good for a little puttering around the house; however, I've come to the age where I need to leave the big jobs to the big kids."

Donna: "Well, we don't have that luxury at the moment. Once we get through this, you can be a lady of leisure. How's your leg feeling? That was a nasty fall you took."

Michelle: "It's much better." She laughed. "We should get matching canes." They both laughed over that, and then she continued, "What are we going to do about our annoying neighbor?"

Donna: "Katy?"

Michelle: "Who else would I be talking about? She was out there all day today, screaming at every car that passed by. You'd think there would be a law about that."

Donna: "Well, there isn't. I already checked. She isn't breaking any laws."

Michelle: "If you say so." She yawned. "We need to get our beauty sleep. Tomorrow's the big day."

Donna: "I wish Baby Girl would come back." Sniff, sniff. "She would be such an adorable ring-bearer."

Michelle: "Don't give up hope. Sometimes dogs turn up months, even years, later."

Donna: "Maybe that could happen, but every day that passes makes it seem more unlikely."

Michelle: "You have to keep the faith."

Donna: "I'll try. But we both know Aunt Nina's never coming home."

Michelle: "We don't know that either, so please don't give up hope. Coming to bed?"

Donna: "Yes, my love. Help me up."

I heard a loud grunt.

Donna: "I'm so stiff. I need to take some ibuprofen."

Michelle: "Me, too. We need to feel good for tomorrow. I think we should get there at least fifteen minutes early. So, leave ten-thirty and get there at ten-forty-five?"

Donna: "Sounds good to me."

A moment passed, and then their voices sounded further away.

Michelle: "Where do you think you're going?"

Donna: "To bed."

Michelle: "Not with me, you aren't. It's bad luck to see the bride before the wedding."

Giggling followed, and then Michelle squealed, "Oh, you bad girl. Screw bad luck."

CHAPTER FORTY

THURSDAY · JULY 23
Posted by Katy McKenna

Haven't posted for a while—time to catch up.
A lot has happened in the last several days!
I hope I remember everything.

Friday, July 17
Part One

Even though the engaged couple wasn't leaving for the courthouse until ten-thirty that morning, I was ready to go at eight. While eating a bowl of oatmeal, I tuned into their morning conversation on my phone.

Donna: "I can't believe the day has finally come."

Michelle: "Neither can I."

Donna: "You want more tea?

Michelle: I better not. I'm so excited, and more tea might wind up upsetting my stomach. You know how I am."

Donna: "I certainly do."

Michelle: "We've been together for a long time. Well, sort of together."

Donna: "Today, we'll be joined in marriage and officially together—forever."

Michelle: "I know it's awful, but I've always been secretly grateful that Gary drove off that cliff."

Donna: "I suppose deep down, I was too. In the end, it sure saved me a lot of grief." She chuckled. "That's so awful. Gary's death made me a widow and saved me grief."

Michelle: "Now we're finally going to have our happily ever after. Till death do us part."

Donna: "I just wish Baby Girl was here. And Aunt Nina, of course. It's so hard not knowing what's happened to either of them. Even if they're dead, at least I'd have closure."

Michelle: "I know. But I truly do believe that they are fine, wherever they are. This time next year, this will all be behind us. Just a bad memory."

Donna: "You have a sneaky look on your face. What have you done?"

Michelle: "Okay. You got me. Can't keep anything from you. I have a little wedding surprise."

Donna: "Really? What?"

Michelle: "I booked us into a romantic bed-and-breakfast cottage. It's on a big cattle ranch and is so charming and cozy."

Donna: "That's wonderful. Where?"

Michelle: "Not far. You'll see. I packed a bag for you while you were taking a shower."

Donna: "Did you put my prescriptions in?"

Michelle: "Of course. Thyroid. Statin. Lisinopril. Clopidogrel —I doubt that's how it's pronounced. Oh, and your diuretic."

Donna: "You know me too well."

Michelle: "The ranch serves a scrumptious breakfast. Eggs Benedict, croissants, fruit salad, and champagne. But there are no restaurants near there, so I've got two bags full of yummy appetizers, wine, and treats for tonight. We'll have a fireside feast with no distractions. No internet. No TV. No phones."

Donna: "No phones?"

Michelle: "There's no cell coverage out there. There's also no idiot waving her stupid sign and yelling at cars—just you and me for one whole blissful day and night. We deserve it. We can even stay a second night if you like. They don't have another booking until the weekend."

Donna: "What if there's an emergency and we don't have a phone?"

Michelle: "If we have an emergency, we'll do what we would have done thirty years ago. We'll walk to the owner's house and use their landline. Feel better now?"

Donna: "Much. I can't wait to get there."

Michelle: "Then go finish getting dressed, silly girl, while I load the car."

I hurried outside and stationed myself in the bushes on Simon's property line. Pretty soon, Michelle came out dragging a blue and white cooler. She looked nice in white pants, gold sandals, and a yellow sweater set that complemented her tan. She set the cooler by the rental car, went back inside, and returned toting a couple grocery bags.

Wow, she wasn't kidding about having a feast.

Another trip to the house, and she came out with an armful of pillows and blankets.

I ran back to my house scolding myself for wasting precious time spying in the bushes when I should have been getting my car out. I grabbed my purse, backed Veronica out of the garage, checked the gas tank—it was three-quarters full, and killed the engine. After a few minutes, I got restless and climbed out to watch from the bushes again.

Everything was in the car and Michelle was smoking a cigarette and clutching two white lacy scarves. Donna stepped onto the porch, looking the best I've ever seen her in an elegant navy pantsuit with a colorful silky scarf arranged around her neck. She'd clipped back her straggly hair and had makeup on. Amazing what a little effort can do.

She called to Michelle. "Do we have everything?"

"Everything except my beautiful blushing bride-to-be."

"You mean the *other* beautiful bride."

Michelle waved the scarves. "Look what I got? Matching scarves to protect our hair. We can pretend they're wedding veils."

I watched them get in the Mustang and tie the scarves under their chins. While they were buckling up, I rushed to my car and edged it out far enough to see which way they would go. Once they were heading down the street, I followed at a discreet distance in my orange car. With hope, they were too excited about getting hitched to notice little old me trailing behind.

CHAPTER FORTY-ONE

THURSDAY· JULY 23
Posted by Katy McKenna

Friday, July 17
Part Two

11:35 a.m.

The blissful newlyweds strolled hand-in-hand through the courthouse parking lot swinging their arms like little girls. They stopped and passionately kissed like very big girls for a long minute. A teenager walking by yelled good-naturedly, "Get a room!"

Michelle hollered, "We're newlyweds! Would you take our picture?"

She gave him her phone and he had some fun with them—encouraging them to do romantic poses, then goofy poses. The scene made me feel rotten about following them.

But I did anyway.

We got onto Highway 101, heading north. Up the long grade and down the other side. The pavement flattened out and we traveled a few miles more with me trailing several cars behind in the slow lane. Her left turn signal blinked. She slowed down and pulled into a turn lane that led to a country road.

I swung onto the gravel road and hung way back until she rounded a curve up ahead. She was driving faster than the twenty-five MPH posted speed limit, and stirring up a dust cloud behind her, which helped camouflage me. An intelligent person would have given up at that point since it was apparent they were going to the place Michelle had talked about. A rustic, cozy cottage on a cattle ranch. The cattle grazing beyond the rusty barbed wire fence that bordered the road confirmed it.

No one has ever accused me of being smart, so I drove on, slowing to a crawl at each bend in the road in case they were right on the other side. If they saw me, they might call the cops. Then I remembered there was no cell service out there, which was hard to believe in this day and age. I can't recall the last time I walked around holding my phone aloft, searching for bars, so maybe Michelle was wrong. I tugged my phone from my purse and checked the screen. No service. However, they could use the land-line at the B & B office.

The further we traveled, the more wooded the rolling hills of parched golden grass became. As I swung around the next curve, I caught of glimpse of their taillights in a shady grove. I reversed direction and backed away until I was out of sight, then parked under the sprawling branches of an oak tree.

My raggedy, faded red baseball cap was on the backseat floor where I tossed it the last time I was "in disguise." A sweatshirt draped around my shoulders (another backseat floor-find) and sunglasses completed my costume. In case I wanted to take some photos, I slipped my phone into my back pocket, got out and locked the door, then felt conflicted. I leaned against the car staring at the cloudless sky.

What the hell am I doing here? What do I hope to accomplish? Obviously, they're here to have the little romantic honeymoon that Michelle planned.

"Time to go home." I was unlocking the car door when I heard screams.

I jogged along the side of a sandstone bank lining the dirt road until it sloped down to ground level, leaving me visible and vulnerable. From there, I sprinted to the closest tree and ducked behind it.

The newlyweds were laughing and screaming boisterously while unloading the car.

I was about to retrace my steps back to Veronica, when my intuition gave me a little nudge. *Oh, hell. In for a penny, in for a pound, as Mom would say.*

I could make out the cottage deep in the shadows of the trees where they'd parked. It looked more like a long abandoned ramshackle old cabin built in the 1800s, than a charming honeymoon cottage.

About twenty-five feet from the cabin, a cluster of giant granite boulders sat in the hip-deep grass. I scrambled to them and hunkered down waiting for my heart rate to slow. When the car was empty, Michelle grabbed the two carry-ons and rushed to the entrance. She set down the suitcases, unlocked the door, and then turned to wait.

Donna closed the trunk, and glanced around for a long moment. Then she picked up the grocery bags and called out to her waiting bride, "Are you planning to carry me over the threshold, my love?"

She left the cooler by the car and climbed the rickety steps to the porch where Michelle was blocking the entrance. Donna set down the bags and approached her with arms wide spread. Michelle started talking and waving her arms. She looked frantic, which made no sense to me. Suddenly, Donna shouted, "Get out of the way!"

"Wait! You don't understand!" Michelle followed her into the cabin and slammed the door. I bolted to the cabin's log and chinked side, and squatted behind a scrubby Scotch broom bush growing in front of a window. I was afraid to peek in, but I could hear them arguing.

"What have you done?" cried Donna. "Aunt Nina! Wake up!"

I had to see what was going on. I spread the Scotch broom's bushy branches apart for a look into the cabin. I could see someone under the covers in the brass bed, but the women's bodies blocked my view of her face.

"Nina can't hear you," said Michelle. "She's dead to the world."

"You killed her?"

"No! She's asleep, that's all."

"What did you give her?" asked Donna.

Michelle picked up a bottle of liquid medicine from the small three-legged bedside table. "SleepWell and sleeping pills. I mix them into protein drinks so she's getting proper nutrition, too. I got the idea from your first book."

"That was fiction! She's old and fragile. You could've killed her." Donna picked up a little prescription bottle on the nightstand and read the label. "This is your Ambien. I thought you quit taking this after you woke up naked one morning in the neighbor's yard."

"I did. But I renewed the prescription at the Walmart in Santa Lucia. I only mixed enough of the Ambien and SleepWell to keep her soundly asleep. It's not that much different from what you were doing at the house."

"She wasn't feeling well, " said Donna.

"Right. The bronchial thing. You told me."

Donna continued. "I also told you she didn't do well with the daytime cold medicine. It made her agitated and she couldn't sleep. That's why I was giving her the nighttime stuff."

"Oh, please, sweetybabe. Be honest. If not with me, then at least with yourself. You were keeping her asleep, because you were worn out. Between the house remodel and your aunt's constant needs—maybe at first it was for her bronchitis, but then—"

Donna hung her head. "I admit that I continued to medicate

her when she probably didn't need it anymore. You know she told me several times she wanted me to leave, but how could I leave without finishing the remodel?" She lifted her head, looking coldly at Michelle. "But I was mixing it with vitamins and fruit juice, not sleeping pills, for God's sake." Donna threw the pill bottle against the wall. "Oh my God! It's just hitting me now. You snuck into the house in the middle of the night and kidnapped her! And then you let me agonize over where my aunt was! I thought she was dead! How could you do that to her? To me?"

"I did it for us. I felt terrible not telling you, but I had to wait for the right time. I've been taking good care of her. I've kept her hydrated and comfortable. I even put a diaper on her and changed it twice a day."

"What do you mean, *you did it for us?*" Donna shook her head, looking incredulous. "Those mysterious errands you've been running. You were coming out here. But why? Why did you do this?"

"You know she's not long for this world. Plus, she basically has no life. Her friends are all dead, except for that obnoxious busy-body neighbor, and she lives with a cat—who ran away. Is that a life you'd wish on someone you love?"

"No, of course not," said Donna. "That's why she was moving to that retirement community. And it's my fault the cat is gone."

"Personally, I don't think she would survive a big move. When she passes, everything goes to you. We can stay in the house and I can take care of you so you can focus on writing."

"But why bring her here? To this awful place? It makes no sense." Donna shook her head. "Never mind. I don't want to hear another word from you. I'm taking her to the hospital, and you're helping me get her to the car." She yanked the blankets off Nina. "Oh, my God! You have her tied to the bed like she's a prisoner!"

I need to call the police. I checked my phone, praying there'd be bars, but it still said "no service."

"I couldn't risk her waking up and trying to leave, could I?" said Michelle. "She might have got lost. Or hurt."

"Oh, Aunt Nina! I swear, I had no idea." Donna reached to untie her aunt's wrists.

"No! Don't wake her." Michelle elbowed in front of Donna, and threw the covers back over Nina. She set her hands on Donna's shoulders, turning her away from the bed. "You have to hear me out! I planned this while I was staying at the hotel. I wanted everything to be perfect for Nina."

Donna backed away from her, looking frightened. "You call this perfect? Drugged and tied to a bed?"

Michelle sighed, then smiled. "There's an ancient oak with widespread branches up on the hill behind the cabin. I've sat for hours under that tree enjoying the magnificent view. You can see the ocean from up there. It's perfect. You're going to love it. I've already dug the grave. We'll take Nina up there and give her a lethal dose at sunset. She will gently and painlessly drift away. I brought champagne to toast a happy ending for Nina, and a new beginning for us."

"No, Michelle. None of that is happening. You're sick and need help." Donna straightened her shoulders, and stepped close to Nina. She laid back a corner of the blue plaid blanket and untied Nina's left wrist. "We're taking Nina to the hospital and then we are going to get you the help you need."

"Stop!" Michelle slipped her hand inside her crossbody bag.

———

That's enough typing for today. I'll continue this tomorrow.

CHAPTER FORTY-TWO

FRIDAY · JULY 24
Posted by Katy McKenna

Friday, July 17
Part Three

I slammed through the cabin door. "Donna—I'll help you take Nina to the hospital!"

Michelle spun around, staring bug-eyed at me, her hand still inside her purse. "What the hell are you doing here?"

"Katy! Oh thank God you're here," said Donna, as she feverishly worked to untie Nina's other wrist. "I've never been so glad to see anyone in my entire life! I'll need help getting her to the car."

I approached the bed shoving Michelle aside, and gazed at my sleeping friend. She looked fragile in her lavender flannel nightgown. "Let me help you untie her."

Donna moved aside. "I'm so shaky I'm all thumbs.

Suddenly, a searing pain stabbed my lower back. I collapsed to my knees and slammed hard on my side, writhing in muscle-ripping spasms that I thought would tear me in half. My brain felt like a marble rattling around inside my empty skull, while a million bees stung my flesh.

After what felt like an eternity of mind-blowing pain, the spasm loosened its grip, leaving me drained and paralyzed.

Michelle's straddled my chest, pointing a pink stun gun at me. "Move and I'll taser you again."

"Leave her alone!" cried Donna.

"She'll live." Then to me, she said, "See what being a Nosy Nellie gets ya?"

I whimpered, and she clamped a gold sandaled foot on my chest, grinding its kitten heel into my ribs. "Donna, get the rope out of the bureau. I put it in the bottom drawer. Then tie her up."

"Why? She can't even move."

"Pretty soon she'll be able to, and I'll have to tase her again." She bent close to my face. "Do you want me to do that?"

I couldn't answer, but the answer was NO!

Michelle pressed her shoe deeper into my chest. "Don't get any funny ideas." She waved her taser. "Still got a lot of juice left. Probably can zap ya two, three more times."

Michelle glanced over her shoulder at Donna. "Hurry up."

In my peripheral vision, I watched Donna drag the rope out of the dresser near the rock fireplace.

"Are you planning to murder her, too?" asked Donna.

"Gently easing your poor old aunt to the pearly gates is hardly what I'd call murder. I hope someone will be as kind to me someday."

Still standing behind Michelle, Donna coiled a section of rope in a loose circle. "But what about Katy?"

With her back to Donna, Michelle continued to stare down at me. "She's an unfortunate complication. Her fault, not ours." She glanced at the palm of the hand not holding the stun gun. "With these blisters I got from digging Nina's grave, there's no way I can dig another hole. So you're going to have to do it, Donna. Or they can share the grave I dug." She smiled sweetly at me. "But don't you worry, Katy. You won't suffer." She slipped her blistered hand into her crossbody purse, withdrew another pill bottle and shook it. "I got lots of sleeping pills. Enough for you and Auntie Nina to go permanently night-night."

Donna stood frozen behind her, her lips clamped in a grim line, clutching the rope loop with both hands. She glanced at me, and I widened my eyes and sputtered, "Please."

Michelle sniggered. "Begging is so pathetic. This is what you get for not minding your own business."

In a flash, Donna raised her arms up and over her bride's head, wrapping the rope around her neck. She snapped it tight, dragging her backward. Michelle's foot slid off my chest, and I sucked in a gulp of revitalizing air.

Michelle whipped around, fighting to loosen the tight coil from her neck with one hand. Her other hand, still clutching the taser, moved towards Donna's abdomen. Donna jerked the rope violently and Michelle dropped the taser. The women lost their balance and landed hard on me.

Screaming and pummeling each other, they slid off me onto the wood floor. Michelle had loosened Donna's stranglehold on the rope. She rolled over onto Donna, planting her rear on her wife's paunchy stomach, and ripped the rope from her neck. Her eyes swept the floor and fixed on the pink taser just inches from my hand. I had to get it before she did. I willed my body to wake up. My fingers twitched a stiff response.

"Don't even think about it," she snarled as she reached for it.

Donna's hand shot out and clawed Michelle's arm with her sharp purple nails, drawing blood.

"You bitch!" She slapped Donna several times, forgetting about the stun gun.

I couldn't take hold of the taser, but I smacked it under the bed, then shimmied away from the women. I hauled myself to a sitting position, leaning against the brass bed frame. I felt a tickle on my head and shifted to meet Nina's eyes. Her other hand pressed a finger over her mouth, warning me to keep quiet. She flicked her eyes at the glass kerosene hurricane lamp on the bedside table. I knew what she was thinking, but could I do it?

Nina slid to the far side of the bed, flattening herself against the log wall. Keeping an eye on the wrestling women, I scooted towards the table and reached up for the lamp. My hand grasped at the round bottom glass base. It was too heavy for a one-handed hold. Using the spindle-legged wood nightstand for leverage, I tried to push myself to my feet. The little table wobbled and the lamp shattered on the wood floor, oozing kerosene. I lost my balance, landing flat on my chest. My cheek slammed into the broken glass and the kerosene puddle.

Michelle thrust herself away from Donna, scrambled to her feet, and started towards me. I heard Nina whisper, "Taser."

Michelle kicked me hard in the side. I slithered under the tall-framed bed—away from the next blow. That brought me within reach of the taser. I seized it with my left hand, then swapped it under my chest to my right hand.

I could see my adversary's gold sandaled feet. "Come out from under there!" she barked.

"No!"

Several feet away, Donna lay on the floor motionless.

"Fine. Stay under there as long as you want while I tie up Donna and Nina. I think a nice spritz of pepper spray ought to keep you in check until I can properly deal with you."

Before she turned away, I jammed the taser into the top of her foot, and she fell like a ton of bricks. I slid out from under the bed, threw a quick glance at Nina, and received a shaky thumbs-up.

"Donna! Wake up!" I searched for a pulse on her neck.

She swatted my hand away. "I'm okay. You need to tie that crazy bitch up before she can move again."

I dangled the rope over Michelle's face. "Lookee what I got." She glared frozen daggers at me. I was still moving slow, but managed to bind her wrists together, then trailed the rope to her feet and wrapped her ankles. I still had several feet left, so I knotted it around a bed frame leg at the foot of the bed. She'd have to be Houdini to get out of the tangled mess I'd made.

After that exertion, I collapsed on the wooden rocker in the corner to catch my breath.

"Katy dear?" said Nina in a tremulous voice. "Are you okay? Your face is bleeding."

I touched my cheek and saw blood on my fingers.

Donna struggled to her feet and sat on the edge of the bed. "I am so, so sorry, Auntie Nina. I swear I knew nothing about any of this. You've got to believe me."

Nina patted her niece's hand. "I know. But why didn't you tell me about that woman?"

She shook her head, looking battered and beat—both physically and emotionally. "I didn't think you would understand."

"Donna, I may be old, but I haven't been living under a rock all these years. If you'd told me, I would've understood."

"Maybe, if I had," Donna's voice choked on a sob, "none of this would've happened."

CHAPTER FORTY-THREE

FRIDAY • JULY 24
Posted by Katy McKenna

Friday, July 17
Part Four

I sat on the bed next to Donna. "I think you both should rest while I go call the police and an ambulance."

Nina nodded. Her skin had a sickly gray pallor, which I feared meant she wasn't getting sufficient oxygen.

Michelle chortled from the floor. "Good luck calling the cops. There's no cell service anywhere out here. I made sure of that."

Donna said, "There's a main house with a landline. Michelle, where is it?"

She sniggered. "Haven't you figured out by now, this is not a B and B? It's an old cabin that no one has used in years. Supposedly a rancher who died in the twenties haunts it. Amazing what you can find on the internet."

Donna shook her head, gazing at her clenched hands in her lap. "I hate you. I really hate you."

"You don't mean that, sweetybabe."

"Never call me that again!"

"What's it going to take to make you realize I did this for us?" said Michelle.

"My God! I thought I knew you. My soulmate. Ha!" Donna wiped her tears on her sleeve. "All these years, I never knew you at all." She sat up straighter, shaking her head. "No more tears for you. You don't deserve them."

I nodded in Michelle's direction. "Really don't want to leave you two with her."

Michelle wiggled her trussed feet. "It's not like I can do anything." She whimpered in a baby voice, "Sweetybabe, I love you with all my heart and you're treating me like some kind of dangerous criminal. I'm your best friend and bride! Till death do us part."

"Shut up! Shut up! Shut up!" Donna stomped to the porch, brought in her carry-on, and removed a pair of red underpants. Then stood over her bride from hell, dangling the panties.

"What're you doing?" I asked.

"I was going to cram these in her mouth to shut her up. But I can't."

"Well, I sure can. Give them to me." I crouched next to Michelle. "Open wide and say ahhh."

"You're not putting those in my mouth, bitch." She spat at me, then clamped her mouth shut.

I wiped her spittle off my chin with the panties, then tickled her into submission, and stuffed them in her mouth.

"Donna, I might have to drive back to the freeway to get cell reception. Will you be okay?"

"I don't think I'll ever be okay again, but yes. I'll be okay."

I opened the door and was about to step out when she said, "Katy? Thank you for being a good neighbor to my aunt."

I wasn't comfortable leaving them, but what choice did I have?

At least with a pair of granny panties jammed in her mouth, Michelle couldn't sweet-talk Donna into untying her.

Stepping down off the porch, I flinched. My side ached where Michelle had kicked me. My chest was sore from her heel digging into my ribs, and my cheek throbbed. My car was just around the bend, and as I hustled to it, I monitored my phone for nonexistent bars.

The car's interior was a sizzling sauna, but it felt good to sit my battered body on the hot leather seat. I got a shock when I glanced in the rearview mirror. My cheek was a bloody congealed mess, and my hair was a matted, sticky snarl. I touched the gunk and sniffed my fingers. SleepWell with a hefty hint of kerosene. I started the engine and drove towards the freeway, keeping one eye on the road and one on my phone.

Finally! One tiny bar! I stopped and the bar winked out. I rolled a little further and it was back. I stopped again and it was gone again. "Come on! What the hell century am I in? The twentieth?"

I floored the accelerator, causing my car to fishtail on the gravelly road and nose-dive into a ditch. I pounded on the steering wheel. "Can this shitty day get any shittier?" I put the car in reverse, spinning my back tires deeper in the loose dirt. "Dammit!" I climbed out and slammed the door.

Clutching my hands to my aching chest, I jogged towards the freeway. It hadn't seemed far when following Donna and Michelle to the cabin, but now it felt like miles.

Finally! I had bars, and the signal looked strong. I pressed Angela Yaeger's number praying she'd answer. It went to voicemail.

"Angela! It's Katy McKenna. I'm in big trouble, and I don't know what to do. Wait! Yes, I do! I'm dialing 911 right now."

"Katy?"

"Angela! Thank God!"

"Try to calm down and tell me what's going on."

Calming down was not going to happen, but I managed to tell her what had happened.

"Where are you?" she asked.

"You know that last country road right before you hit the grade heading back to Santa Lucia? I can't think of the name. I just saw it a while ago, and now I'm totally blank."

"I know the road you're talking about. Hold on a sec—let me look at a map. Does Granada Road ring a bell?"

"That's it!"

"I'm heading to my car right now. An ambulance will be on its way, too. Hold tight, and we'll get you, Katy."

Even though I knew they would arrive before I could reach the cabin, I headed back, shifting between walking and trotting, with an occasional stop to hang my head over my knees and catch my breath. During my third panting break, I heard sirens in the distance. Moments later, they were in sight, and I waited to hitch a ride.

Angela drove the lead car with two squad cars behind her, an ambulance, and a fire truck in the rear. She jumped out and hustled me into the front seat, clucking like a Police Chief mother-hen. Back in the driver's seat, she said, "Katy, you look awful. Your poor face." She touched my head. "What's this goo in your hair?"

"Mostly SleepWell syrup."

"Of course."

"I don't think you'll need all the backup. I have Michelle tied up good. No way is she going anywhere."

"Police protocol, Katy. Tell me where to go."

"Follow the road. I'll tell you when to stop."

We passed by Veronica. "We'll get your car towed later," she said.

I pointed through the windshield. "This is where I parked and continued on foot. We're almost there. Just around the bend. There! In those trees. That's where the cabin is."

We parked. Angela rolled down the windows, then pulled out her gun.

"You don't need that," I said.

"Until I know the area is secure, I do."

I opened the car door.

"No." She set her hand on my arm, shaking her head. "I want you to stay put. Got that?"

"But—"

"That's an order."

The expression on her face shut me up. I closed the door, feeling relieved that everything was beyond my control now.

The cops quietly surrounded the cabin, guns pointed at the cottage. It was like watching a crime show, except this was for real. The EMTs were standing by until it was safe to enter the building. Once everyone was in place, Angela called, "Donna Baxter? I need you to come out, please."

The door opened, and she poked her head out, looking terrified.

"It's all right, Donna. No one is going to hurt you. We need you safely out here before we go in. Can your aunt walk?"

"No. She'll need help." Donna stepped onto the porch holding up her hands.

"You're not under arrest," said Angela.

Donna crumpled over, sobbing. "I didn't mean to do it! I swear to God, I didn't mean to do it."

———

Friday, July 17th was a very long day and I can't type another word. I'll pick up where I left off tomorrow.

CHAPTER FORTY-FOUR

SATURDAY · JULY 25
Posted by Katy McKenna

Friday, July 17
Part Five

Still catching up! I feel like I'm writing a book!

"Come down off the porch," commanded Angela.

Donna struggled to her feet and then her knees buckled. Angela motioned two officers to assist her.

I had to know what was going on. I got out of the car and crouched behind it, surveying the scene. Then moved slowly towards the group, remaining far enough away not to annoy the chief, yet close enough to hear what was happening. Her eyes flicked in my direction. She frowned, but she didn't order me back to the car.

The chief holstered her gun as the police officers guided Donna toward her.

"Chief?" yelled an officer from the cabin door. "You need to see this."

Donna broke into choking sobs again. "I didn't mean to do it. I swear to God, I didn't mean to."

Angela told a cop to stay with Donna. With another glance in my direction, she strode to the cabin. I held my breath as she stepped inside. All was quiet, save for Donna's weeping. Several minutes ticked by, and then the chief yelled from the door, "Bring her in."

Donna cried, "No. Please don't make me go in there! Please, I'm begging you. It was an accident. I didn't mean to hurt her."

The officers that had helped her down the cabin steps steered her back to the cabin. No one was watching me, so I crept over to the side window and peered in. Nina was seated on the rocker, looking like she'd seen a ghost. Angela had draped the cardigan she'd been wearing over her shoulders. My gaze swept the gloomy room and landed on Michelle's legs, still trussed up like a rodeo calf. I wondered why no one was untying her.

Is she dead? Did I suffocate her with the granny pants? Am I a murderer? My head tingled, and a wave of nausea engulfed me. I bent over trying not to heave.

"Katy?" Angela set her hand on my back. "Are you all right?"

I jumped, startled by the sound of her voice behind me and the touch of her hand. I turned to face her. "I didn't mean to do it. I swear." I felt faint, and squatted, hanging my head. "I feel like I'm going to pass out."

"You're probably dehydrated," she said, then yelled, "I need water here."

An EMT dashed over with a cold bottle of water.

Angela uncapped it. "Here. Drink. It'll make you feel better."

I remained hunkered over as I drank half the bottle. Within

seconds, the faintness passed, and I stood. "Thank you. I guess it's been hours since I had any water."

"We need to talk about what happened in there," she said.

"Well, um, I tied her up and—" I sucked in some air. "Do I need a lawyer?"

Angela cocked an eyebrow. "I don't know. Do you?" She watched Donna being escorted out of the cabin in handcuffs. "We're all going to the station now. We'll need your statement, Katy."

At that moment, the EMTs were carrying Nina down the cabin steps on a gurney. "Hold on, Angela." I dashed over to check on my friend and was assured by the first responders that she was doing well.

"Her vitals are all within normal range. We're taking her to the hospital now where she will get a thorough evaluation."

Nina smiled at me, and I squeezed her hand. "I'll check in on you as soon as I can."

———

I didn't ride to the station with Angela. Instead, I rode with two young male cops. I wasn't under arrest or treated like a criminal by the amiable officers; however, sitting in the rock-hard molded gray plastic backseat in the squad car sure made me feel like a felon. When I went on a police ride-along a while back, Sergeant Crowley told me the seats are like that for easy cleaning and disinfecting. The drunks often vomit. Some perps deliberately defecate and then smear the feces on the seat. Knowing that, I kept my hands primly folded on my lap.

They escorted me to an interrogation room at the station and left me there with a chilled bottle of water. I watch enough crime shows to know the police often collect DNA from cups and water bottles. Since I'm not a criminal, I didn't fret about it, and I needed more hydration.

Glancing at the one-way window, I wondered if anyone was observing me. Finally, Angela walked in. "I'm sorry I kept you waiting, Katy." She handed me a Baby Ruth candy bar. "I thought you might need some sugar."

"Thank you. I do, but first, I desperately need to pee."

"You know where it is. I'll wait here."

Clenching my pelvis muscles, I scurried down the hall praying I'd make it. I did. Barely. While sitting on the toilet, my ankle vibrated a few times. I'd forgotten that I had on my FitTrim. Confetti was flying across its tiny screen. I had hit 10,000 steps!

Returning to the interrogation room, I found Angela sitting at the table with Lieutenant Joann Yee. The attractive, raven-haired woman stood and gave me a quick embrace. "Good to see you again, Katy. Although I wish it was under different circumstances."

"Yes," said Angela. "Trouble seems to have a way of finding our Katy."

I sat down, unwrapped the candy bar, and took a bite. "Mmm, so good. I haven't had a Baby Ruth since I was a kid. This brings back happy memories. It was my grandpa's favorite candy bar." I glanced around the room. "Are we doing an official interrogation? I ask, because this is an interrogation room, right?"

"It is," said Angela. "Although, we use it for other things, too. It's a quiet place to talk—hopefully with no interruptions. When you called for help, you gave me a brief rundown of the events. Now we need a concise timeline. Everything you can recall."

Joann pushed a small digital recorder towards me. Then set a legal pad on the table.

Angela's hand hovered over the recorder, prepared to switch it on. "Are you ready?"

"Hold on. I have a question that I hope you'll answer."

She folded her hands on the green laminate-topped table. "All right."

"Back at the cabin, Donna screamed, *I didn't mean to do it.* When I saw you crouched beside Michelle, I couldn't see her face."

She cocked her head. "You mean when you were watching through the window instead of staying in the car like I told you to do?"

"Yes. I know I wasn't supposed to be there, but…is she all right?"

Angela shook her head. "No, she is not. I assumed you knew. She's dead."

"I wasn't sure." It scared me to ask my next question because I didn't want to find out that I caused her death. "How did she die, if I may ask?"

"You may. There was a pair of red panties—"

My hands slapped the table. "I swear. I didn't mean to do it! You have to believe me."

Angela's brows shot up. "I didn't think you had. Now you're saying you did?"

"Do I need a lawyer?"

"Let's back up a moment, Katy, and get on the same page. Tell me exactly what you did that you didn't mean to do."

I stared at the recorder, still not on. Was I about to crucify myself? I needed to measure my words carefully. I took a swig of water and cleared my throat. Angela turned on the damned recorder.

"I was the one who gagged Michelle with the panties. She was screaming awful, vile things. Donna was basically in shock, and Nina had already been through so much, so I…" I paused when she grinned. "What?"

"She wasn't gagged with the panties. She was strangled."

"With the panties," added Joann with a smirk.

"Oh, thank God." I blew out a relieved breath. "I mean, I'm not thankful she's dead, but I'm thankful that I didn't do it. When I left, Michelle was fine. Tied up and gagged, but totally fine." Then it hit me. "Are you saying Donna killed her? Because it sure wasn't Nina."

"It appears that way. Let's begin at the beginning. Why did you follow them to the cabin?"

We began the arduous task of documenting the hours leading up to me going for help. I was reasonably sure of the timeline since I had listened to their conversation the night before. Michelle said they should leave at ten-thirty to get to City Hall by ten-forty-five, making them fifteen minutes early for their appointment. Luckily, I didn't let it leak that I'd overheard that conversation with an illegal listening device. However, I had to have a reason why I would have followed them.

"I was outside this morning puttering in the yard when I saw them stowing suitcases in their car. Like for a trip, or something."

"How did you see that if you were in your yard? They're two doors down."

"All right. You got me. I've been keeping a close eye on them. You know, for Nina's sake."

"Like when you crawled through the dog door, right?" said the chief.

Joann giggled. "That photo of you is so funny."

"I guess I'll never live that down. I swear I haven't been in Nina's house uninvited since." Yes, I fibbed. "But I had a feeling they knew where she was. It turns out one of them did."

I paused for a bite of candy. "Anyway, I was curious where they would go at a time like this—all dressed up. I mean, taking a vacation when your aunt is missing? Who does that?" I unscrewed the cap from my water bottle and chugged a few swallows. "I heard Donna say, 'Do we have everything?' and then Michelle says, 'Everything except the bride-to-be.' That's when I realized that they were getting married. So I followed them to city hall. I remember seeing the time on the dashboard clock after we parked in the lot. A little before ten-forty-five."

I continued to detail the day's events with occasional questions from Angela and Joann. Finally, we were back to me getting into Angela's car on Granada Road.

"So you think Donna strangled Michelle?" I said.

"We're collecting evidence at this time," said Yee.

"Oh, come on! On the porch, Donna yelled that she didn't mean to do it. If not her, then it was either me or Nina."

Angela glanced pointedly at Joann, then said to me, "Of course, Nina didn't do it."

"So am I under suspicion?"

She gazed at me long enough to make me squirm in my seat. "No. Because of you, we found Nina Lowen alive."

"You mean, *I* found her alive."

She nodded, looking irked. "Yes, Katy. That's what I meant.

"Am I free to go?"

"Of course. Now go home. Have a good dinner, put your feet up, and relax. You earned it."

We all stood. Angela hugged me and thanked me again. I took my water bottle with me. Better safe than sorry, I always say.

CHAPTER FORTY-FIVE

SATURDAY • JULY 25
Posted by Katy McKenna

Friday, July 17
Part Six

Lieutenant Yee gave me a ride home. Driving down my street, we saw my man-crazy neighbor, Maddie, jogging slow-mo past Simon's home in an outrageously low-cut red spandex jogging suit. Her boobs bounced in perfect tempo with each step. The bare midriff top showed off her tanned, tight abs, and I swear the bottoms had a padded derrière because I didn't remember her packing a curvy Kim Kardashian fanny before.

"Wow," said Joann. "She looks like she just stepped out of one of those housewives shows."

I glanced at her. "That's Maddie, my new neighbor. She's hoping that my other new neighbor is looking out his upstairs window."

We stopped in front of my house.

"Is he a hottie?" asked Joann.

"Depends on your definition of hottie. He's a techie gazillion-aire from New York, so that may be her definition."

"Living in this neighborhood? No offense, but this is middle-class suburbia. Shouldn't he be living in a castle somewhere?"

"Simon is working on a project that would enable us commoners to live off the grid right here in suburbia."

"Is his name Simon Richard, by any chance?"

"Prichard. Why? Do you know him?"

"I've read about him. He's a lot like Elon Musk. No wonder she's on the prowl. What about you? Is he your type?"

"He's a nice guy, although a bit odd. The more time I spend with him, the more I like him. As a friend. Definitely not my type, whatever that is. Uh-oh. She's watching us and probably wondering why I'm in a cop car. I'd better say hi to her."

"And bye to me." She set a hand on my arm. "Good work today, Katy. You're a hero, you know."

I grinned, feeling gratified. "All in a day's work, ma'am." I climbed out, and she pulled away with a honk-honk.

Maddie stood at the edge of my property staying in view of Simon's windows—working a perfected red carpet pose.

"Hi, Maddie," I called with a wave.

She followed me up my walk. "Good grief. What happened to you?"

"I'm fine. My car broke down and Joann gave me a ride home."

"You sure don't look fine. The side of your face is grazed pretty bad." She pointed at my rib cage. "You have a footprint on your chest, and what's that stuff in your hair?"

"I fell."

Maddie looked genuinely concerned. "This is more than a fall." She moved close and inspected my face. "It looks like there are some tiny pieces of glass embedded in your cheek." She wrinkled her nose. "You smell like gasoline."

"It's kerosene. It's definitely been a rough day." I glanced over her shoulder and saw Simon approaching. Maddie's eyes trailed my glance, and she instantly shifted back into manhunt mode.

She twiddled her fingers at him. "Hi there."

With a quick nod in her direction, he said, "I saw your arrival in a squad car. What the hell happened to you?" At that moment, Simon only had eyes for me, and I observed Maddie's posture slump a bit. He gently touched my cheek, and her boobs literally deflated. I kid you not!

"Looks like you've been in a fight. Did you win?" he asked.

With hands-on-hips, I proudly said, "As a matter of fact, I did! I found Nina! She is alive and well."

"You're kidding!" exclaimed Maddie. "That's wonderful. Ethan will be so happy."

"Where was she?" asked Simon.

"Tied up in a cabin. It's a long story."

Daisy must've heard me, because she was barking like a maniac in the house. "I wish I could chat longer, but I gotta go feed the kids. I promise to fill you both in, later."

I started for the door and Simon hollered, "Hold on. I've had a lot of first aid training. How about you let me practice on your face."

"Gee, that sounds super."

He followed me to the door, and as we walked into the house, I glanced back at Maddie and waved. She twiddled her fingers, looking like someone had stolen her puppy. One of these days, I need to tell her that Simon and I are just friends.

Before Nurse Simon attended to my wound, I started a pot of coffee, and fed my starving pets. While Nina's cat chowed down on his kibble, I stroked his back. "Guess what? Pretty soon, you can go home to your momma." He nudged his head into my hand and purred softly. "She will be so happy to see her baby." I snapped a picture of him sitting next to Tabitha. They've become pals, and Tabby will miss him.

It was going to take a few more minutes for the coffee to perk to perfection, so I made Simon wait while I took a quick shower. When I pulled off my filthy top, I was astounded at the blossoming bruises on my sternum and side. "No wonder I hurt." Then, when dressed, I stuck my head out the bathroom door, intending to shout I was ready, and found him standing there holding two mugs of coffee.

"I couldn't remember if you like three or four teaspoons of sugar, so I went with three-and-a-half," he said. "I put a straw in yours, thinking it might hurt to drink."

I tried a sip without the straw, and he was right.

Simon cleaned my cheek, plucked out the bits of glass (ouch!!!), and dressed the wound. Once done, it was more of a bad scrape with no deep cuts, so he gently taped a gauze pad over it and called it good to go.

After Simon went home, I checked my phone. The screen was littered with messages from Ruby. I leaned against a pile of pillows on my bed and called her.

"Where the hell have you been all day?" she hollered.

"Nice way to answer your phone, Grandma."

"Don't you ever check your voice messages? Texts? Smoke signals? I was afraid you were dead in a ditch somewhere."

"I don't check my phone when I'm in the middle of super-hero-crime-fighter duties, or don't have cell service. Both would apply today."

"Oh, God. Now, what have you done?"

Ben yelled in the background. "Are you okay, Katy?"

"I'm fine, Ben. However, I need to ask Ruby a favor."

"What?" she grumped.

"I need a ride to the hospital."

"What's wrong? Are you hurt? Were you climbing on a ladder? I've told you not to do that when you're alone. You could fall and break your neck, and no one would know. You should wear one of those 'home-alone' bracelets."

"Ruby. I'm thirty-two. Not one hundred and two."

"Anyone can fall, ya know. One of the old geezers here tripped over his cat in his kitchen, and nobody knew until he didn't show up for breakfast. It was Waffle Wednesday, and Owen is always first in line."

"Is he okay?"

"He cracked his elbow and broke a front tooth. He could've starved to death if he didn't keep cookies in a bottom drawer."

"I doubt he would have starved to death in one night, but you're right about anyone can fall. Can you give me a ride to see someone in the hospital? Veronica is out of commission."

"Did you have a car accident?"

"No. I slid into a ditch," I said.

"I knew it! All day long I've been getting bad vibes. I knew you were in a ditch. You could've been killed."

"But I wasn't. I need to go see someone in the hospital and I asked you first because I think you'll want to see who I'm visiting, too. But I can ask Mom or Pop if you're not up to it."

"I'm up to it, but I expect to hear the full story when I get there."

CHAPTER FORTY-SIX

SUNDAY · JULY 26
Posted by Katy McKenna

Friday, July 17
Part Seven

Last Friday was an incredibly long day!

While I was waiting on the curb for Ruby, I spotted the boys across the street sitting in a cloud of smoke on the porch. They waved me over. I expected to find them flying high, but they were burning sage.

"We smudged the entire house, and thought we'd burn some out here, too," said Earl.

Randy stood and waved the sage bundle overhead. "Purifies the air. Removes the toxins."

"So you're purifying the neighborhood?" I said.

Earl pointed at Nina's house. "We're were thinking about going over there and waving the sage around the yard." He shrugged. "If Donna doesn't like it, too bad."

Randy said, "What happened to your face?"

I touched the gauze pad. "Long story short: I found Nina and got into a fight. I'll fill you in when I have more time. My grandma is picking me up any minute now. We're going to see Nina at the hospital."

"That's awesome," said Randy. "Is she all right?"

"I think so, but they want to keep her overnight for observation. Oh, and those toxins across the street will no longer be in the neighborhood. One is totally eliminated——"

Randy's eyes widened. "Whoa. Like dead?"

"Yup. And Donna will probably be in prison."

"Wow. That's a lot to take in. Sounds like Karma caught up with them," said Randy.

"It definitely did for Michelle. But I don't think Donna deserves to go to prison, so we'll see."

Randy placed the sage in a bowl and moved to the porch rail, gazing at Nina's house. "How can Nina live there now? It's a shambles. Just getting to the porch would be risky for her."

"You're right. She'll need to stay with me until we figure something out."

Ruby rolled to a screeching stop in her little red spitfire convertible and honked the horn. "Your Uber's here," she yelled.

"Gotta go, guys." As I jogged to her car, I heard Randy say, "I didn't know her grandma was an Uber driver. Wonder how much she makes?"

I waved at them from the car, thinking what adorable goofballs they are, then climbed in, gave Ruby a smooch on the cheek, and buckled up. "Where's Ben?"

"Watching a ball game with BeeGee. That dog is a sports fanatic. Go figure." The engine idled while she stared at me.

"Are you going to start moving, or are we going to sit here and chit-chat while your motor pollutes the entire neighborhood?"

"What the hell happened to your face? The last time it looked like that, you were learning how to ride a two-wheeler, and you did a face-plant on the sidewalk."

"You will not believe this, but I found Nina today, and—"

"What?" she shouted. "Why did it take you so long to tell me?"

"I wanted to tell you in person."

"I'm all ears." She shifted into first gear and hit the gas.

My tale ended as we pulled into the hospital parking lot. At the lobby reception desk, the on-duty volunteer escorted us to Nina's room. Before allowing us in, he checked to see if Nina was awake and wanting guests, then ushered us into the room.

Nina's face lit up when she saw us. She held out her hands and I grasped them, getting drawn in for an embrace. "My dear, dear friend. You saved my life." She pulled back. "Your poor, pretty face."

"It'll heal."

"I hope there won't be a scar," she said. "Maybe a doctor should look at it."

Ruby stepped closer to the bed. "It's such a relief to see you alive and well, Nina. You had us all worried. I can't begin to imagine what you've been through."

"Thank you, Ruby. The truth is, I slept through most of it. In fact, I've slumbered through the last few weeks or so. I feel like Rip Van Winkle." She motioned to the visitor chairs. We pulled them close to the bed and sat. "It started with taking medicine for a cold that was coming on. Colds have a tendency to turn into bronchitis for me, and twice led to pneumonia. The daytime medicine makes me feel cruddy and shaky."

"I remember when you came for brunch and you'd taken cold medicine. You were jittery."

"Makes my heart race, too. I do fine with the nighttime stuff, probably because it knocks me out. Obviously, Donna was very, uh, generous with the SleepWell and I must've been too dopey most of the time to realize it."

"That's putting it mildly," I said.

She shrugged, shaking her head. "With all the commotion in the house, maybe she thought I was better off asleep. I don't know what I was thinking when I agreed to her plans to update the house." She paused. "No, I *do* know what I was thinking. I thought she meant updating with trending paint colors, and a good cleanup in the yard. You know. Trim the bushes, prune the trees." She stifled a choked sob. "My garden. Decades of love and work, not to mention money spent, gone in a matter of days. I can't begin to tell you how devastated I was when I saw it. I wanted to die right then and there."

"I'm so sorry. I didn't know if you knew about that," I said.

"One day, when Donna wasn't home, I managed to get to a window to see what all the noise was about. I cried and cried." I gave her a tissue to catch the tears dribbling down her cheeks. "Why she did that, I'll never know. It was as if she just wiped out my life in one fell swoop."

"She told me that's what families want these days," I said. "A low maintenance yard."

"Utter nonsense," said Ruby. "Your yard was like a fairytale. What child wouldn't love to live in that?"

Nina smiled. "I often thought if I had grandkids, how they would have loved playing hide and seek in the garden."

"Katy never gave up on you," said Ruby. "In fact, when you're feeling better, we have some crazy stories to tell."

I patted Grammy's arm. "Ruby, her boyfriend, Ben, and my best friend Samantha, helped, too. Even the boys across the street."

Nina shook her head. "I didn't know, although I have a couple foggy recollections of you, Katy." She sighed. "You were in my bedroom, but I thought I was dreaming."

"You weren't dreaming.

She sipped a few swallows of water. "My mind is still reeling from what took place after you left the cabin. I've never been so frightened in my life."

"But first—how did Michelle get you to the cabin?" I asked.

"Donna asked Michelle that question, too. She said she slipped into the house in the wee hours of the morning and rousted me out of bed. I was so dopey I thought she was Donna. I just walked out to the car with her and wound up at the cabin. It's hard to believe that I did that."

"You were probably practically sleepwalking," I said. "Although getting you through the torn up yard had to be a challenge for Michelle."

Nina went on. "After you left the cabin, Katy, Donna was hysterical. Begging for my forgiveness. She kept screaming at Michelle, *Why did you do this to my aunt?* Michelle was gagged and trying to talk, but couldn't, so Donna pulled the panties out of her mouth, and the woman went wild."

I leaned closer in my seat, picturing the scene in my head.

Nina glanced up at the ceiling. "Oh, my. I could hardly believe the things she said." She held out her cup. "Would you pour me some more water, dear? I'm so thirsty."

I did, and after a few sips, she continued her story.

"It turns out that Michelle murdered Donna's husband all those years ago. Ran him off the road. Can you believe it?"

"What a horrible shock for Donna," I said.

Her lips puckered, and she teared up. "She drove straight at him, and he swerved and went off the cliff. He was a louse, but he certainly didn't deserve that. She... She..." Nina broke into sobs, and I embraced her, feeling her delicate shoulders quiver spasmodically.

"Is that when Donna strangled Michelle?"

"No. I wish she had, though, so I wouldn't have heard what she said next. It was as if that woman came unhinged, just screaming about how she had done what she had to do so they could be together."

"What else did she do? I mean, what else could she have done? She killed Donna's husband and was going to kill you."

"That dreadful woman murdered Linda. My sister."

I pulled back to see her anguished face. "Why?"

Ruby said, "If this is too much for you to talk about, Nina, we understand."

"No. I can talk about it. I *need* to talk about it." Nina shook her head, looking desolate. "Linda had been sick for a long time, and Donna moved in to take care of her. I think I told you that."

"I remember," I said.

"Michelle was tired of waiting. Tired of being kept in the shadows. So, one day while Donna was grocery shopping, she slipped into the house and…and…smothered Linda. With her pillow."

"Oh my God. That's so awful," said Ruby.

"My sister was suffering terribly, and I know she wanted to be gone because she'd asked me to help her die. But assisted suicide was illegal, and I was afraid I'd wind up in prison." She laughed ruefully. "I heard Michelle say something along that line about me. You know, giving me death with dignity."

"But you're not dying."

She patted my arm. "You're damned right, I'm not."

"Then what happened?"

"Donna stood over Michelle, clutching those wretched panties in her fist while Michelle confessed her sins—as if she was proud of the things she'd done." Nina drew a deep, ragged breath. "After that woman told Donna she'd killed her mother. Donna…" She gazed at her hands that were twisting her top sheet into a knot. "Donna went berserk and screamed, 'I'm going to kill you!'"

Nina shrugged. "In that terrible moment, her despair and rage took over any rational thought. In the blink of an eye, she wrapped the panties around Michelle's neck and kept jerking on them. Tighter and tighter. I begged her to stop, but she didn't hear me. She was out of her mind making these horrible guttural sounds—almost inhuman. Michelle struggled hard." Nina covered her mouth, shaking her head. "Her feet thumped the floor. Over and over. All of this was happening just an arm's length from me. I managed to get to my feet. I tried to pull Donna away from

Michelle. But I knew I was too late when Michelle's feet stopped banging the floor." Nina sighed. "It's a lot to process, as they say, these days."

She dropped her hands to her lap, staring down at them, as silent sobs wracked her chest. Then, finally, she spoke again, and that's when I knew she was a survivor with a lot of life still to live. "You know. If ever there was a time to have dementia, this would be it." She gazed at us with a tiny smile. "Probably going to need some therapy."

Ruby stood. "Will you two excuse me? I have a quick call to make. I'll just be out in the hallway."

"I hope this wasn't too much for her to hear," Nina said.

"She's a tough lady."

"So is her granddaughter. Katy, you risked your life to save mine."

"Donna would have taken care of you. Although I must admit, I had my suspicions about her."

"The chief told me you never stopped trying to find me," she said.

"I had a gut feeling. Intuition. That's all. One thing I've learned over the years is to trust my intuition. Every time I don't, I usually regret it."

Ruby returned. "I realize we don't know each other well, Nina, but I have a proposition for you, and I won't take no for an answer." She laughed. "I guess that means it's not a proposition."

"Sounds more like an order to me," I said.

"Anyhoo, I have a comfy guest room, and I want you to stay with me."

"I can't impose on you like that," said Nina.

"It is not an imposition. I've seen the outside of your house and can't begin to imagine the mess inside. You can't possibly stay there."

"I was going to offer the same thing," I said. "But I bet you'd be more comfortable at my grandmother's. Especially since you'll be moving to Shady Acres one of these days."

Ruby went on, "Speaking of that, I have some good news that I think you will like. There's a lovely ground-level apartment in the complex that will be available in ten days. The current occupant is moving in with her daughter's family in El Paso. The apartment has a nice master and a guest room. A perfect size kitchen with a newer stove and refrigerator and a private patio surrounded by lovely flowering shrubbery. There's been a lot of interest in it, but I took the liberty of submitting your name for it just now, and was told it's yours if you want it."

Nina burst into tears. Happy tears. "Oh, I do. I really do."

"Then it's settled. Tomorrow, we'll pick you up and take you to my place. Katy? Can you go to her house in the morning and pack some things so Nina has something to wear when they release her?"

"I'm sure the house is locked," said Nina.

"I'll figure something out," I said. *Dog door.*

Ruby had read my mind and winked. "We should get going. Let our friend rest."

We were leaving the room when Nina said, "Oh! Katy, will you feed Mr. Snickers and check his water?"

CHAPTER FORTY-SEVEN

SUNDAY · JULY 26
Posted by Katy McKenna

Saturday, July 18
Part One

In the late morning, the hospital released Nina. Ben gave us a ride to Ruby's house. On the way, I told her that Baby Girl is now living with my grandmother. I didn't tell Nina that I had dognapped the mutt because I'd seen Donna mistreating her. Didn't matter now anyway, since Donna is in custody.

"That is so kind of Ruby to give her a home, instead of the poor thing winding up at the pound. You know what? I think Baby Girl will be much happier with your grandmother. Donna smothered that dog."

"We changed Baby Girl's name, though. It's now BeeGee."

"I like that so much better," she said. "That name annoyed me to no end. Every time she called her, it set my teeth on edge." She imitated Donna's doggy-baby-talk voice. "Baby Girl! Baby Girl!" She snorted. "So annoying. I shouldn't make fun, though. Donna is going to miss that dog so much. And she certainly does not belong in prison."

"If she does time, I don't think it will be a long sentence," said Ben. "Given the circumstances."

He parked in Ruby's driveway, and we held Nina's arms as we escorted her to the front door. Ruby opened it before we knocked.

"Welcome to Shady Acres, Nina!" said Ruby. "I have the dog in my bedroom until we get you settled. I was afraid she might be too rambunctious and knock you over in her excitement."

Nina sat on the couch, and I laid the blue chenille throw over her lap. "I'm ready. Release the hound!"

Ruby opened her bedroom door. BeeGee tore out and practically flew through the air to get to Nina.

"Baby Girl, I mean BeeGee!" Nina cuddled the excited, wriggly pup. "I'm so happy to see you. Yes, I am!"

———

Ruby doesn't want the chaos that would ensue by adding Mr. Snickers to her household, so I'll keep the cat until Nina is moved into her new apartment. However, we did want Nina to have a little reunion with Snickers, so Ben drove me home to get him. I tucked Snickers into Tabitha's carrier, and told him he was about to be the happiest kitty in the world. He didn't believe me and yowled in hissy protest when I snapped the door shut. "Maybe not so much right now, but just you wait."

At the Shady Acres entrance, Gatekeeper George saw me coming and raised the gate with a salute for the second time that day. Nina's rescue had been on the evening and morning news, and now he thinks I'm a hero.

Ruby was waiting on the porch. "I put BeeGee on the patio with the dog door closed." She led the way into the living room. "Nina? We have a surprise guest here to see you."

I set the carrier on the floor, pulled the cat out, and set him in his mother's lap.

Nina burst into joyful tears, cuddling him close. "Mr. Snickers! I am so sorry about everything. You must've wondered why I wasn't taking care of you."

"I have a confession to make," I said. "Mr. Snickers got lose one day. Daisy and I were walking by the house and when Daisy saw him in the front yard, she barked and he ran off. I nearly lost my mind trying to find him. Finally, I found him in Josh's house when I went over to complain about the late night party noise. You know his cousin Dillon is staying there now. Anyway, I knew Donna would not keep him safe for you, so he's been staying with me. My plan was to keep him until Donna left town."

"I wasn't aware he was gone. I think I would've lost my mind if I'd known. That's one thing I can be thankful I missed out on."

"I have one more surprise for you." I opened the photos on my phone. "When you get settled in your apartment, I have some plants for your patio that I think you'll like."

She gazed at the picture of the red, pink, and peach colored roses that I had potted for her. "Oh my. Are those my roses?"

"They are. I couldn't save them all, but think I got the best."

She wrapped me in a warm embrace. "Katy. *You* are the best."

CHAPTER FORTY-EIGHT

SUNDAY · JULY 26
Posted by Katy McKenna

Saturday, July 18
Part Two

Last Saturday, after the happy pet reunion at Ruby's, I loaded up Snickers and went home. Oh, how I wished I hadn't.

I rounded the corner onto Sycamore Lane and discovered a giant RV parked in front of Josh's house. I knew he'd bought a fancy home-on-wheels, and he and Nicole had recently embarked on an extended road trip since getting remarried—so my first thought was, *Did Nicole die?*

As I passed by the house, it relieved me to see her sitting on the porch steps. Josh was standing, facing her, and he glanced over his shoulder when she waved at me. I waved back and continued to my driveway clicking the garage door opener as I made the turn. Halfway in, I hit it again to close the door.

I turned off the engine and sat there feeling sick. "What should I do?"

You know what you have to do, said the exasperating voice in my head. *Walk over there and act pleased to see them.*

"No. I'm going to my bedroom and hide under the covers."

You have to face them. Sooner or later.

"Later works for me. In fact, I just remembered I forgot something at Ruby's. Yeah, that's it. I forgot something."

Really? What did you forget? asked my conscience.

"Nothing." I crawled out of the car. My legs felt like lead weights. My heart was twisted into a knot, and I felt close to losing the snickerdoodles I'd enjoyed at Ruby's. I opened the back door, picked up the cat carrier, and went inside.

Daisy knew I wasn't in good shape when I walked through the garage door into the laundry room. I closed the dog door, let the cat loose, then sat on the floor leaning against the dryer while my girl whined and kissed my face.

"I can't go out there, Daisy. They're married now. How am I supposed to be all, yay—I'm so happy to see you two! How's married life treating you?"

She tilted her head, gazing at me with her big brown eyes.

"Okay, I don't have to say anything like that. But I have to be friendly."

The doorbell rang, and Daisy dashed for it, barking her head off.

"I can't deal with this." I shuffled to the foyer. "Daisy, sit." I sucked in a deep breath of air, and opened the door.

"Hello, Katy," he said in a solemn tone. "How are you?"

"I, uh... Not so good at the moment to be honest."

Clad in jeans and a black t-shirt, he reached down and patted Daisy's head. "Knowing your history with your neighbor, I thought you might need a little moral support. Am I overstepping?"

Pressing my lips tight, trying to hold back threatening tears, I shook my head.

"How about we walk over together, and you can introduce me?"

I grimaced, feeling like I was about to get a booster shot in the butt.

Simon gave me a brotherly smile. "You can do this." He took my hand, pulled me onto the porch, told Daisy to stay, and shut the door. "I know how you feel. Someday, I'll tell you about my broken heart."

At the bottom of the steps, I said, "I look awful."

"You look fine—"

I made a "yuck" face at that. Fine is not good. Fine is average, mediocre, meh.

"I meant to say you look very nice."

Yeah, right.

He released my hand, and we headed next door. Josh saw us coming and met us halfway on the sidewalk.

"Hi, Josh."

"Hey." He took a tentative step towards me as if to embrace me, and I subconsciously stepped back.

Simon threw an arm around my shoulders and held his hand out to shake Josh's. "I'm your new neighbor. Simon Prichard. I live on the other side of Katy."

Josh's brows furrowed briefly, and he half-smiled. "Nice to meet you. I didn't know the Millers moved."

Simon grinned at me. "Lucky for me they did."

"Katy, what happened to your cheek?" said Josh.

"It's a long story," I said.

"Our neighbor is the town hero." Simon hugged me closer. "The story is online, Josh. You should check it out. It's on all the local news sites."

Nicole strolled over with a tiny Yorkie tucked under one arm. She looked healthy and way too much like a blushing bride. "Hi, Katy."

I forced what I hoped looked like a friendly smile. "Hello. Cute dog."

"Thank you. This is our new baby." She waved one of the dog's tiny paws. "Snookie, say hello to Katy."

"She's adorable," I said.

I wasn't sure if I was happy with Simon's arm around me. I thought it might be sending the wrong message. Then Nicole slipped her left arm through Josh's, resting her hand on his forearm. The sun glinted off her diamond wedding ring. Suddenly, I was grateful for Simon's supportive arm, and decided they could read into it whatever they wanted.

"Hello," said Nicole to Simon. "I'm Nicole. Josh's wife. You look familiar. Have we met?"

"No. I'm Simon Prichard. Nice to meet you, Nicole."

Her eyes widened, and I knew she knew exactly who he is. "Didn't I see an article about you in *People* magazine?" she asked.

Simon said, "I don't know if you saw it, but yes, there was an article not too long ago."

Josh looked baffled. "What are you talking about?"

"I'll tell you later," said Nicole.

"What brings you to the neighborhood, Josh?" I said, feeling Simon's fingers squeeze my shoulder.

"We were heading back to Los Angeles. Nickie has decided to resume chemo."

"I thought you were done with that, Nicole," I said.

"I'm sure not looking forward to it." She patted Josh's arm. "But I have a lot to live for now."

"Anyway," said Josh. "Devin called when we were on the I-5 passing through Fresno and said the water heater is on the fritz. So we cut over to see if I need to get a new one."

"And do you?" asked Simon.

"Yeah. I'm heading to Home Depot in a few minutes."

"We better get going, Josh," said Nicole. "Good seeing you, Katy."

"Yes, same here. You look great." I swallowed hard. "Really happy for you."

When we reached my steps, Simon reclaimed his arm, and we sat on the porch swing. "You want a glass of wine?" he asked.

"Huh?"

"Wine?"

I nodded.

"Be right back."

I was deep into moping mode and wasn't aware he'd left and returned until he handed me a goblet of red. He set the bottle on the table, sat beside me, and we gently swung in silence for a while.

"This is hard." I sighed.

"Seems like a nice guy," said Simon.

"He is. Maybe too nice." I pivoted to face him. "Thank you for the moral support."

"I hope putting my arm around you wasn't too much. I knew you were hurting, and it just happened. I don't want your friend to get the wrong impression."

"You mean my ex. I know how guilty Josh feels about leaving me. So if he got the wrong impression and thinks I'm dating—then good. It'll probably make him feel better thinking I've moved on." I shrugged with a little snort. "At least one of us will feel better. Clearly, I have not moved on. And I'm not ready to date. Not even close, even though my grandmother keeps pushing me to get out there. I'll probably become the old neighborhood busybody spinster living with a houseful of cats."

"Poor Daisy." Simon topped off our glasses, then leaned back, and we returned to congenial swinging. A few minutes later, he tapped his glass against mine. "Here's to good neighbors and crazy cat ladies."

Dinner Time

I was in the kitchen making a salad that I didn't want, but figured if I ate something healthy, then I could justify finishing off the ice cream in the freezer.

The doorbell rang, and Daisy beat me to the door. I wasn't expecting anyone, and prayed it wasn't Josh. I considered not answering, but then Nicole called out, "Katy? Can we talk?"

I opened the door and didn't invite her in.

"I wanted to tell you how happy I am that you've found someone. Simon Prichard is quite the catch. The man is a billionaire."

"We're…" I was about to say we're not a couple. "He's a wonderful guy, however, I'm not interested in his money." I wanted to add that I'm not a gold digger, but kept my mouth shut and let her talk.

"But still. It is nice. I mean, who knows? Maybe you'll wind up living in New York on the family estate. Wouldn't that be something?"

"That would certainly be something."

"Katy. I just want you to be as happy as I am. I feel like a have a new lease on life." Her narrowed eyes drilled into mine. "A very long life. With Josh. I finally have back what I lost when we broke up, and I will never let him go again. One of these days, Josh and I will be living next door, and I know that might be hard for you. You know, seeing how happy we are."

"Well, as you say, maybe I'll be living in New York, although I think I'd prefer his country estate in England."

She reached down to pet Daisy, and my loyal dog backed away. "If things go as I expect them to, I plan to have a baby."

"I'm sure Josh would be a good father."

"Yes. A very loving father, and a devoted, loyal, *loving* husband." She turned to leave, then stopped. "I'm glad we had this little chat."

Lucky for Nicole that I didn't have a pair of Donna's granny panties in my hands.

CHAPTER FORTY-NINE

SATURDAY · AUGUST 8
Posted by Katy McKenna

The fundraiser trail ride was scheduled at ten a.m. at the Beaver Lake Ranger Station, about fifteen miles out of town.

On the drive to the lake, Sam said, "I haven't been horseback riding since your twelfth birthday."

"Best birthday ever! I wonder if the "Little Cowpokes Dude Ranch" is still in operation. It'd be fun to take Casey and Chelsea."

"We should check it out—but sooner rather than later." She patted her belly. "Won't be long before this little cowpoke is too big for Mommy to sit on a saddle."

"There's the turn! Watch out for the turkeys!"

About a dozen turkeys were milling around on the narrow road, totally oblivious of us.

"Look how cute they are. I love turkeys."

"Me, too," said Samantha. "On a plate with lots of gravy. Gobble! Gobble!"

I gave her the expected scowl and Sam tapped the horn. The gobblers cleared out, and we continued to the ranger station.

———

We lined up on our assigned horses in a big corral. Our tall, dark, and drop-dead handsome ranger stood in the dirt, gripping the reins of a magnificent shiny palomino. He was the ultimate rugged, hunky cowboy of my daydreams. A total Hollywood heartthrob.

Sam leaned towards me and whispered, "Oh, my God. Be still my heart."

And then he spoke. I expected a commanding voice that would leave me weak-kneed. A Sam Elliott—Morgan Freeman—George Clooney mashup with a dash of Clint Eastwood—*Go ahead, make my day.*

Nope. Our sexy heartthrob sounded like a falsetto version of Roseanne Barr with a dash of Gilbert Gottfried.

Sam leaned towards me again. "Oh, my God."

"Hello! I'm Ranger Kyle Cruise," he screeched. "No relation. Ha, ha, ha. Thank you for coming out today for our fundraiser. It's going to be a *fun* day." He petted two black short-haired Labrador-mix mutts standing next to him. "And these two handsome fellas are Ranger Tippy and Ranger Toby."

Tippy was about thirty pounds and Toby around seventy. A couple of goofy cuties.

"They live at the station and are a big help around here. They keep our beds warm, chase pesky squirrels, and go on rounds with us. Today, they will act as tour guides."

I raised my hand. "Uh, just to be clear. You'll be with us too, right?" My lame attempt at humor.

Ranger Kyle brayed a hearty, honking laugh that ended with a snort. "Yep. But these guys are the bosses. Everyone ready to hit the trail?"

I stroked my horse's silky neck. "Are you ready, Suzy Belle?"

She nickered softly, and I took that as a "yes."

Kyle mounted his horse. "Let's move out!"

Everyone rode through the corral gate except me. My pretty

brown mare wouldn't budge. "Come on, Suzy Belle. Time to hit the old trail."

Kyle turned in his saddle and yelled, "Give her a little kick."

I nudged her gently with my sneakered feet. "Giddy up. Pretty please?"

"That's not a kick," hollered the ranger. "Toby, go help her!"

The dog dashed behind me, and nipped my horse's back foot, then dodged the quick kick that followed. The trick worked, and we were off to a sluggish walk.

Toby must've figured I would require further assistance because he hung back with me. His buddy Tippy stayed at the head of the line, leading the way down the trail.

Sam, who was several horses ahead, called back to me, "Looks like you got a new friend."

I glanced down at my grinning sidekick. "You said I might meet a cute guy today."

"And you certainly did!"

That got a round of laughs from the other riders.

We were on a woodsy trail that ran alongside the lake. The sky was cloudless, a soft breeze was blowing, and hawks drifting overhead called, "Kee-aah, kee-aah."

About thirty minutes into the trail ride, Suzy Belle, Toby, and I were lagging behind by about thirty yards. I kept encouraging my horse to catch up, but she wasn't having it.

"Oh, well. Let's just enjoy the day. No need to rush." I glanced at Toby. "Right, buddy?"

Suddenly, Suzy stopped and snorted. Her ears twitched back and forth. A skunk was about four or five yards ahead, staring us down, his bushy tail flicking.

"Uh-oh. Stay calm, Suzy, " I murmured. "We'll just wait right here until Mr. Skunk toddles off."

But Toby had other plans. "Grrr," he said, wagging his tail furiously.

"Shh, Toby. We're in no hurry. He'll leave in a sec."

Then I swear, the dog said, "No worries, Katy. I'll clear the trail for you."

He trotted ahead, barking his head off. The skunk skittered towards him, and as the dog moved in, the animal spun around, stamping his feet. His tail shot up stiff, and he sprayed Toby. And my horse. And me. Not once, but several times at lightning speed.

Suzy Belle reared up, spun around, bucked like a rodeo horse, and broke into a run. I hung onto the saddle horn with one hand while jerking back on the reins as hard as I could with the other. She was sneezing and banging her nose on the ground as we careened down the trail all the way back to the corral. She skidded to a halt, quivering, stomping her hooves, and still sneezing.

Toby caught up and barked for help. A slim, middle-aged woman ran out of the office shielding her eyes against the sun. She froze when she got a whiff of us. "Dammit, Toby! Not again! When will you learn not to mess with skunks?"

I shakily dismounted and spewed my breakfast in the dirt.

Toby approached her. She pointed a finger at him and sternly shouted, "Stay!"

He flopped in the dirt and rolled around, trying to scrub off the stink.

Keeping her distance, she asked if I was all right.

"Yeah. Can't believe I stayed on."

The rest of the group returned, and Kyle ordered everyone to stay out of the corral. "Tie your horses to the fence, folks, and head over to the picnic area under the oaks." Then to me, "I've never seen Suzy Belle move like that. You okay?"

"Pretty shaky, but I'll live."

Sam tied up her pinto and started towards me. "You scared me half to death, Katy."

I held out a hand. "Stay back. Trust me, you do not want to get near me. The stink could start your labor."

She took a couple more steps and plugged her nose. "Wow. You're not kidding. That's terrible."

"Tell me about it." I rubbed my burning eyes. "We'll have to miss the lunch. I've got to go home and shower about a hundred times."

Ranger Kyle, looking contrite, apologized for the skunking.

"These things happen." I shrugged. "Nature. What're ya gonna do?" I looked at Sam. "I feel sick. We need to leave now."

Kyle said, "Not like that, you're not. Your car will be ruined."

"You mean *my* car will be ruined," said Sam. "But Katy needs to get home."

"We have a special solution that we keep on hand for this," he said. "You'll need to strip off everything and take a long shower. You won't smell like roses, but it will bring the reek level down to bearable so you can get in the car without ruining it. I don't suppose you brought an extra set of clothes with you?"

"No. Why would I?" I was snippy, but I couldn't breathe and was trying not to upchuck whatever was left in my stomach.

"I have some scrubs in the car, Katy," said Sam. "They're dirty, but they're better than what you got on now."

While everyone gathered in the picnic area for lunch, I removed my clothes in a private outdoor enclosure at the back of the station. I put them in a plastic bag that the office lady took away—probably to be burned.

Then my BFF hosed me down. "Never thought I'd be doing this to you."

"Neither did I. Goodbye dignity. Hello humiliation." When I was properly drenched, I scrubbed down with the skunk odor remover several times—getting rinsed with chilly hose water between latherings. Lather, rinse, repeat. Over and over. Several times it seeped into my eyes and burned like hell. Finally, when I felt like I'd removed the top layer of my epidermis, I dried off and donned Sam's scrubs, which were decorated with a schmear of dried infant vomit on the left shoulder.

Ranger Kyle escorted us to Sam's car. "I've been sprayed a few times. The smell will wear off, but if you have any dates planned over the next few days, you might want to cancel."

I kept my answer short because I was trying to breathe through my mouth. "No. No dates."

"Oh?" He shuffled his boots, kicking up a little cloud of dust. "May I call you? Maybe we could have coffee sometime?"

I glanced at Sam who had turned her back to us—trying to stifle a giggle, no doubt.

He was so hot, and yet, so not. But he seemed like a nice guy. *Maybe he's a man of few words. The strong, silent type. Oh, what the heck.*

"Sure. Give me a few days, though. I won't be going out in public for a while."

He cackled, and I cringed.

AFTERWORD

Life would be tragic if it weren't funny.
~ *Stephen Hawking* ~

Dear Readers,

If you've read the previous books in *The Murder Blog Mysteries*, you know I often incorporate scenes from my personal life. Everyone's life is a mixture of good times and bad, and mine is no exception. But without the heartbreaks, you won't appreciate the joys.

Cuss Scene

Several years ago, we lived on a quiet residential street in our town's village area. There was a charming little house across the street that two young men had recently rented.

At first, there weren't any problems, but then a few more people moved in—and that's when the cussing started. Plus, the new move-ins were running a motorcycle repair shop in the front yard during the day when the official rent-paying tenants were at work.

One day, while I was trimming the daisies, the language got so crude that I lost it. "Enough!" I threw down my clippers, marched into my house, grabbed the dictionary, then went across the street and stood on their lawn screaming like a crazy woman. I seldom say the "F" word, but boy, I sure did that day, just like the scene in this book.

I didn't realize that many of my neighbors had come out to watch. When I finished my tirade, I got an ovation, and a few shouted, "Encores and bravos."

Later that day, the actual renters came over with a bouquet of flowers and apologized.

Skunk Scene

When I was a teenager, I had a sweet horse named Mandy. One day, we were on the trail with our canine pals, Tippy and Toby, a couple of sweet mutts who lived on the ranch where I boarded Mandy. When we encountered a skunk on the path, both dogs took it upon themselves to shoo the skunk away. I begged them not to, but they assured me they had everything under control. They did not.

Poor Mandy got sprayed in the face. She reared up, spun around, bucked several times, and broke into a dead run—sneezing all the way home. I didn't think I would survive that wild ride.

If you've heard that tomato juice removes skunk odor, I'm here to tell you it does not.

Character Names

I've been asked why I use certain names repeatedly in my books. They are names of friends and family, and they get a kick out of seeing their names in my stories. Like Samantha's son, Casey. And her husband, Spencer. I have two sons. Guess what their names are?

Respectfully yours,
Pam

P.S. Indie writers live for your kind reviews.
If you enjoyed *While She Slumbered* and have a moment to leave
a rating or write a short comment, it would mean the world to me.

amazon.com/author/pamelafrostdennis

ABOUT THE AUTHOR

I live on the California Central Coast with my husband, Mike, and our sweet dog, Emma. Along with my writing career, Mike and I have been partners in the restaurant business for eons - Klondike Pizza.

Links to my Website, Blog, Facebook, and Instagram.
https://linktr.ee/pamelafrostdennis

DEAD GIRLS DON'T BLOG
Book #1 in the Murder Blog Mysteries

Katy McKenna's life takes a dramatic turn when she stumbles upon a newspaper story about the upcoming parole hearing for one of the men who raped and murdered her high school friend, sixteen years ago. Fearing he could soon be set free to prey on other innocent young girls, Katy sets out to make sure this doesn't happen, not realizing she might not survive to blog about it.

BETTER DEAD THAN WED
Book #2 in the Murder Blog Mysteries

Katy McKenna has had enough near-death experiences and heartache to last a lifetime. Now all she wants to do is get her career back on track, find a nice guy, and live happily-ever-after. But when she hears about a man maliciously exposing innocent young women to HIV, she is compelled to put her plans on hold to stop him.

Meanwhile, Katy's mother is forced to reveal a shattering child-hood trauma that has come back to haunt her; her obnoxious baby sister is moving in, and her scuzzy was-band is stalking her.

And she's beginning to wonder why every rotten person she has recently heard about has suddenly dropped dead. Is it divine providence? Or is it murder?

COINS AND CADAVERS
Book #3 in the Murder Blog Mysteries

While battling a furry vermin invasion in the spooky attic of her old house, Katy discovers a vintage wooden chest hidden behind a wall. Although everyone assures her the box is legally hers, its incredible contents compel Katy to search for the rightful owner. Meanwhile, she takes a temp job assisting her hunky P.I. neighbor, Josh Draper. The assignment: Trap a sleazy wife-cheater. Something Katy knows about all too well from personal experience. During a cozy stakeout in Draper's two-seater, things get awkward as the sizzling tension builds. Who will make the first move?

Since she's already been searching online for past owners of her home, Grandma Ruby asks Katy to use her sleuthing skills to discover what happened to her bigamist great-great grandfather. Katy's quest leads her to find an extended family she never knew existed.

Family secrets are revealed, for better or worse....
Romance blossoms, for better or worse....
And Katy's good intentions lead her into
a terrifying dilemma she may not survive.

WAS IT MURDER?

Book #4 in the Murder Blog Mysteries

Nothing bad ever happens in the peaceful English village of Bridleford—except for murder, that is.

A dear family member has met an untimely end. Now Katy and Grandma Ruby must travel to the Cotswolds of England to sort out legal matters. When they arrive, they're overwhelmed by the friendly villagers who offer help and moral support.

However, when Katy and Ruby become the target of vandals, they realize that not everyone in town is pleased about their presence.

Is murder next on the list?

Made in United States
North Haven, CT
27 January 2024

47988067R00163